Toska

Toska

Toska

If Not Now, When?

Sara Al-Haider

PARTRIDGE
A Penguin Random House Company

To order additional copies of this book, contact
Toll Free 800 101 2657 (Singapore)
Toll Free 1 800 81 7340 (Malaysia)
orders.singapore@partridgepublishing.com

www.partridgepublishing.com/singapore

To you.
The one who encouraged me the most.

"Toska - noun /'tō-skə/ - Russian word roughly translated as sadness, melancholia, lugubriousness.

> "No single word in English renders all the shades of toska. At its deepest and most painful, it is a sensation of great spiritual anguish, often without any specific cause. At less morbid levels it is a dull ache of the soul, a longing with nothing to long for, a sick pining, a vague restlessness, mental throes, yearning. In particular cases it may be the desire for somebody of something specific, nostalgia, love-sickness. At the lowest level it grades into ennui, boredom."

– Vladimir Nabokov

Chapter One

I do not love the sun, or ever remember looking up to the sky for any kind of happiness. And, when I was younger, people often would not look at me, especially when they noticed the bruises, or the swollen lips. I was called every nickname under that sun, every bad name you wouldn't want your kids to be called. Which made me hate anything bright, or blue, or gold with a dark, black passion.

I'm eighteen now.

And I'm walking down the street, in front of hotels, not far from the park. Near to the relative safety of other pedestrians, casually inhaling the gas of heavy air and staring blankly at the cars and taxis.

Listening to kids full of energy and laughter playing happily with their parents.

Trying to imagine myself sitting on a swing, or anything that would bring joy to my dead soul.

And today, like every day, I am unlucky.

I hate waiting, but here I am waiting.

Waiting.

Then suddenly, Laura rushes up to me. She smiles, and kisses my cheek.

"Hey, sorry for being late, I had lots to do" she stammers apologetically, then adds:

"You look superb today."

I know she's lying. She does this more often lately.

"Thanks" I answer, a little coldly.

She nods and we start walking. I don't bother to ask where we are going. Probably to the park she kept talking about yesterday. She starts telling me that everything in my profile is progressing, but my face isn't even close to happiness and she shrugs a tired 'sorry'.

"It is kind of true though." Her voice trails off.

It takes us five long minutes to arrive at the grill in Millennium Park. A young Chinese guy guides us to a table, and I notice people staring at Laura, probably wondering why is she walking around with some kind of freak. I bow my head when a little kid points at me, pulling his mom's hands and crying;

"Look mom, look!"

Laura doesn't notice and sits down. I automatically sit with my back to the kid. In the shelter I never look at myself, and I just take a glimpse now and then whenever Laura takes me to a hotel where mirrors are hanging.

Laura smiles at me, the kind of smiles that tells you that everything is great. I don't feel like smiling but I do it anyway. It never reaches my eyes.

"Alright", she says firmly, opening her black book.

"I've never been anywhere like this", I whisper so no one has to hear me. And just whispering makes me sad. Angry. Hateful. I hate the people judging me with their filthy looks, hate the loud kid, and particularly hate my father for turning me into a monster.

Right now, I hate everything.

"It's alright. I'll help you with whatever you need", Laura reassures me.

I nod. She nods back, flashing her pretty smile.

The Chinese guy returns, and Laura orders two Cajun chicken breasts, with fries on the side, and organic beer. The annoying sun lights up Laura, particularly her eyes so blue like the sky. Her beautiful light brown hair is so shiny that it seems alive. I feel a pinch of jealousy. No, I feel straight envy. I envy her amazing clean skin, her smile, and her skinny body. Not like mine isn't skinny, but hers is like a model I've been seeing constantly on my TV for the past few weeks.

Since I arrived so dramatically in the shelter

Laura clears her throat, a sure sign that she is going to get more formal.

"We are here to discuss how everything is going for you".

I look down at my knotted fingers. Just talking about me fills me with pain.

3

"Yes. We sure are".

"Okay. I've just signed some papers that mean that I can take you with me wherever I go, in order to keep up with your progress. And I also signed you up for some English tuition lessons. I think it would be good for you to learn a language. The lessons would start sometime next week".

She stops talking, and waits for my response. I don't say a word, so she continues;

"I already feel as though you're my little sister or daughter. I just want to take you to beauty salons and go shopping and help you see all the amazing places you couldn't see when. Well. You know".

Her voice trails off, as if she is embarrassed for me. For even mentioning my past. Then she smiles, showing off her perfect white teeth.

I can't react. I'm too angry. Angry that my family that is not a normal family. In any world. Angry to be in this situation. But I don't jet it show, and I nod, and Laura claps with glee.

The food arrives, some kind of sandwiches I've never seen and a large sized beer, and I only know this because my dad used to drink the same beer all the time whilst pretending he was working.

We start eating, and I gulp the food down nervously. Chewing. Chewing harder. Swallowing.

Laura acts like she isn't watching me, eating slowly, carefully. Elegantly. Drinking beer. Reading the newspaper, making sly glances at me to se if I'm okay.

As ever, I feel that the people walking by are staring at. Judging me with silence. I hate myself. I hate that I make everyone everywhere stare at me with hatred and contempt.

God, why did you do this to me? Why?

I finish my sandwich. Sauce stains all over my face, hands and some on my grey pants that are too big for me now. I hate those too. Make me look like a freak kid. Laura hands me a napkin and motions toward my mouth and face. Great. Now I feel exactly like a kid.

Just a fucked up freak kid.

I wipe my face, my hands, and my pants but the stains don't go away.

They never do.

I sigh.

"It's fine, we're going shopping anyway" smiles Laura. She stands, grabs her purse and my hand in one fluent movement. Makes me stand too.

I like Laura so much, not just because she's taken good care of me in the past, but also because she isn't embarrassed to be with me. Or maybe she is, but isn't showing it. Which also makes her a good person. And she never stops caring. She pulls cash lightly from her purse and hands it to the man at the door. He nods and wishes us a nice day.

As we stroll along I see families, and couples all over each other, old people walking alone, teenagers laughing, trees, dogs, girls hugging guys. Little babies in buggies, people listening to music and smiling in a world of their own.

Everything I'm seeing is wordless, pictures, snippets of happiness, pretty and full of love.

And everything I see needs words to describe them that I don't even know.

It's a world full of love. A love I will never know.

But it's gorgeous, and wonderful, and full of love and that's all that matters.

I smile to myself, for the first time in a long time.

"What's so amusing?" Laura asks.

"All this," I say, staring ahead.

She furrows her brows.

"The people, the love. I can feel the love," I say.

I stop and turn to her.

"Yes." She smiles. "You're right."

We keep on walking until we get to a main street busy with cars, buses and cabs. Laura raises her hand and one of the cabs pulls up in front of us. She gets in first, into the back seat, and waves for me to come after her.

It smells like old red roses.

On the way she shows me all the hotels she's been to, the shops she'd love to visit, and a lot of things I didn't even know existed.

The cab stops somewhere called Michigan Avenue. Laura calls it the magnificent mile, and all the time that we walk she wears the widest grin. I wonder why she always seems so incredibly happy.

Laura walks into a small place, a blue place, with trendy white chairs. A man walks over and greets us immediately.

"Mrs. Allen, nice to see you again," he says, as if he's known her forever.

"Hi Eduardo, how's everything going"? she replies happily.

"And who's this pretty young lady," he adds. Staring at me.

I stare back at him. Just stare.

Laura speaks. "She's my new little sister. She's called Eva." She places her arm around me protectively.

Squeezes me.

"Hi new sister." Eduardo winks.

I simply nod. He creeps me out a little.

"We want to change her look," says Laura. "Something that will make her look more her age."

"Okay baby," oozes Eduardo. "Let's see what I can do to help you."

He points at the black leather chair. I sit. There's a mirror. I avoid mirrors.

I still hear the voice. It's inside my head.

"Don't ever stare at the mirror. You bitch".

Laura knows about my struggle with mirrors. She taps on my shoulder and whispers.

"It's alright. That's you".

With a little smile that's supposed to reassure me, she steps back. I still avoid the mirror. Eduardo starts saying things like; "this will show her cheekbones" and "this will make her diamond face even more beautiful" and "this color will show off her eyes."

I interrupt him savagely.

7

"I don't want to change my hair color. I like it as it is!" I shout.

And then I stare at my lap. I'm ashamed at my outburst. The man is only trying to be kind.

"Fine! Then no color change Eduardo," shouts Laura.

She claps her hands together and sits next to me.

He nods. There are only a few older women here, sitting with wrappers on their head like they're roasting a chicken. I chuckle. Laura raises her eyebrows and smiles. Eduardo takes my hair and snips his scissors. I shudder. Laura takes my hand and nods.

Scissors remind me of a man that my dad once gave me to. He tried to cut off my eyelashes when I told him to go to hell. He used to get way too close, and hold me tight. Hold my arms until he saw his finger marks on my arm.

He would smile as he hurt me.

I forget sometimes how painful it was.

Eduardo takes a water sprayer and sprays my hair until it drips on my pants. And all over my face. He is combing my hair. No one has ever touched my hair in this way before, in a gentle way.

My hair has often been pulled.

Hard.

I'm still looking at my lap. He grabs the scissors again and Laura squeezes my hand. I don't move. But I listen to the sounds. Cut. Cut. Cut.

Hair is falling, long strands of black hair.

Falling from me like the black raiment of a darker memory.

"Voila," Eduardo says, with a theatrical flourish. He spins my chair towards the mirror. "But we haven't finished yet. Oh no, madam". He pulls out a black object, switches it on and I jump as a weird noise emerges from it.

Laura giggles.

"It's okay, Eva, it's only a hair dryer," she laughs. Kindly.

In a few minutes, Eduardo stops, stands back and stares at me like a proud mom.

I've never had a proud mom.

He turns me around to look in the mirror.

I don't stare. I don't stare.

"Look, Eva", says Laura.

I slowly began raising my eyes until I can see my hair. But I avoid staring at my face. I look at my long black hair. Not as long as it used to be. Black hair that now reaches my breasts, where it used to reach the bottom of my back.

It's nice. It's wavy at the ends.

It's a great change.

"I like it", I say. Smiling to Laura. And then back to Eduardo.

"Thank you. Thank you both".

"It's a pleasure". He nods.

"No problem you deserve the best". Laura says, standing up. She walks with Eduardo. He writes down on a paper. She pays.

Again. "See you next time". Laura said and we walked out again.

I feel different. It is a good feeling.

"I took all of your belongings to my apartment," says Laura.

"To your hotel?" I asked.

"No, to my apartment. Not the hotel".

So. She has an apartment. That's nice.

We start shopping. She tosses shirts, pants, jeans, beanies, jackets, more shirts, fancy clothes, dresses that would suit for a night out, shorts, everything at me. I check the tags and it is all pretty expensive. Costly.

Suddenly we're pulling two heavy bags, full of brand new, girly clothes.

I can't quite believe my luck.

We go to the fitting room and I try them all on. I don't check the mirror though. I avoid mirrors. Laura says they all look perfect. She likes my skinny body and curves. She'd love to have my skinny, curvy body.

I don't love my body. I don't like it at all. But I know that Laura is slowly teaching me how to do that.

"You're going to wear these right now and dump those old clothes, alright?" she asks, passing me some skinny black jeans and a white pale shirt with no sleeves. I love it.

I look new. I don't look like me.

After buying all the clothes, we go into underwear shops. And she talks about falling in love, especially when I eventually get a boyfriend. I blush. Hate the idea. But she buys everything she likes. And everything I like.

I still like black. I feel like I can hide in that kind of darkness.

"Okay, let's go, it's getting late" Laura says, and hails a cab to take us back to her apartment. "And I must to introduce you to someone", she adds happily and I nod.

The entire drive back is quiet, except for Laura talking on phone. As she speaks so kindly to relatives, I wonder why I wasn't born into a normal family like hers.

Loving. Caring.

Rich.

"We're here," Laura says.

We climb out and I grab some of the bags whilst she takes care of the others. We walk into what they call a 'lobby', no people, but it's very wide, very grand, and full of light. She presses a button and a door opens. We get in, and in what seems like seconds later, we are at her place. She beckons me in.

"Follow me, Eva, I'll show you to your room." We walk up some stairs, and pass a door. Two doors. Three doors.

We enter through the fourth door and the room is impossibly huge, and very white.

I feel like I'm standing on the edge of heaven.

There is a big bed, and a beautiful view to the sea.

This place is enormous.

"Wow," I whisper, and turn around as Laura places the bags on the floor, just staring at me with that beautiful smile.

"You sure you like it?"

I nod.

"Thank you so much. I'll take good care of it. I promise."

"No need for promises. You deserve it. Now, take as much time as you want to fold your new clothes in the closet, there's the bathroom, with everything you'll need and don't hesitate to come and ask me if you do need anything. When it's time for dinner I'll call you. Got all that"?

I thank her again and again until she pulls me into her arms and hugs me.

It is the first time I've ever been hugged like that.

Laura smiles, finally releases me, and leaves, closing the door behind her.

I sit on the big bed and stare out of the window. It's so pretty that tears begin to roll down my cheeks. Suddenly, I'm crying. Not from the pain, but from the certain knowledge that God has blessed me by giving me the chance to know someone as wonderful as Laura.

And I cry some more because she didn't seem to be embarrassed when I looked so bad.

I wipe my tears and stand up. I head to the closet, which is as big as my old room.

I called it the rat room.

I shudder at the memory. I feel cold and I start to cry.

Lamenting my deplorable, useless, injured soul.

I hide my face in my hands.

And cry.

I try to breathe to calm the anxiety, exactly the way I've been taught.

"Be strong," I tell myself. The tears stop, and I take everything we've just bought and fold it in the closet or hang it up. Then I walk to the bathroom.

There's a vast mirror.

And I can't avoid mirrors forever.

I stand before the giant faucet and slowly, so slowly, begin to examine my face.

My lips look red and full. Normal.

My eyes are green. Normal.

My cheeks are clean and the bruises are fading.

Normal.

My hair is fabulous, a real transformation. My nose is finally straight, and my diamond face has a healthy glow.

For the first time in forever, I look normal.

I notice that my eyes are red from crying and I wash my face. As I turn and walk out of the bathroom, I see a small bookshelf, with about ten books in all. I open one of them. I recognize it. "All Passion Spent".

It is a great old book.

I've loved reading since I was seven. I adore the voyage it provides into a world far away.

I adore the joyous journey of reading, and the joy of escape.

I open the first page and read the introduction, even though I hate introductions. I start reading the story proper.

"Henry Lyulph Holland".

A knock on the door scares me, I jump and the book falls from my hand on to my face. "Shit", I curse loudly, sitting up straight.

"Can I come in?". Laura knocks on the door again. "Yes, of course" I reply.

"Hey, how are you doing?" Laura says and comes over. I show her the book. "Oh". She nods.

"I used to love books, but I don't have time to read now."

She takes the book and fans through the pages.

"I never knew you could read," she says.

"Oh yes," I reply. "Almost every time I am free." She hands it back. "Anyway, dinner is served," she announces, and leads me down the stairs, to another pretty room with a square table, six chairs, and the table is literally full of food. A vase of flowers, glasses. Wine. Silverware. Napkins.

And a guy standing next to the big window holds out a glass.

"Hello," he says, and his deep voice startles me. I hide behind Laura.

Laura walks next to him and that prevents me from hiding more. "Eva, I want you to meet Jacob". Laura said placing her hands around him. He is tall next to her. "Jacob this is Eva, the girl I've been telling you about".

He nods and opens his arms for me. I don't want to hug him. I don't move. "Alright, so you hate hugs. But I'm really happy to see you at last," he smiles. We shake hands. "Yeah," I mutter.

Laura motions to the chair next to her and I sit. Jacob sits next to Laura on the other side. An elderly woman enters carrying plates and places them in front of each one of us. It smells so good. I love that smell. Food. Real food. Finally.

I'm famished. Ravenous. Starving. Jacob starts eating. I grab my spoon and fork. Laura coughs.

"Oh, I'm sorry. I forgot", Jacob murmurs, placing back his spoon. I do the same.

"Prayers", Laura says, firmly.

They close their eyes and hold hands together, Laura offers me hers and I place mine lightly on it.

"God, we thank you for this food, for rest and our home and all things good, for wind and rain and sun above, but most of all for those we love".

"Amen". They both say it at exactly the same time. That was beautiful, and it makes me appreciate her existence even more - a precious human being.

We begin eating and Jacob talks about his English class, and how everything had gone great that day.

"And all the students were so happy to finish the semester and ready to start a new one," he adds. "Are you ready to begin studying, Eva"?

"Yeah, I am,' I reply distractedly. This chicken tastes heavenly, and if I ever get to heaven, I am sure the food will taste like this. I chuckle at my own thought, laugh out loud. Both Laura and Jacob stare at me. Laura smiles. I mouth sorry to them. And they both laugh.

It's so weird that my thoughts can be so funny when everything has been so disastrous recently. I think it's a good thing. A kind of progress.

We finish what we have, and now I'm bloated, like I'll explode any second. I stand. Laura asks me if I'm interested in watching a movie with them, but I apologize and say no thanks. "I'm so tired from all that shopping," I say, and they both wish me a good night.

Before I leave, I pause. I thank them for allowing me to stay with them.

For sheltering, and feeding me.

I thank them for everything.

"No problem," they both say, again almost at the same time.

I walk back to the room.

My room.

I go into the bathroom, brush my teeth, and wash my face. Avoiding my thoughts as I approach that closet.

Avoiding the demons.

Shelving the hate.

I climb into the soft bed, and turn out the lights.

And, finally, drift away.

Chapter Two

I'm sitting on the couch, it's nearly seven in the evening, and my mother isn't home. Dad isn't home either. My brother, Luke is somewhere in one of the rooms. I'm reading a book, bothering no one.

Then he walks in.

He just pulls me from the couch by my hair, and the book falls to the ground in what seems like slow motion.

He stinks of alcohol. I cry out in pain.

"No! Stop it, you're hurting me"!

I try to resist, but he pushes me roughly to the ground. "You little rat," he screams. Then he kicks me hard in the ribs. I crawl to the corner, and cover my face. He keeps on kicking and kicking. And kicking.

I whine as the breath is forced out of me and my lungs start to collapse.

17

Whine because this is my father.

Whine because I'm just six years old.

Luke rushes in and tries to push him away, but he turns around and punches Luke so hard that it causes him to lose his balance. I hear a sharp crack as Luke hits his head on the floor.

Father pulls me across the floor by my hair again, and throws me next to Luke. I smash my nose on the floor.

"If you move again, or even speak, I'll cut your fucking heads off", he growls through gritted teeth.

He storms out of the house, slamming the door as he leaves. I sob. I howl. It hurts to the point I want to cut my head off to stop the blinding pain.

I'm shaking and sweating.

I can't escape.

I'm trapped in a world full of pain.

Suddenly, I open my eyes. It is pitch dark, and it takes me some seconds to remember that I'm in a luxurious apartment with Laura. It's just a nightmare.

It is a nightmare that was once my everyday reality.

I climb out of bed and go into the bathroom. I stare at myself and I see a familiar pair of dark green eyes. Eyes once bloodshot from weeping. Eyes often surrounded by bruises, fading now. I wash my face. Once. Twice.

"Just a nightmare", I whisper to myself.

I walk back to the bed and fall into its delicious softness.

And the next thing I know, the rays of the sun have become an unexpected guest.

I step into the shower, it's wonderfully hot and I switch it to the rain setting and simply stand under it, naked.

It feels like bliss upon my recently bruised skin, like a caress.

I wash my hair, face and body. Like I've done so many times before, I try to wash the memories away.

I try to wash the violence down the drain, into my past, and away from my present.

The violence I have known my entire life.

And yet, although I try and try, and scrub my skin until it tingles, I can't ever imagine washing it all away.

I step out, and wrap a towel around my hair. I feel the tiniest crumb of comfort from being able to walk in any room naked.

I walk to the closet, put on a cool pair of sweatpants and a black shirt with an Oxford logo on. I dry my hair and let it hang loose. I walk down to the living room and Jacob is sitting on the couch holding a newspaper and a cup of coffee, which smells fantastic.

"Good morning," I say.

"Good morning Eva, did you sleep well"?

I shudder at the thought of the nightmare but I nod yes. I think he notices that I am not exactly being truthful, because he says kindly "I'll be here if you need anything."

"Thank you," I reply. I walk through to the dining room and Laura is there. "Good morning, I wanted to ask you something,' she asks cheerily.

"Sure," I say, and sit down next to her. She pushes some pancakes towards me.

"How did you sleep?" she asks.

"Oh, I had a bad dream in the middle of the night, but other than that everything was wonderful," I reply and start to eat.

Once again, I eat as if I am starving. I make a mental note to myself to try and slow down.

"Want to discuss it?"

"No its alright, I don't want to go there twice. If you don't mind," I say weakly.

"It's okay. Don't worry. I'm always here if you want to talk about anything".

I begin to chew more slowly on the pancakes. They are so good. Laura produces some papers and begins to shuffle through them slowly. She peers up at me from them. I sense she is trying to tell me something.

"Was there anything else?" I ask.

"Well, only to say that Jacob provides great English lessons for students like yourself who come over to the USA to study. So I was wondering if you would ever be interested in studying English again".

"Uh," I begin to blurt.

Instantly, she interrupts me.

"But I would totally understand if you don't want to."

"No. Please. I'd be so grateful. Yes. That would be great."

"Excellent," she replies happily. "Sorry, I must get on with these papers. Enjoy your breakfast," she adds, and leaves the dining room.

"She is so graceful," I think. "Like an elegant cat, the way she walks."

I would love to be that comfortable in my own skin one day.

I pour myself an orange juice, and eat once again without even thinking of anything else, just the food.

In a little while, once I'm finished, both Laura and Jacob call me and they walk me down the street to his car.

We climb in, and they explain that today we are visiting the big city. Chicago! The windy city, as it is often nicknamed. It's so unfamiliar I may as well be going to the moon, but for once, I'm not afraid.

"We're going to show you the place where Jacob works," says Laura.

"You'll love the people, and the place. I guarantee you," Jacob joins in.

"Bet I will," I say happily, staring out of the window, awed by the sheer size of the roads and the numbers of the people traveling in their cars, swarming, working, moving.

Always moving.

It takes fifteen minutes to get through the morning traffic, and we talk and listen to the morning news on the radio until we finally arrive at Jacob's workplace. It is a beautiful, large modern building, with huge windows whose glass reflects the early morning sun like a giant mirror.

I don't like mirrors.

We get in an elevator with two other men wearing suits who nod when they see us. I've never been this close to men wearing suits. They look cool, just like characters in the books I've read. Salesmen. Or gangsters. I'm wondering which when we get to the fifth floor. This is where Jacob's classroom is, and he ushers us into his office, which is off to the side of the teaching area.

There's only two people in there, and I glance at the large clock on the wall It's only eight o'clock, which gives the rest of the students half an hour to get ready for class. One guy is seated, abstractedly gazing out of the window. He must hear us enter, because he turns and says "Hello, Jacob."

Jacob wishes him a good morning, and greets the lady in the corner too. She's wearing a long red skirt, a burgundy blouse, and her hair is done up in a bun. She doesn't answer back.

"She's new, she doesn't understand English too well. Yet," Jacob explains to me, and grins.

"Oh, okay," I nod.

"And this fine fellow is Benjamin."

Jacob introduces me to a tall guy with dark brown hair.

And the most beautiful blue eyes.

They are dark water blue.

A blue you could swim in.

"Hallo." He smiles at me. We shake hands. "Hi there. I'm Eva," I reply feebly. Smile weakly.

I don't know what else to say.

Laura is engaged in conversation with a man I have never seen before, so I stand there awkwardly. I truly don't know what to say, and Benjamin picks up on this and moves away slowly, making some polite excuse about needing to find some more books.

He moves over to a shelf a few meters away.

And I'm feeling angrier and angrier.

Finally, Laura walks over. I start on her immediately.

"Can you please ask Jacob not to introduce me to anyone. I'm not here to make friends," I say, very coldly. I start to pat my lashes in the weird way that I hate. Playing with my hair, twirling it around my index finger.

I hate meeting new people. I absolutely hate it.

"Oh, I see. I'm sorry, Eva. He introduced you Benjamin, yeah? He's a German boy. He really is a lovely guy. It wouldn't do any harm getting to know him," she adds, hopefully.

She walks over to Jacob and starts talking to him softly.

I walk to one of the chairs, right in a far corner, sit down, and hide my face in my arms. I don't know why I'm being like this, I know it's getting better. I know I should be thankful. I know I should show so much more happiness.

But I also know that my father is still alive.

And his last words to me still haunt my every moment.

I still remember what he said.

"I will come back and I will find you. If it takes me a hundred years," he had hissed.

I know he will.

Someone touches my shoulder, and I raise my head so fast that my heart beats violently. My heart just went all the way up to my mouth! For a split second, I think it's my dad. But it's only Benjamin.

I start breathing slower, trying to get my breath back to normal.

"Hey, I'm so sorry for scaring you". He says, in English.

"I thought you were Dutch,' I say.

"No I'm not. I'm German, from Germany". He smiles a dazzling smile.

"I thought they were the same anyway," I say, stupidly. I remember I never did pay enough attention at geography class.

"No, they aren't". He laughs. I laugh weakly. Oh, my. This is getting awkward.

"Oh, okay". I say. "But you know English".

And I'm dying inside and thinking:

"Why did I just say that? Why am I so rude? Of course he does, he already lives in America. I'm so stupid!"

"Yeah, I should do, I've been here for nearly two years."

He sits on the chair next to mine, and I see Laura in the corner of my eye, watching me, but I don't let on.

"That is pretty cool. Do you like it?"

"Oh yes. This country is awesome. What about you? What brought you here"?

"I'm afraid that it's a long story".

"How long?"

"Seventeen years too long."

He laughs. "That is long," he says. "Maybe you will allow me the time to hear it one day."

He smiles and turns around. Perhaps he's wondering when the class will start.

"Maybe, maybe not," I reply.

He turns back and smiles again.

People start entering the class, until it is over half full. I turn and Laura is standing outside the classroom, waving goodbye to me. Just when I went to school as a child, when mothers used to wave all the time to their kids and I wished so badly for a mom who would wave to me or hug me goodbye. Or just kiss me goodbye.

A mom who could make sure I arrived safely at school. A mom that could keep me safe.

A mom who could give me anything

Any scrap of love in an empty world.

Tears gather in my eyes, and I wave goodbye to Laura. They run down my cheek, and I wipe them away quickly and concentrate on Jacob. He seems to notice me, smiles, then turns to the board and starts teaching.

Teaching has always fascinated me. Passing on the power of English.

Handing on the power of precious words.

Showing your love through teaching.

The class finishes, and everyone starts leaving, either alone or with classmates. Benjamin is still sitting, and he turns around and asks me if I'd like to walk out with him, and I say, "sure why not?"

One of the things they are trying to teach me these days is to trust others. So why should I not trust this guy?

We walk out of the class and down the stairs, and he starts telling me that he came to the States because he lost both his parents in Germany. His mom was an American, so he came here to live with relatives and bought his own apartment with the money that his mom left him. He wants to start his own business someday. He asks me about my interests and I shrug. She says, "What's your favorite movie?"

I told him that the last time I saw a movie I was around six years old. It was a film about war.

I didn't go on to explain that even the films I was forced to watch were violent.

"How can a girl of your age not have seen a movie in years?" he asks, laughing.

I can't hide my sadness.

"I told you. It's a long story," I say.

"I'm sorry," he mutters. "I didn't mean,"

I interrupt him.

"My dad didn't allow me to."

"I'm so sorry, I didn't mean to be rude."

"It's alright." I smiled. Sure he didn't know. Of course he didn't know.

"So. Maybe I'll see you tomorrow?"

He beams once more and walks away, waving back to me.

His smile is as bright as the sun.

I smile back, and for once, it is a genuine smile.

I turn around and suddenly remember that I'm here with Jacob, so I run back upstairs to the fifth floor, and when I reach it, I am exhausted. I bend down, trying to breathe.

I am still out of condition. I think it is the hidden legacy of all the beatings.

When I feel better, I find Jacob sitting on his chair, reading papers.

"Hey Eva! Come here." He motions to me and I walk over to him.

"Yeah?"

"Are you alright?"

"Yes, actually. I'm great," I smile.

He grins back. Looks relieved.

"Great. Laura will be here in a few minutes to pick you up. Feel free to go and get a coffee."

I nod and sit on the same chair I was sitting on before. I stare at the signs on the wall, all about loving English, praising English, enjoying English.

I remember when I used to go to school, simply happy that I was away from home. I was happy that the teachers would care for me, almost love me, even. They were always ready to help if I had a problem.

The memory vanished as I remembered the day I went to school barefoot because my dad stole all the shoes that I owned - I only had four pairs - and sold them. I had cried the entire night. I didn't have anything to put on my feet for a whole week, and my teacher kept asking me why, and was anything wrong at home.

I could not speak for shame.

The teacher bought me a new pair of shoes. I hid them under a pile of boxes so my dad wouldn't find them and take them away. Or worse.

Laura rushes in. "Sorry, I had a meeting," she apologizes. I say goodbye and thank you to Jacob, who is still reading his papers, and we leave. "Let's go to the center and talk," says Laura, "and then we can go to wherever you want."

"Why the center?" I ask, trying to hide my fear of the place. I hate it. It reminds me of everything that I went through, and how, when I first arrived there, I was suffering with wounds that hadn't healed. Laura says they will be healed very soon. She says that if I hold on, I will heal soon. I trust her.

"I may as well be honest," she says hurriedly. "You have to go back to answer some more questions about your father."

She turns the engine on.

All my fears are back. Hammered into that big building. Built into every brick in that skyscraper.

It's close to where my dad lives and I don't want him to see me.

I don't want to go back. He'll kill me.

Or I'll kill me.

Chapter Three

We arrive at the center, and the halls are so bright. Stark. There are white walls, with patients sitting alone wearing white or blue gowns, and nurses roam the corridors. I shudder, hiding behind Laura. But to be honest, this place gives me the feeling that there is nowhere left to hide.

We enter a bright room with a big comfortable chair in the middle, one you can easily rest on for a long time. There are a couple of chairs next to it. A man in yet another white coat strolls in. Calm Relaxed.

Inquisitive.

"Hey there, Eva, I'm Doctor Stevenson, " announces a light haired doctor in his forties. He shakes hands with me. I nod.

"Lie down if you would be so kind."

I do as I am told, and he opens a notebook and scans some papers. Laura sits on a chair next to him.

I stare at the ceiling. Willing myself away from this place. Anywhere. But nothing emerges from the slow shadows of my injured mind.

And I just know what is coming.

He speaks softly into some kind of recording device.

"Listening Session Number 2. This is Doctor Stevenson accompanied by psychiatric doctor Laura Allen, and her current patient, Eva."

He looks directly at me.

"Eva, could we start with just a few memories of that unfortunate period of your life? Nothing too complicated. Just let your mind wander and speak when you feel comfortable".

I close my eyes. Hard. Re-open them.

It's like a stream trying to force its way through a small pipe that is blocked somehow.

Maybe it is blocked for self-preservation.

I shake my head, willing the blockage to go.

I look at Laura. I stare at her sad, kind eyes.

And suddenly, it happens. The pipe unblocks and the words flow out.

"I remember when I used to wake up in the morning, and my dad told us not to go to school today. I wouldn't want to go anyway, for many reasons. I didn't have any shoes or any clean clothes to wear. I would walk to the small dirty kitchen, barefoot. Walk to my mother and ask her if there was anything for me to eat. She would just shake her head, or sob into her hands. Helpless.

31

But still she would cook for him, whenever he demanded

I try to open the fridge, the door sticks, and all I can hear is the clicking of bottles. The alcohol he buys, instead of food for his own children. I feel tears rolling down on the sides of my face. My throat starts hurting.

Eventually, he stumbles into the house. He is drunk. Again. He starts yelling at my mom because she hasn't served the food on the table, right there and then. Exactly when he wants it, as if she is some kind of mind reader, and can tell when he's going to show up.

He falls into a chair at the table, and she takes whatever she's cooked and places it in front of him. She stares in silence at the floor, waiting for him to react.

He starts eating. First spoon. Second one. And suddenly, with extreme force, he picks up everything in front of him and throws it at her. The plate smashes on her outstretched arm, as she instinctively tries to shield her face, so he pulls her arm away and hits her flush in the face with a beer bottle. Smashes her nose.

Stunned, she falls to her knees, sobbing and gathering up the broken pieces. I see blood dripping from her nose, a red fountain, mixed with tears. He staggers to his feet to go to his room, singing something incomprehensible.

I start crying because mom is crying. He turns, walks back and stomps on her neck so she will fall into the broken glass. I protest loudly so he comes back to me. I stare at his hand. He is carrying another bottle. I try to sob quietly, so quietly. But his face is close to me now.

"Why are you crying?'. He says it gently, and I think he is being nice to me for the first time.

He isn't. He swings the bottle wide and high.

And smacks me straight in the face with it.

Hard.

I fall to the floor alongside my sobbing, shaking mother. Clutching my bleeding face.

"Sick weak fucks!' he screams, and storms out of the house, slamming the door behind him.

The whole house shakes, and we do too, for a long time. Because we know that he will be back after nightfall.

And that is when he will start doing the other things to us.

"Okay. Okay Eva. That's enough. Thank you," Doctor Stevenson says softly, and I sit up straight. Wipe my tears.

When I look at Laura she's crying quietly.

"That's all for this session, Eva. See you next week, same time, yes?"

I nod my assent, and the doctor leaves. Laura wipes her face quickly and comes towards me. Wraps her arms around me. No one has hugged me since eleventh grade. I hug her back.

No words are necessary.

I stand and almost run out of the office.

"We should leave this place, it's haunting me," I say under my breath and I make for the lobby quickly. I can't wait for Laura. I need air. Clean air. Clean thoughts. I run.

It's so pale outside. The sun is starting to leave like the light is leaving my world once again.

Then I fall to the ground, and sob.

Fuck you Dad. And fuck you Mom.

What a fucking life you led me.

Seconds later I feel Laura's hand on my arm. I stand up and wipe my face.

"Are you alright?"

I nod and walk with her back to the car.

We sit in silence for a while.

"I'm here if you want to talk to me, " she says eventually.

"I know."

She nods. So do I.

Nodding is the only answer I need right now.

Later, the thoughts come again.

I'm cowering under dirty clothes in a dark room overwhelmed by freezing cold and the loud voices.

Fighting voices.

Shattering glass.

Sobs. Begging.

That drunken voice, the one that sends shivers through my body.

Then abruptly, there is the sound of a gun.

A single shot.

I shake. Petrified with fear now. I cannot move.

One of them must have died.

And it is either the drunken evil guy, or the weak, begging helpless mother.

I cannot move. I shrink under the disgusting, rancid clothes I'm hiding in.

Finally, the door slams.

I emerge slowly, fearfully, like a rat, and enter the living room.

A room that now looks like a bombsite.

I crawl slowly to the body.

The blood is pooling under my mother's head.

Tears burn my cheeks, and my throat aches. Sobs escape in the silence. I fall right next to her.

There is a small circle, right in the middle of her forehead.

That fucking monster has killed her.

He's murdered a helpless woman.

A woman he once loved.

I quickly turn away.

Dead as she is, I feel nothing.

All I feel for her - all I have ever felt - is contempt for her betrayal.

I cannot say I ever loved her. She was poor, useless, and weak.

And she never raised a single finger to defend us when he treated us bad.

When he kicked me to sleep.

When he threw every empty bottle he had drained at me.

And when he did the other things. The things she knew about, and never told anyone.

I move mechanically back to the room, like some kind of zombie.

Closing the door on my mothers twisted corpse.

I go back to the vile clothes and throw myself on them.

I shake from the shock. And then the tears begin.

Not for her.

The ghosts of every emotion I ever had rise up and possess me with fear and disgust and loathing. I wrap my own arms around myself in a vain attempt to cease shaking and stop my teeth from chattering.

I want to strangle the memories, and stop my soul shattering into little pieces.

Suddenly I cry out loud. I scream at the horror of what has just happened.

And, just as suddenly, someone is shaking me hard and I awake once more.

My eyes open wide.

Laura is hugging me and I burst into tears and bury my terrified face in her shoulder. I'm crying again, sweaty, full of tears, all fucked up.

Again.

"It's okay" she whispers softly. "I'm here. You're safe."

Jacob enters with a glass of water. He hands it to me, and I drink like a girl who has been in the desert for years.

And in a way, I have.

I've been lost in a desert where the sand hides terrifying memories that could swallow me up at any time.

I drain the glass, pass it back to Jacob, and collapse back on the bed. I close my eyes, completely mortified with embarrassment.

"It's okay," says Laura softly. "Take your time."

I screw up the courage to speak. I have never spoken of this to another living soul.

Then suddenly, words pour out of my mouth.

"I remember! I saw it! He killed her. The bullet went right through her forehead into her brain. I really did see the pool of blood and her mouth open with cuts all over her lips. Some looked fresh but most were old because he slapped her hard all the time. Her eyes were half closed even before she died, with purple bulges around them. She looked just like a boxer that never fought back.

My voice trails off.

"Go on," says Jacob.

"Well, her jaw was obviously broken or something and she looked ugly, like a car crash victim, but I know she wasn't always ugly. I know she was once the prettiest girl in our area because that motherfucker never loved her for herself. He loved her for her beauty. Then, she was like a trophy to him. A jewel. That fucker didn't just kill my mother. He killed her fucking beauty."

I cover my face and begin to sob.

"He ruined our lives. And he ended hers," I stammer through floods of tears.

Laura's places her elegant hand gently on my thigh.

"It's okay now. He's not here and you're staying with us. Forever if you want to. I don't mind"

Her voice cracks, and Jacob continues, softly.

"Eva, believe me, I've been through some tough times too. Not like yours, nowhere near as bad, but I was trapped and I escaped too. And look at me now! I know it is hard, but I want you to try your best to think positive thoughts. They will wipe out your past with their light."

I suddenly realize why Laura likes him.

He goes on.

"Trust me. Shiny new memories will burst like a star in your mind. Just help us lead you into that light."

He comes closer and strokes my hot forehead. Tenderly. Kisses my hair like a real father.

"Now sleep, Eva. Nothing can harm you now. I won't let it."

I sigh. I close my eyes. And I wait until they close the door behind them before sleep steals my tired soul like a thief in the night.

Chapter Four

I open my eyes with a start and I glance at the clock. It's only six thirty. A whole hour until Jacob goes to work, and I go with him. I walk to the bathroom. Do the usual. Wash my face. Brush my teeth. Comb my hair. Stare at my green eyes.

Feel vulgar. Accept the feeling and walk to the closet. Think of wearing something I always wanted to wear, like the other girls at school. Normal girls.

Girls that make me feel worse about myself just by being themselves.

I pull out black skinny jeans and a white crop top and put them on.

I stare at my reflection and, for the first time in my life, I like what I see. The white has made a real difference. My eyes look brighter and my hair looks shinier. I look so much healthier.

I try to smile but it's not that easy.

Someone knocks on the door and I pad to the door in my new pair of black converse. Open it and Laura is there, wearing a long pink dress and a white top. "You're up," she smiles. "I am" I say, and smile back.

We both walk down the stairs to the dining room. I love coming down the stairs, I feel like a princess in a film.

But I am a damaged princess, of a lost and lonely kingdom.

Jacob is finishing eating, and he smiles, nods, and I sit on the same stool as the previous day.

"I didn't think you would attend lessons today," he says.

"Why not?" I say, pouring an orange juice. I don't feel hungry after last night.

"I wasn't sure if you liked having class mates yet," he says kindly.

"Well, I haven't talked to them all, but I like that guy who laughs a lot, what was his name again"?

I feel a little guilty. I already know his name. His smile is a lovely picture behind my sad eyes.

"Oh you mean Ben," he says. "Yeah. That poor guy lost his parents in a terrible accident. I'm surprised he's still studying English to be honest. He was so sad when he came to us."

"Yes," I mutter. "That is terribly sad. I'm sorry about last night, by the way."

Laura shakes her head. "No need to apologize, Eva. I'm so glad we were there for you."

"Well, I'm going to be late, ready Eva?" says Jacob, walking to the door.

I drain the glass quickly and pick up my bags, following Jacob.

"Have a great day. And make new friends," urges Laura.

As I leave, I reflect on how weird it is to actually have the feeling that someone really does care for me. Even though it's Laura's job to care, and record everything about me over the next few months, I still can't get used to it.

I may be leaving her eventually because I'm too fucked up to help, because the nightmares never end, or because the fear and depression makes me slit my own throat.

Either way, I'm grateful.

We arrive at class and I sit in exactly the same chair that I sat in last time. Ben smiles at me and I smile back. He is so nice.

But I daren't become attracted.

"You look pretty today, if you don't mind me saying," he says, trying to start a conversation.

"Thank you," I answer politely, opening my notebook without even glancing up at him.

He doesn't reply, and starts to pay more attention to Jacob, who has started talking about ancient literature, how it began, and who could have been the first writer. I enjoy the lesson, but it also makes me feel like shit when I remember how I dropped out of school in my senior year.

I wasn't supposed to. I once harbored an overwhelming desire to study hard, get my qualifications, and fly away to another country to study something worthwhile like medicine.

I wanted to bring hope to others.

Others like me, who had been abused.

Ben was still trying to make conversation after the lesson had finished, and once everyone had left. He kept asking random questions like:

"Is Jacob your dad?"

"Why didn't you come here from the beginning of the semester?"

"Do you love burgers?"

"Which parent did you inherit your lovely eyes from"?

I laughed when he finally gave up asking and went silent.

"Okay. I'll bite," I said, smiling at him. "Jacob is my psychiatrist's boyfriend. I was in the psychology care unit for three months before Laura took me out so I could engage with the world. And, yes, I do love burgers! I've only eaten them four times before but they totally taste like paradise. And I have my mother's eyes."

With that, my jaw wobbled and my voice trailed off. That final answer has made me sick to the point that my smile faded away and the thought of eating burgers filled with as much dread as eating a live cow.

"I'm so sorry if I made you feel bad," he said, placing his hand on my shoulder.

I shake my head.

"You really do have the most beautiful eyes"

"Thank you," I mumble.

"And you should smile more often."

"I will try, " I reply shyly.

He stands abruptly, as if he's had an idea.

"Hey, listen. There's a new shop down the street that sells the most fantastic ice cream I've ever tasted. Would you like to join me? My treat!"

He winks.

I'm just about to answer when Jacob wanders over.

"I don't think," Jacob interrupts.

I look at him pleadingly.

"Okay then Eva," he says. "You go. I'll be here when you get back."

Ben is already moving. I follow and we walk down the stairs and enter the fresh air outside.

People are everywhere. Walking and laughing, running to work or as lost as a puppy, for all I know. Ben is chattering happily, telling me about the first time he ate ice cream at this place, when he found it, and about his favorite flavors. Then he stops, and looks right at me.

"Tell me more about you," he says.

"There's nothing much to know." I shrug and look ahead.

"Well, I think there is. I think you're very interesting. Remember when you started to tell me about being seventeen?"

"Yeah, I remember," I reply, but think silently that if I tell him the whole truth he may never speak to me again.

"I'm not sure I could," I say weakly.

43

"Well, just start from year one then. We have lots of time." He smiles again, that winning smile.

He's smiling, but he doesn't realize that he's just asked me to describe hell itself.

I freeze. If I tell him the whole truth, he will most likely run as far away from me as he can. Or, even worse, simply pity me.

"I will tell you when I'm ready to," I say, finally, and he nods.

Then he quickly changes the subject.

"Okay. No worries. Hey, on Friday night some friends and I are going to that new club on the end of the block, just down from here, would you like to come?"

He's asked me out on a freaking date?

I don't even know what I'm supposed to say!

"Um, I don't think I can," I tell him and look down at my knotted fingers.

He takes my chin gently in his hands and lifts my face higher so that my eyes meet his. The touch of his warm fingers on my skin is so nice.

"Hey. Don't worry. It's fine," he says softly. "Maybe another day."

He smiles sweetly at me, and we get in the line to order.

I've never been to an ice cream parlor.

I'm kind of excited that I'll finally get the chance to taste ice cream. I used to dream of moments like this in my rat hole.

And just like a kid visiting Disney Land, I start to grin with anticipation.

Benjamin starts to order.

"I'd love strawberry and vanilla, what would you like Eva?"

I shrug. I don't know.

"There's so many to choose from," I say.

He smiles, and mouths "Don't worry."

"She would like a vanilla and chocolate flavor please, " he says.

"I'll bring it right to your table sir," she nods, and we take a table in the corner.

This place is as colorful as anything I've ever seen. There's no black. It's like a kaleidoscope of fun. I relax.

We sit down, and he sits in front of me, pulls out his phone and places it on the table. I suddenly realize that I don't actually have a phone.

I've never had the chance to hold one.

I smile shyly at him. His eyes are shining, and so beautiful. Again, I calm myself.

How can I have feelings for him? I only just met him.

"I've never tasted an ice-cream, " I say, shaking my head and going red with embarrassment.

His eyes widen with surprise.

"What, not even as a child?"

"Nope."

Especially not as a child, I think, but I giggle anyway.

He stands, and with a flourish, performs a mock bow, just like a waiter.

"Well, madam, I'm so honored that I am the first person ever to buy you an ice-cream. My life is now complete."

I start to laugh. He looks so funny.

I haven't laughed like this in a long time.

He sits, smiling. Long eyelashes. Lips curved seductively.

Everything about his face is kind and beautiful.

Moments later the vendor brings the ice-cream bowls and places them in front of us. She gives us one yellow spoon each. I love it here! Everything about this place is cheerful.

"Okay then," says Benjamin. "Do me a huge favor. Close your eyes and taste it, then tell me what it's like to taste ice cream for the very first time."

I take a full spoon full of vanilla and raise it slowly to my lips.

I feel an instant moment of freezing cold, then a rush of fabulous, intense sweetness.

"It's perfect," I say, and he smiles with relief.

"It's delicious, yes?"

"Oh yes,' I say, and silently think that it's so good, and so pure.

Like everything I've been missing for so many years.

"I'm not sure there is a word to describe it," I say, my eyes widening. In an instant, he raises his phone and I hear the camera capture sound.

Defensively, I furrow my brows.

"Why did you take a picture of me?" I mutter.

"Because you looked so happy just then," he replies. "I can delete it if you want though."

"It's okay. It's fine," I say, looking down at the table.

"I'd love to keep it. If that's okay with you?' he adds, embarrassed.

'Why?" I ask him, genuinely puzzled that anyone would want a photo of me.

"Because every time I look at it, your happiness will make me happy too."

That's such a beautiful answer. I make a mental note to try and remember this moment.

No one has ever taken a picture of me.

There are a lot of things in life that I haven't experienced and I'm experiencing them all the time now time I'm with Laura, Jacob, and now Ben.

I smile. For once, it's a real smile.

"Oh shit. Jacob!" I say loudly. I had literally forgotten, and it's probably been an hour since we left him. I'm so scared that he will get angry. "I'm sorry, Ben, I'm late for Jacob" I blurt out, standing. Ben's spoon is mid-way to his mouth, but he nods, puts it down, leaves money on the table for the vendor and we walk quickly out of the shop.

"He'll be so mad" I say.

"No he won't. Don't worry, I'll talk to him, and besides Jacob is quite possibly the nicest guy I've ever met since I came to the States," he says, reassuringly.

"Well yeah. He is very nice," I murmur.

But I still speed up.

We make it to the building, climb the stairs two steps at a time. I'm thankful that I don't stumble and fall in front of Ben, and even more thankful as I see that Jacob is still in the room, working on his laptop.

I stand still. Silent. Motionless.

Terrified that he will be angry with me. That he had something important to do at home, while I've been eating ice-cream with this hot new guy.

I feel Benjamin's hands on my shoulders, and I shudder and he takes them off me. Fast. I stand still until Jacob looks up, smiles and waves at me. He takes his earphones out.

"Want to go back home or stay some more?" he asks, rather sweetly.

I look at Benjamin and he is watching me carefully, his blue eyes still and sparkling.

I am so relieved!

"Can we stay a little longer, Jacob?" I reply, with the most innocent smile.

"You can stay as long as you want to," Jacob says, "I have plenty of preparation to do here, so just come back and see me when you are ready to go home".

Home. That's such a lovely word. I suddenly feel so much happiness that Jacob is in my life, and I can't quite believe that he is being so nice to me.

"Well, now what?" Benjamin asks as we walk back down stairs. I shrug nervously, twice. It's like I have something wrong with me. I think it's the adrenalin from being so scared.

Until Ben places his hands on my shoulders to hold them still, and we're standing in total silence. Some people would find this awkward but I don't.

It's comforting and amazing.

I look into his eyes for reassurance. He nods, and then we sit on a low wall at the bottom of the stairs. There is no one else around.

"Tell me why you were so frightened," he whispers softly.

I let it all out.

"When I was only six years old, my father was so insane with drink and anger that he would get mentally and physically abusive. We would be sitting on our old couch watching an ugly old TV and he would just crash into the house, crazy drunk and yelling at us or my mom for literally any reason."

I pause, gasping for breath. Apart from Laura and Jacob, no one knows this stuff.

"Go on," says Ben. He takes my hand gently.

49

"Well, the first time he ever yelled at me he was so drunk and he smelled like dead animals, or worse. He got right into my face until I could not breathe for the stench of him, and I thought my lungs would collapse. But he never noticed my pain, just kept on yelling and yelling, curses that I didn't understand because I was way too young.

I remember he used the word 'bitch' a lot.

I stop again, looking at the floor. My lips are trembling.

"It's okay," said Ben softly. "Let it all out."

I look back up at him.

"So, when he finished yelling, he would just spit at me and walk to his room, or storm right out of the house."

I don't tell Ben the whole truth. Not yet.

He really would be shocked if he knew more.

But he just squeezes my hand.

"I'm so sorry about that. He really does sound like a first class douche bag. How could anyone do that to a child?"

His tone is angry, and his eyes connect to mine. It's a powerful connection, like electricity. I like it. Then, his indignation at what he just heard turns slowly to sadness.

What I've told him is nothing compared to the whole truth.

He is still looking at me with such tenderness, and now I see pity in his eyes, and I don't want anyone's pity because I'm better now that I'm away from that monster.

"If you want to know the rest of my story, promise me not to feel sorry for me. I don't need your pity, honestly," I say, as nicely as I can.

He nods, and we leave the building and walk some more until we find a chair under the forgiving shade of a large, old tree. I sit and he sits next to me.

I can feel him wanting more, either to get closer to me, which I don't think he would want to if he knew the whole truth, or just to talk.

I know he wants to tell me something about himself.

I gaze at him and smile. I want his smile back.

"Well, I guess my life wasn't as terrible as yours, but I was bullied at school for years. I was the fat and ugly kid, the one with horrible, decayed teeth. They used to call me hässlichefett, which is German for ugly fatty. I couldn't help the way I was. It wasn't my fault."

His voice trails off. He is almost in tears at the memory. Then he flashes that brilliant smile again, and his teeth look as perfect as those of a model. They are so perfect they remind me of Laura' dazzling smile.

Now it's my turn to understand, so I angle my head towards him and take his hand.

"Well, you sure do look great now," I say. "How did you get over it all?"

"It wasn't easy, but I lost a great deal of weight when I went to high school, and got braces for a year which helped to fix my crooked teeth. My looks improved so much that I actually got to date a girl in my senior year!But she turned out not to be so nice. Have you ever dated anyone?" he asks, gently.

His question surprises and pains me. No. I've never dated anyone. But I've been in love. I've never dated anyone, but I've been hurt.

I've never dated anyone, but I know what it is to be heartbroken.

"No, I've never dated anyone" I shake my head in denial, and that's true.

I have never dated anyone in my life.

"You said something about a club," I say, trying to change the subject.

"Yes, what about it, you interested?"

"Of course. The trouble is, I'm only eighteen."

"You are?" he says, and I nod. "Well, no worries, we can always go somewhere else. We could go and watch a movie," he says then stutters.

"Not on a date, you understand. Just as friends," he says quickly.

Yeah, right, I muse silently.

I wouldn't date me too.

"Can I think about it? " I look at him quizzically, and he smiles. I love his smile. I love his eyes. And it is weird because I don't know him that well. It is weird because we're almost strangers.

Weird because I already feel better when I'm with him.

He is the kind of guy who can make any girl fall in love with him with a wink.

He is my kind of guy.

There is an awkward silence.

I change the subject completely.

"What was it like where you grew up?" I ask.

"Oh, small, and quiet. Most of the people in my city are older so it's quite boring. What about yours?"

"Oh, it was nothing like that. I wish! Mine was ugly, you know the scary neighborhood you'd freak if you had to go out at night because it's way too dark and people are drunk on every corner. Most people were homeless. They wouldn't care if you got beaten or worse, because they were so fucked up in their own way. It wasn't cool." I shake my head and giggle nervously at the memory.

"Oh, hey, here comes Jacob." He points to the building and I see Jacob standing there, looking around.

"Yup, looks like it's time to go home," I say, standing and walking towards the building.

I don't move too quickly - I don't want to seem like a little kid.

We get to Jacob, and Benjamin says he'll see me tomorrow. As he walks away, I know I'm going to miss him already.

"Okay. Ready to go back home?" Jacob asks.

"Yep." I love thinking about the fact that I now have a new home.

And I really love knowing that I have a loving home.

"Did you have fun?" asks Jacob as we walk back to the car.

"Yes. I really did."

"Do you like him?"

"I guess so."

I look away, embarrassed.

"Sorry Eva, I don't mean to pry. Even though I know he is a great guy I've never seen him take such an interest in a girl before."

"Are you trying to protect me?" I say, and giggle.

"Something like that,' he says, smiling to himself.

"Well I don't mind," I say.

It's good to feel safe.

The entire way back Jacob talks on his phone with several people, all related to work. I gaze at the afternoon traffic, thinking of Benjamin's invite to watch a movie with him. I like him. I think I may have fallen for him already. But I don't know if I'm strong enough. I don't know if I am able to give myself to any boy just yet.

Emotionally, I can't afford to get hurt. Not like before.

We finally arrive at the apartment and Jacob is still talking on the phone. I grab my bag, and his, and head into the elevator.

When we get in, Laura is sitting at the kitchen table studying some papers.

"Hello honey," she says, and wraps one arm around me as I lean into her. She squeezes tightly.

"Alright, enough already" I smile, playfully pushing her away.

"How's your day? I see you guys are an hour late." She glances at her watch.

I shrug and sit next to her.

"Was the traffic bad?" she says, smiling a little.

"No, I gave Eva time to make a new friend," says Jacob, smiling.

"Oh. Really?" Laura smiles, and I know she is going to tease me, so I decide to tell her before she starts. I give Jacob a 'thank-you-for-opening-that line of enquiry" look. He just laughs.

"Well, yeah, I got to know this German guy you told me about a little better. I actually sat with him for an entire two hours. He was fun," I say, pulling the bowl of fruit towards me.

"And?" she says, raising her perfectly shaped eyebrows a little.

"Nothing that interesting!" I giggle. "He just told me about himself and I tried to tell him about my amazing life so far."

She laughs at my sarcasm, and waves her hand at me to continue.

"But you know, even though I was afraid he'd leave me as soon as I told him some things about my past, he didn't. He's really quite sweet."

I give her the goofiest smile I can manage.

Laura takes my face in both her hands.

"Well, I think that's just perfect. Well done. I'm so proud of you, Eva."

Then she plants a huge kiss in the middle of my forehead.

"Okay, people, dinner will be ready in ten minutes." She directs it to me as Jacob is still deep in phone conversation. I would love to know what he is talking about, but I remember what curiosity did to the cat.

I walk back to the room that is now mine. And as soon as I enter I throw myself on the bed, and cover my face as the power of love hits me, possibly for the first time.

And I am suddenly so thankful for the beautiful things that have already happened since Laura took me in.

I'm thankful for her love.

I'm thankful for Jacob's protection.

I'm thankful that I have finally started to live.

I turn my face to the window and the sunset goes from yellow to pink to blue. Finally, there is beauty in my life, and by recognizing that, I am learning to see all the beauty that surrounds me everyday.

I stand, walk to the big glass door, and gently push it open. I step out on to the balcony, and it's pretty huge. I love everything about this place! My hair flies like gossamer on the breeze and I remember the day I first went to the shelter and ran into Laura. My long hair was just a horrible mess, covering my face, and my filthy clothes were covered with dirt. I was in the worst condition a girl could ever be. And the first thing she ever told me was that she would take care of me, and be my friend, as well as my, doctor for as long as it took for me to get better.

At first I was too afraid to even talk to her. A part of me feared that if I told her anything personal, she would call child services, and they would immediately arrest my dad for all the terrible things he had done to me. And for the things he did to my mother. Don't get me wrong, I want him arrested, but I know he would hunt me down like a dog and kill me.

That wasthe exact phrase he used after he had done bad things to me, to keep me quiet.

But I refuse to let him spoil this moment.

So I hold my hands out wide, forget the bad memories, and embrace the setting sun.

After dinner, I change into something more comfy for bed, and climb under the covers. I am about to drift away when Laura enters quietly.

"Jacob wanted to give you something," she says, sitting next to me on the bed. "And I agreed, because you badly deserve the best of everything. We want to give you this."

She hands me a small box, beautifully wrapped with white gift ribbons, and I open it carefully. It is a smart phone, the same model that Benjamin took a picture of me with. This is a freaking perfect gift, but I instantly feel guilty.

"This is too much, Laura. I can't take it," I say, trying to give it back.

"No, not at all, it's one of mine, I hope you can use it. I'm not particularly good on this model, but Jacob will teach you how to use it. It's practically new."

I am lost for words. I don't know what to say.

She flashes her beautiful, wide smile.

"Eva, please take it. I want you to be the amazing daughter that I never had. I want you to have the best life that anyone could ever have." She strokes my cheek and stands up.

"I will see you in the morning. Jacob will show you how it works at breakfast."

She turns to leave, but I call her back.

"Laura?"

"Yeah?"

"Thank you so much."

"It's nothing. Honestly, " she says, shaking her head.

"Before you go, can I tell you something?"

"Sure."

"Remember that guy at school? Benjamin?" I say, hesitantly.

"Yes, what about him?"

"Well, he's kind of asked me out twice. The first time he invited me to go to a night club with some of his friends, but I told him I'm only eighteen so he suggested that we could go watch a movie instead?"

I look down at my hands, waiting for the refusal.

"Well, this is marvelous!" yells Laura in surprise. She grins and claps her hands with glee.

"I'm sorry," she says, I was hoping he would ask you out I think you really suit each other".

"I still didn't say yes," I tell her.

"Oh, you should say yes!" She is so excited! It is kind of infectious.

"Mmm, I don't know."

"Please say yes! I insist!"

I just shrug and give her a big smile.

"Fine, don't worry, we'll talk about it in the morning. I'm so proud that you made a friend, and who knows? Maybe someone more important than that!" She giggles happily and leaves, closing the door behind her.

I place the phone carefully on the table and get back under the warm cover. I want to say yes. I want to say yes so badly. I want to go out and watch a movie. I want to have dinner with him because I think he can make me happy. I want a lot more, and all of it with him.

But I don't want to be left alone again.

I don't want to be hurt.

I just want to feel life. Love. Beautiful times.

I drift into sleep, and his beautiful eyes smile into my mind.

Chapter Five

I open my eyes and I am in a place that looks like a basement, or an attic. I can't tell, but there's no furniture. Nothing. It's empty. Cold. Dead.

It's loathsome. I feel like spewing my empty stomach out. I try to stand but I can't feel my feet. I think they're broken. I crawl to the wall and I know someone peed here because it smells so bad of urine. And worse.

I back off and start screaming for help but no one answers. So I just sit huddled in the corner, in the smell and the dirt. I hate my life. I hug my knees and hide my face between them. I wonder what happened to my mother. What happened to Luke?

And what will happen to me.

I sit there in silence. I can't manage any more tears. I've cried enough in the past few years trying to survive the misery. I guess no one can ever survive it. My mother sure didn't.

I hear the lock being turned and I stand up. A big muscular man with dirty blonde hair and a bruised face strolls in.

I take a deep breath and stare at him. I feel my eyes widen and I can hear my own heart beat. I know I look scared, and something tells me that looking scared will make him worse.

I know that acting like a pussy won't save me. I know if I utter just one word that he doesn't like he could decide to kill me. I actually want myself dead, but I daren't say it. My tongue is frozen with fear.

"I hear you're a little virgin," he spits. His voice is hoarse. I shudder at the last word.

"A fresh, tight little virgin."

"Who are you?" My voice fails me. "Please don't hurt me." Tears sting my vision, and my throat aches so badly. I want to yell. Scream. Cut him down, but instead I just shake my head at him.

"That's none of your business, you slut" he says, and moves closer to me. He grabs my hair and pulls my face towards him. His breath stinks.

"I'll cut your fucking tongue out if you ask any more damn questions."

He licks my ear with his stinking tongue. My tears are burning my cheeks. I don't protest or even fight him. I just give up on everything that is going to happen to this little girl.

I am eleven years old.

And I know that I am going to be abused, and treated like a worthless piece of shit.

He pulls me all the way up the stairs by my hair, and for a second I feel like he is scalping me. He throws me hard into a room with a large bed and a sink, and nothing else. I crawl on the floor and hug my legs to my chest.

"Take off your disgusting clothes. There's something new in that sink."

He stands there staring at me. I don't move. I hate him as much as I hate that fucker that gave me to him.

I try to stand but I fall. I try again, and this time he slaps me across the face.

"Hurry. We haven't got all day,' he curses.

I stumble to the sink, terrified, my face ringing with pain. What is he going to do to me? I take my shirt off and my oversized pants. Whatever this is, at least it will be cleaner than what I have on. I dress, and it feels so soft against my skin, but it's not at all suitable for my age. It's some kind of very short, see through dress, not covering my legs at all. My skinny legs are exposed and my breasts are showing. I hate it how I have such big curves and I'm not even a proper teenager yet.

I turn around and he is lying on the bed.

"Are you coming or should I come and help you," he growls.

I don't want him. Not like this. I pray silently.

"Please, God please take my soul away."

"I said are you coming, bitch, or do I have to drag you here." I walk towards him, ashamed that he can see my nakedness under this thin outfit. I hate it. I hate him.

"Very nice," he murmurs lasciviously, "turn around so I can see all of you."

I do as I am told, and turn my back on him. Suddenly, swiftly, he is behind me. He bites my ear again.

"Yes. I love fresh meat," he whispers.

I shut my eyes hard, as hard as I can. I am frozen with fear. I think I will pee myself.

He starts to touch me all over, his rough, wrinkled hands exploring my pale young skin. I start to cry as he lifts the dress above my breasts and his strong fingers squeeze my flesh.

I start to sob and he turns me around and slaps me hard.

"Shut up, you slut. Shut up and take it."

He throws me forcefully on the bed.

Tears the dress off me.

So I shut up.

And I take it.

I wake up and sweat is running from me like a river. My heart is racing.

And then, once again, I realize that I am in the big beautiful bed. I am safe in Laura's apartment.

The nightmare is over.

I get up, change and wash and after breakfast, we leave and I spend one more day in class with Jacob.

No Ben.

He hasn't showed.

It becomes a very long day without him.

On the way home, stuck in Chicago's evening traffic, I'm wondering why Ben didn't come to class today. Is it because of what I told him? Or am I being negative again?

The memory of the big dirty blonde man and the unspeakable things he did to me is clouding my brain again. I showered in the middle of the night, but I couldn't wash away that memory. Because of him, once again, I haven't paid any attention in class. I hate myself for doing this.

The entire drive back, my thoughts are about Benjamin. Was he cool with everything, or has he decided to ditch me already? If he has, is it about me, or is it something wrong with his own family? Is it his life, not mine? Is it, is it, is it?

The questions are driving me insane so I close my eyes and try to think of something happy like his eyes, or his smile. But the dirty blonde man pulls me back into my own prison with his strong, cruel, filthy hands. The prison I fear the most.

My past.

I'm suffocating. Tears well in my eyes again. I want to get out of the car.

And I want crawl into some distant hole for the rest of my life.

Jacob, who has been quiet throughout the whole journey back, suddenly turns to me. He notices my tears.

"Eva," he says, "what's wrong?"

He sounds quite worried.

We are seconds away from the apartment, but I can't bear the memories anymore, so I just cry. Snivel. Sob. Hold my hair tight.

Bang my head hard on the dashboard.

I need to shout and let it all out of me. Laura told me crying might help, but right here and now, it's not helping me.

So I scream. Just scream.

Seconds later the car skids noisily into its parking slot, the door opens and strong arms carry me out of the vehicle.

They are gentle arms, not filthy ones.

They are Jacob's arms.

I hear him yelling something,

And then I black out.

The next voice I hear is Laura's, but everything is dark.

"She'll work it out. I believe in her, " she says softly.

My eyes open slowly and I can see Jacob, Laura and another woman in her mid-thirties.

"Hey, you're back," smiles Jacob. I don't remember much after the car, but I do know I have had a shot in my arm, as it throbs a little. I've felt it before.

And I know that something has happened because I am in my pajamas.

"Do you know what happened, Eva?" Laura asks.

I shake my head and shrug at the same time. I really have no idea.

"Did I have a fit or something?" I croak. My mouth is very dry, like I've been in the desert for a while.

"Not exactly. We had to call the doctor. She gave you an injection to calm you down"

"What was it?" I ask, concerned.

"Benzodiazepine," says the lady doctor, with a sad look in her eyes.

I nod in understanding. Yes. I've had it before.

She nods. And she knows. She will have seen my records before giving me anything.

"Well, have a little rest now, and we'll be here if you need anything more. Just call my name honey," says Laura.

"Jacob? " I say before he leaves the room, I need to ask him about Ben.

"Yeah? What is it Eva?"

The women leave. It's just me, and him.

"Thank you so much for helping me out of the car," I stammer.

"It's no problem. Really. Anything else?"

It's almost like he knows. I do like Jacob. He is such a kind man.

"Yes, did you know why Ben didn't attend class today?"

I feel a little foolish, but it is out there now.

"I mean it's kind of weird, " I add, trying not to sound too interested in Ben, but Jacob just smiles and shakes his head.

"No worries. I'll try to find out what's going on with him." He winks at me.

I smile and mouth thank you to him, and he blows me a kiss and closes the door behind him.

I try to remember what actually happened but I can't. All I remember is that I freaked out, and then it all went black. This always frustrates me. My memories are so bad they shut my brain down like a computer being put to sleep.

Maybe it's a good thing. Maybe I don't really want to remember.

I want to get out of bed but my head feels too heavy, so I grab the book I'm reading and take myself away to another world.

Time goes by really quickly while I read and I don't realize that it's already nine in the evening. I'm really thirsty after the injection, and Laura goes to bed at that time, so I sneak quietly out of bed and go downstairs. I am surprised to see Jacob sitting there, quietly, working on his laptop. He is under a spotlight that just surrounds him.

"Hey," I say, and sit next him.

"Hi Eva, are you feeling any better?" He clears his throat and takes off his glasses. He looks stressed out.

"Much better," I say.

"Well, I went to the office and got Benjamin's number for you, even though it's against the rules. As you know, we are not supposed to give away student numbers, but I just want you to be happy. No more panic attacks, I hope." He tries to smile but looks serious. I shake my head.

"Honestly, I'm fine," I say, aiming to reassure him. He smiles.

"I hope you don't mind, but you are becoming like a daughter to me," he adds.

Then he passes me a piece of paper with a cell number on it.

"Thank you so much, that is so sweet of you" I say. "And I don't mind that you feel like that. It's so nice to be cared for."

I go back to my room as Jacob has more work to do, and as it's not too late in the evening, I just dial Benjamin's number and hope for a response. It just keeps ringing, then goes to voice mail. It's a huge step, but I dial again and, finally, he answers. The voice is deep and hoarse, and sounds tired.

"Who's that?" he says. He sounds irritated.

"Hey, um, it's uh Eva" I tell him, and for some reason I shrug apologetically, even though I know he is not watching me.

"Eva from English class?" He sounds surprised. No wonder. He never gave me his number.

"Yep, that's me," I say, trying to sound relaxed.

"Hey, Eva, what's going on?"

"Well I was going to ask you the same question, since you didn't appear today, " I joke.

"Right, I see. I didn't think you'd notice I wasn't there!" I can feel him smiling down the phone.

"Oh really? That would be difficult seeing as you sit right next to me." I roll my eyes as if he is there

"Yeah, I'm sorry, the truth is I've just moved to a bigger apartment so I haven't slept much. Actually, I thought of taking a couple days off."

"You won't be there tomorrow then?" I ask, trying not to sound too desperate.

"Yeah. I mean, no. No, I won't be there. Sorry."

I clear my throat.

"Oh, that's too bad. I just wanted to see if we were still cool for Friday night.

"Ah right, the movie?"

"Yep."

"Cool! I can't wait. You just made my day," he says and sounds genuinely happy.

His voice makes me want to talk to him all night.

And we do talk for ages, until my head is way too heavy and I drift away, just listening to while he tells me all about his move. He tells me about his roommate, who is called Aiden, and his new apartment, and stupid things. Like the fact that, when he first moved to America, he didn't understand English, so he just signed to people, like a deaf, mute person. For weeks, everyone thought he really was deaf, or mute, or both. I laugh, picturing his comical smile and him goofing around. He laughs too. He says that the way I laugh is making him laugh.

It's a first for me just to talk to anyone for this length of time, and I enjoy every second of it. He really is a kind and funny guy. I feel badly tired, but I don't want to hang up.

"Then don't," he says.

"Well, I went through some kind of panic attack today, and they had to give me a lot of drugs to sedate me. They are kind of kicking in on me now," I sigh.

"Hey, I didn't realize that I was so boring," he jokes, and I laugh again.

"Are you in bed?" he asks.

"Yeah," I whisper.

"Well, listen Eva. Before you fall asleep on me, I want you to know that I'm there for you anytime you want to call. Have a rest now and I'll try my best to see you tomorrow. Okay?

"Yeah, that would be great," I say.

"And if I can't make it, I will at least call you back and let you know. Is that okay?" His voice sounds so tender that my heart skips a beat.

"Yeah. Totally. Totally fine," I mutter, taken aback by my feelings for this handsome stranger that I've only just met. "Okay. Good night Ben. And thanks for listening."

I don't want to hang up, but my eyes are so heavy.

"Good night then babe" he whispers, and I want to shout with joy at that. I bite my lip instead.

I hang up the phone and there's a feeling in my stomach that I've never really felt before. I don't really know how to deal with this, but I think that I'm falling for him. Really.

Falling for a guy who is way out of my league.

Dark midnight thoughts start to intrude like an unwelcome guest, but I try to push them away and try to will myself to sleep. Can a girl fall in love by just talking to someone for a long time? By goofing around?

Maybe, just maybe, this girl can.

Chapter Six

I'm being moved or carried. I feel it. I know that I'm not in Laura's, but sometime in the morning, I got up for the bathroom and then fell to the floor as my brain blacked out again. My eyes seem glued together, and I can't seem to open them. I can hear Laura and Jacob but my mouth feels like it is sealed shut, and I can't reply.

"Okay, whatever we gave her last night made it worse," Laura is saying. "But let her rest and she can wake up whenever she feels like waking up." Doesn't she know I am awake? What is going on?

"Okay, I'll go without her today" Jacob says. Oh my, he is going to the class and I need to go with him. Ben said he'd try to show up, especially for me. I will my eyes to open but it's too hard. I try to move but my body feels like there's a rock on top of it. I can't do anything right now. I'm helpless.

I can't even cry, and yet I feel myself full of tears.

I left school because some guy decided to buy me from my father. I can't live my life the way girls at my age live it and it is slowly breaking me.

When I open my eyes it's noon, and I'm in the living room on a couch. Everything seems to be working again - my eyes, my legs, or my mouth. No one is here, and I'm alone. They probably haven't come back from work yet. I feel nasty so I go upstairs to shower before dinner.

Once I'm clean again they still haven't arrived, I have no idea what to do so I just grab a bottle of water and go to the main balcony. It's even bigger than the one in my room. I see people walking, driving, or meeting up for coffee or a dinner.

From here they look like ants. The breeze is cool and comforting. I'd say I'm at my most peaceful right in moments like these.

I have learned from experience that when times are bad they eventually turn around and become almost better. I have slept for almost a whole day, and it may have changed my perspective a little, but not entirely. I still remember how it was and how it used to be. And I know that the only reason I'm here is that they finally got my murdering father arrested.

I still suffer from paranoia. One of my biggest fears is that my dad is still out there. Still looking for me.

And whenever feel this way, I remember how used to treat me. Just like yesterday.

The way he kicked my ribcage. The hard, sharp punches. The slaps.

The way he used to pull me across an entire room by my hair.

But the memories of the other man are even worse.

73

The man my father sold me to after he killed my mother.

Who handcuffed me in a cold empty room so that I couldn't escape the terrible power he had over my body and soul.

The monster tortured me beyond belief.

He burned me with cigarettes, beat me every day with a belt, and abused me for filthy gratification.

A rapist.

Who abused and degraded me endlessly.

Intolerable. Insufferable.

Unforgettable.

"Oh look who's here!" Laura interrupts my train of negative thoughts.

"Hey Laura. You're home!"

"How do you feel now sweetie," she says, moving a strand of hair away from my face and placing it behind my ear

"I'm good. I think the injection is starting to wear off."

"I was so worried about you. I kept on calling you," she says, apologetically.

"Oh really, I'm so sorry, I never checked my phone. I showered and drank plenty of water like the doctor said the last time this happened. I thought it would make my brain lighter, but it's not working."

Laura laughs, and I laugh too.

"Alright. Okay, so we bought burgers for dinner, and Jacob has something to tell you." She pulls me gently inside.

We walk back inside and Jacob is already eating.

"Hey you could've waited for us" Laura chides him. I giggle.

As we enjoy the meal, I remember today is what we call a 'professional' day, where I have tell her more about myself in her official capacity as a psychiatric doctor. It's kind of weird, but she says it will help so I can't really say no.

"Eva are you going out with Ben tomorrow?" Jacob asked.

"Yeah, I guess so" I frown. I didn't know Laura had told him about it.

"Well, he's a good guy, I know that. But remember to take things steady."

He gives me such a loving look of total protection.

It's such a strange feeling to be cared for like this, and I look at them sitting there, holding hands and gazing at each other adoringly, and hope that I too will know that kind of love.

The kind of love they share.

It is a special kind of love.

One day.

"Great, let's watch some TV," says Jacob, but I pull a funny face because I know Laura will have to call me upstairs now for therapy.

"Can you give me a few more minutes, Eva? Just go in my office and make yourself comfortable," she says, and I nod.

"Aw, just me for TV then," sighs Jacob. "Guess I'll watch the sport!"

"Yeah, that's a shame, what a sacrifice," I joke at him, rolling my eyes.

I wait for Laura in her office. I've never been in this room. Pictures everywhere. Pictures in fancy frames, all matching gold colors.

There are different people in them, posing with her. There is one of Laura with an old man, one with Jacob, and another with two other women. One of those women is very old. Jacob and Laura. There are other pictures of Laura with a couple of cute kids.

I love the way she surrounds herself with pictures of the people in her life. In my opinion, people keep them to remind themselves of the good times. It's as if the camera records those moments of happiness and then freezes them in paper. I'd love to have my own house one day, with pictures of great moments in my life.

Frozen happiness everywhere.

It would be so great to be happy forever, but I am not sure it is possible.

"Those are pictures of my dad." Laura comes in and points to the picture of the older man. "He got lung cancer when I was twenty six, and passed away shortly after his diagnosis. He only lasted a month after they told him it was terminal."

"I'm so sorry," I stammer. I don't know what to say.

"Ah, well, he was very old and in so much pain, so it was a blessing at the end. But it was incredibly painful to watch a once physically powerful man become so weak."

She puts on her glasses and looks down at her papers. I think she is hiding her tears.

I feel guilty because, every time my father abused me I wished him dead from cancer.

"Oh I'm sorry," is all I manage to say.

"Yeah. He was one of the good guys," she says then moves on. Picks up her notepad and pen. "So, what would you like to talk about tonight, Eva?" she says.

"Oh, I thought you're going to tell me," I answer.

"Okay, let's talk about your nightmares. You're in so much pain and discomfort at night" she says, and I try to remember.

"The dreams really began when he killed my mother," I begin.

Sometimes, I cannot believe I am uttering the words.

"Yes, after she died, my dad sold me to that disgusting pervert. He used to just chain me up a tiny, damp, dark room that was always locked. The only time I would see him, apart from when he shoved food and water through a hole in the door, was when he would do bad things to me. Like that time I was handcuffed to a pipe in total darkness. He woke me from a fitful sleep by crashing into the room and belting me so hard that my naked breasts bled."

The memory of his studded belt on my nipples brings me out in a cold sweat right now. It is exactly like he is here, in the room, right now.

"It's okay, Eva. Let it all out," says Laura.

"I'm afraid that's easier said than done," I whine, showing her my outstretched hand. It is trembling.

"Go on. I promise, these talks will help you," she says.

I nod.

"Okay. So. When he hears me cry, it just excites him. He beats me more and more and more until I stop. Until I make no sound at all. Until I am completely still. Broken. Then he lays his filthy lips on me. Everywhere.

He licks me with his rough, disgusting tongue, all over my face. Neck. All down my body, and all over my private places. Then he just gets in those private places, all of them.

He just gets in me like a fucking monster."

I start to shudder and sob loudly and Laura is shedding a tear too, but I don't want to stop talking because I need her to know.

"Whenever he rapes me and tears me up inside, he steals yet another part of me that I think is mine. As he is doing it to me, I often black out, but he doesn't allow that. He just slaps my face hard until I wake up. "Look me in the in the eyes, you little bitch," he says, so I have to fix my gaze on him as he pierces me over and over. Nowhere is private to me anymore. No piece of my body is off limits to him. He enters and degrades every single part of me."

I think that even Laura, with all her experience in psychology, has never heard anything as bad as this. She struggles to keep her composure, but I can tell she is disturbed by my words.

"How on earth did you cope with that?" she stammers. "Looking him in the eye while he committed these...these atrocities?"

"I just went away," I reply. "I became an expert in gazing at him, but actually going away. Somewhere else, any place in my imagination that could take me away from his horrible stare."

"What kind of places?" she asks.

"Well, that bit wasn't easy, a there had been so few in my life up to that point. Like going to school and learning English. Or into the stories in the books I had read. I could be Robinson Crusoe on a faraway beach. Or Kathy, high on the English moors in Wuthering Heights. Anywhere away from the monster that left me with no food, often for up to three days, locked in like I was some kind of animal. Starving me. Making me feel pain in every part of me, from starvation, from being whipped by his belt, from mindless torture. Pain from being raped everywhere. I was in so much terror. It was truly unbearable."

I feel my tears stinging my face.

"Stop, now" Laura says, and wraps her arms around me really tight. I hug her back just as tightly. I clink to her like a girl drowning in a sea of terrible memories. We stand there for a while, me crying, her crying. I hear a footfall and turn to see Jacob standing behind us, so I pull away and see that Jacob too is in tears.

"I'm so sorry, I didn't mean to listen but I did and I'm so sorry. You know that we love you and cherish you, right?" Jacob came over and hugged me too. And I let him.

Which is some kind of progress. He is the first man that I have allowed to hug me properly. I forgive him, because I like him, and, judging by his evident distress, he's obviously never heard from a rape victim before.

Why would he? Many of us never tell.

We certainly never speak.

It is the crime that has no name.

A couple of hours later, after the movie we are all watching has finished, Jacob looks up and says,

"Hey. I have to tell you both something"

"What?" Laura says.

"I'm going to Atlanta for a couple of weeks, and wondered if you guys wanted to go too."

Laura sighs. "I'm sorry Jacob, no can do. There's just too much work for me to do at the moment. Sorry sweetie. I'd love to come."

"It's just a couple of weeks babe." He makes a baby pout then kisses her.

"Hey. Guys. Get a room!" I smile. "I'm going to read my book" I walk out of the office and hear them giggling like teenagers. I check my new phone and there are a lot of missed calls from Benjamin. Shit, I totally forgot about him. I call him back and he answers right away.

"Hi Eva. Something wrong? How do you feel?" He is talking fast, but in a low voice.

"I'm fine, why are you talking like that?"

"Sorry. I was just worried, I came to the class today but didn't attend, I just showed up at the end to maybe go for a walk walking with you but I couldn't find you, so I asked Jacob and he said you were way too tired to even move your hand."

He sounds really concerned.

"He did?" I whisper more to myself than anyone else.

"I really was worried." he mumbles.

"Yes, I can tell. Please don't worry."

"Are you going to class tomorrow? I'll be there for sure."

"Of course. If I manage to wake up," I say, teasing him.

"What do you mean?"

"Oh, nothing" I say, casually.

"I'm afraid that nothing isn't in my dictionary. I would really love to see you."

I chuckle.

"I'll be there don't worry"

"I love it when you laugh, Eva. It makes your eyes light up because I'm sure your eyes are sparkling at this moment. I wish I could be there to see them. I haven't actually seen you since Tuesday, you know." He's flirty now.

"Yeah, well you'll see enough of me tomorrow," I blush and thank God he can't really see me.

One day, maybe he will.

Really see me.

Chapter Seven

I feel an uncontrollable urge to vomit, push myself out of bed to the bathroom and throw up everything from last night. It feels like my stomach is burning. I stop throwing up but the gagging action is still there.

I manage to drink a glass of water it and wash my mouth out with it. I place the glass back and look in the mirror. My lips are red like they're bleeding. My nose has totally healed from all the bruises that used to be there. I avoid my eyes, out of habit. I don't like to stare into their particular kind of hell. It may come back to get me.

It's probably the medication I took yesterday. I walk back to the bed and see that it is just four o'clock in the morning. I sneak downstairs carefully, hoping I don't wake anyone. It's dark. Really dark, and quite scary I run back to my room and shut the door calmly.

"Eva, Wake up." Suddenly Laura is shaking me, and my eyes spring open like I've seen a ghost.

"Huh? What?" I snap.

"You're going to be late for your class, even though Jacob won't be there, you still have to go. Come on. Let's go, Eva!"

She claps her hands.

"Yeah, right."

A few minutes later I'm ready.

"Are you scared, Eva? " Laura asks softly, as we get in the car. "Of going to class without Jacob?"

I frown. "No."

"Well, if it's not that, maybe of dating someone" she adds.

"Oh, yes. Well. Kind of," I say. "I'm not scared of him, but of the power that men have had over me."

"Ben is not going to hurt you like they did" she says, and shakes her head.

"Yeah. I hope so. I really do like him," murmur, and look out of the window.

We fall silent for a while. It is a beautiful day, and I feel my mood lighten the closer we get to the school.

"Okay, your stop! Take care honey."

Laura gives me a brief hug and a kiss.

"Same to you." I climb out of the car and walk to the building alone today for the first time ever.

I see men everywhere dressed in sharp business suits, baggy sweat pants, or just relaxing, sipping coffee. This is a busy place where people don't really care about others around them, where men aren't abusive but are respectful to their job and others, and I love it.

I walk all the way up three flights of stairs then remember that I could have used the elevator. I shake my head and enter the class. To my total relief, Benjamin is sitting there with his head lowered, writing. I smile and he smiles when he sees me. When I get closer he stands, and wraps his arms around me. I shudder a little at the unsolicited contact, and he feels me back off and locks eyes with me.

"I will never ever dare to hurt you, I promise on my life," he whispers.

I try to drink this in. This kindness. This love. Maybe it is a fantasy, something that a man in a work of fiction tells his girl and they both end up together, or die. It's both exciting and terrifying. It's both loving and caring.

"I miss you. I really missed you, " he says.

He's taking a big step. I admire his sincerity, and bravery.

"I do too," I tell him, and I blush.

This is not supposed to happen to me!

We sit down and his chair is closer to mine this time. Jacob isn't here, but there's an overweight guy literally asleep on the chair, I feel Ben's eyes fixed on me.

"What the?" I laugh.

"Just looking at you," he smirks.

"I know, why?" I roll my eyes.

"Just enjoying the view."

"What's up with him?" I point at the man snoring on Jacob's chair.

Ben laughs. "He's Jacob's temporary replacement. He won't teach anyway, by the look of him, I think he must have been out all night, so we have the next three hours just talking or reading." He points at some of the others in the class and he is right. Some are reading, and many are sleeping.

"What are you writing?" I pull the book out from under his arm, and he stares at me, smiling. I look at him and his eyes are soft, and blue like peaceful water. It's like they are looking right into my soul, and I fear him knowing everything. So I just look down at the book.

"Well, that is one of the most incredible books I've ever read, so I was just writing my thoughts about it," he says.

"Nineteen Eighty Four" I read aloud from the cover. "I've read this book once, but I just read the first twenty pages."

"I can loan it to you, if you want," he says kindly.

"That's nice," I say, and give it back to him. "So you read?"

"I'm not a massive reader, but I do enjoy it. I just love learning."

His eyes are beautiful when he speaks about things he loves. "And you?"

"I love it so much. I want to buy as many books as I can, then read them all."

"You know when I was a little kid," he says and moves his hands to his lap, "I used to hide in the trees almost all the time if I felt pissed over something. Or angry."

"Why was that?" I giggle. "Like, why in a tree?"

"Because they didn't know that I could climb that tree! And they probably still don't know that I was hiding in the tree the entire time. They would just go and scream my name out. Sometimes the entire house would go searching for me."

"I don't know if that is kind of funny or sad." I laugh.

"Well, I wasn't a cool kid, or the local nerd either. I was that stupid, desperate boy that would hang out with anyone."

"I think that's okay. Cool even. I only had one friend and she left me alone all of a sudden, even though she was aware of everything I was going through."

I try to hide my disappointment but my voice is showing it.

"That's rude, she should at least have give you a reason."

"She did. She told me I wasn't the kind of person who could be her friend." I shrug.

"That's just plain mean," he says.

Protectively.

We then have the longest conversation I've had with anyone in my entire life, mostly about my school or his school, like the time when he got suspended for three weeks and failed math twice. I laugh. I laugh like I've never laughed before to the point that the fat replacement wakes up and stares at me like an eagle needing to hunt something.

"I can't wait for tonight," says Ben, finally.

"Me neither," I reply, and smile.

"Okay, class dismissed!" The replacement yawns, stands and just leaves Do they pay him for this? I shake my head and grab my bag. Ben packs his books and I dial Laura, who picks up right away, just like she has been waiting for my call.

"Hey Laura, I'm done."

"Thanks Eva, I'll come right away," she says, and I hang up.

"Ready?" Benjamin stands.

"Yep."

He walks me downstairs to the parking lot, and I walk with him.

"Well, that's my ride babe, want me to take you home?" he offers, pointing at a car.

"Thank you, but Laura is already on her way" I tell him.

"Maybe next time?"

"Yes. Maybe next time."

He places his bag in the car and stands next to me, we're facing nothing but cars parked under the burning sun and feeling the cool breeze of Chicago's evening. It's a pretty place. Benjamin pulls a cigarette and lights it up. I almost flinch, but I have learned in these past months not to fear everything that I used to be hurt with.

Cigarettes. Belts.

Men.

The smell. The ember. Glowing.

Takes me back to when I was burned on almost a daily basis, in several places on my body. I don't fear Benjamin. I fear the thing in his hand. I fear that it takes away souls. Even though I have to admit he looks extremely hot, I still won't be comfortable next to him while he is smoking it.

"I know I shouldn't say it, but those things will kill you," I say, and he just grins. I look away from him and stare at the cars passing by.

People rush to their cars before the evening traffic. This place is nice, yet crowded. Benjamin stands in front of me, looking at me with furrowed brows. His eyes aren't clear blue anymore they are dark. Then he throws the cigarette on the ground and steps on it.

"Okay. If it makes you feel better then it makes me feel better," he says quietly, looking right into my eyes. He looks hurt. His look isn't the funny, tough guy look I've spent the past week with.

"It will kill you, it's true," I mumble.

He laughs. Hurt. Wounds opened.

"It isn't funny," I say, frowning at him.

"I know. I'm sorry. I won't smoke anymore. At least not with you." He run his hand through his hair, and turns his face away. I keep my eyes on him, he reminded me so much of my brother, he would just run his hands through his hair whenever he was angry or frustrated. Benjamin's eyes say frustration but his clenched fist says anger. I don't want him to do anything that he or I would regret. I just feel so amazing with him and if he did anything out of line, it would push me right back to the start and I would struggle to engage with people anymore.

Luckily, my phone starts ringing and I answer. Laura is waiting for me.

"I have to go," I tell him and he does not reply. He just turns away, and gets in his car. Silent treatment.

I walk towards the building where Laura is waiting for me. If I fucked it up with him he'll have an excuse for not meeting me tonight. I get in the car and Laura is smiling. She is always smiling.

"How's everything?" she asks.

"Not so good. We didn't have a real class today because Jacob's replacement is a fat lazy ass," I snort, my brows knotted.

"Oh dear."

"Yeah, and I might have pushed some buttons I wasn't supposed to push with Benjamin."

"What did he do?"

"It's more what I did. I just asked him not to smoke and he got kind of frustrated and angry." I shrug.

"Its fine, he'll get over it."

I nod and she smiles.

While we drive to the restaurant Laura tells me we are meeting a friend that is coming to visit her for a couple of days. I receive a text. No one texts me but people who have my number, and there aren't that many people. I see the message, and it is from Benjamin. "I'll be there at seven princess". With the dumbest winking face I've seen in my life. "I'll be ready," I text back. Things aren't bad with him. I'm he isn't sulking too much.

After lunch with Laura's friend, who is lovely and welcoming, we go back home. I have a few hours to kill before my date, so I have a shower and then call Laura.

"Yes," she says breathlessly. She has just run up the stairs, she probably thought something was wrong with me. "Is everything alright?" she asks.

"Yes, cool, I just hoped that you could help me get ready."

"Sure."

She opens the closet and pulls out several dresses, then chooses a short black sleeveless one. I put it on and it fits perfectly. It looks amazing. I glance at Laura from the mirror and she is looking at me like I'm her daughter who is going to the prom.

"C'mon" I say.

"Sorry. It's just that I never had the chance to have a daughter. You know."

I walk over and hug her.

"I am your daughter then," I smile up at her.

"Yes. Yes you are. I would love you to be."

"Then I would love to be your daughter too."

I sit on the small round chair in front of the mirror and she starts straightening my hair. Tears are falling on her cheeks, but she keeps going, makes my hair look great then puts some makeup on my face. I ask about every single thing she uses and their names too. "In case I need them myself one day," I say, and she laughs.

"You look like a princess," she says, and hugs me. "Now wear these heels, and if you need anything else you call me. Benjamin is a great guy and I trust him. So you should too."

"I will. Thank you so much. I feel so pretty."

I have no idea what happens on a date, but have heard things at high school. I take my purse and walk with Laura down the stairs, I'm not used to the heels, and I'm nervous of all the possibilities that might happen tonight. As the time gets closer I get more anxious. Nervous. Agitated. I just want everything to be okay, and fun. The bell rings and I walk towards the door. And Laura is walking with me like she is invited too!

Chapter Eight

I open the door and he looks so smart and handsome in a suit. His hair is combed backwards and he is holding a bouquet.

"Hi," I say and he offers me the flowers. I take them trying to act normal and cool but I'm freaking and my blood is rushing like it's in a race.

"Thank you so much," I say and Laura takes the flowers from me.

"I have no idea of your favorite color, so I grabbed everything. Mostly red, it appears, " he stammers, running a hand through his hair. Nervous.

"Have a great night both of you and remember, Benjamin. I know how to shoot." Laura winks at him and I gasp.

"Laura!" I say, and Benjamin laughs.

Puts his hand up in mock surrender.

"Ok, I will take care of her. I promise. Now, we have to go or we'll miss the movie," he says.

"Bye," I tell Laura and walk out, trying to be calm.

We walk to his car and he opens the door for me, I get inside and wait for him to get in the drivers seat.

"You look beautiful. I don't think I'll be able to take my eyes away from you all evening," he says looking at me. I look down at my lap because I don't want him to see me blush.

"Well, I hope you keep your eyes on the road until we get there," I joke.

He laughs and drives away. At first there is an awkward silence.

"I thought we could watch the movie and after that, go eat dinner wherever you want," he says, peering down the highway. He is a careful driver. That's good to know.

"Yes, that'll be great. Of course it will," I tell him. I should've worn something more comfy.

We arrive at the theater and walk right inside. There are a lot of seats and I could get lost easily, it is so dark. Cavernous. There are many seats but the place is empty. We go to our seats that are right in the middle. We sit down.

"We are probably fools for wearing such fancy clothes to an empty theater," he jokes, and I laugh.

"What do you like? Soda? Beer? Popcorn? You know what I'll just surprise you!" I open my mouth to speak but I close it again and nod and he heads off to the refreshment area.

At the same time people start entering. A group of teenagers come in noisily and sit far away from us. I try to exhale and inhale to avoid anxiety or panic. A much older couple take two seats, further away. I check my texts, Laura wishing me good luck with a heart emoji. Jacob has also sent a text, just a lot of exclamation marks. I love how both of them worry about me like I'm their real daughter.

"No phones allowed in here," Ben says sternly, freaking me out. I frown and he points at the screen.

"Yeah, I'm just checking some texts not actually trying to communicate with anyone!" I put the phone back in the purse, shrugging.

"I brought us popcorn to share, and two cokes. Wasn't sure if you would drink all mine," he jokes and I roll my eyes.

The lights go off, and the screen is huge, I bet my mouth is in the shape of an O I really love it even though the movie hasn't started yet.

"Is it a horror?" I whisper in Ben's ear.

"Yep," he nods. I try to act like I'm fine with horror movies.

In the middle of the movie I realize that the movie isn't scary if we mute the voice. Which is stupid, because the scary sound track is the reason we nearly crap ourselves. I hold Ben's hand three times during the movie, and he smiles widely every time my hand touches his.

"Do you want to leave?" he asks me.

I yawn, teasing him. He laughs, but he looks bored. And I'm bored too.

"Yes let's do it," I stand, walking after him.

We sneak out. We literally just sat the entire time, with me freaking out and nearly jumping on him, and him laughing at me because my facial expressions were priceless.

We walk out of the theater and there is no sign of the sun.

"Aren't we going to the car?" I ask.

"I prefer walking, if you don't mind. It's a lovely evening."

"No, that's fine" I smile, and while we are walking my hand touches his. He act like he didn't notice and I get little bit farther. He walks near me, his hand brushes mine, his fingers touch mine, I try to move my hand away but he holds it. His touch is soft and nice. I interlock my fingers with his and act normal. I catch his smile.

"You didn't like the movie," he asks.

"I did actually. The effects were good but the story was a little boring."

"I watched it last week, that's why I was bored," he shrugs.

"Why did you book it again then?" I ask, staring at him.

"Because I watched you all the time instead of the movie. Your face is a way better view," he laughs.

"You're weird." I push him playfully and he lets go of my hand. Actually, I wasn't even watching the film. I was watching him too. The way he held my hand. Everything.

95

If I'm not feeling happiness now, when will I?

And I think he is one of the people that will help me find it. I've heard a lot of people saying that I will never stand up again and start fighting all the difficulties I've went through, and I kind of believed them. I used to believe that I would not survive, and yet I have and I'm here today smiling and walking with one of the most handsome guys in the city. Guys have only ever shown me pain

I'm so glad I didn't walk to the end of the bridge and end all this. I'm glad that things are finally turning around.

"Here we are. This is the place I've always wanted to take you ever since I laid my eyes on you." He says it in a way that I feel every muscle in my heart tighten, in a way that every hair on my body stands up, not just because of him, but because of the place.

It's beautiful. Ben says something to the waitress and they walk us to the back where tables are lined next to the river, and the view is amazing. We sit, there is a candle in the middle, and he sits facing me and I gaze right into his eyes, smiling.

"Thank you so much" I whisper so it is only him who can listen. "This is so pretty." I shake my head in disbelief.

He reaches out for my hands, and I place my hand in his.

"I would love to do anything in this world to make you happy," he whispers. "I don't know you well enough yet, but I feel like there is something in you that will light up my entire world if you're happy, and I will do my best to make that happen for you."

"I like everything about you Benjamin," I smile widely, and he smiles back and eyes are sparkling and lighting with hope and love and it's getting to me.

I feel like I'm something. I feel like I'm really a part of this world. The waitress returns and our hands break apart, and his eyes break away from mine, but I am still looking at him and thinking how handsome he is.

I'll be eternally thankful for Laura and Jacob, and all the others who the police about the guy that had trapped and tortured me for over seven years.

"Hope you like wine and steak" Ben says, looking anxious.

"I eat anything that tastes good." He laughs at the way I say it and I laugh with him.

"Well that's good, because that's all they serve here!" he says.

I must look a little sad because his expression changes.

"What's bothering you?" he says, furrowing his brows.

"Nothing. I'm just thinking how warm hearted you are and thankful for having such a good time with you," I tell him, and take a sip of my wine.

"Tell me more about you," he says clearing his throat. "You said you didn't have much love for your mother. Why was that?"

His question bothered me, not just because it was so direct but also because it reminded me of her death. And that reminded me of how stupid she was.

"She was weak, and she was helpless. She didn't do anything to stop my father from abusing her and me and my older brother. She was not a person who would save you if you were drowning. She would just drown with you instead of swimming to the shore." I look down, ashamed to be speaking about her like this.

"Maybe he gave her no choice" said Ben. "Maybe he took away all of her strength and beauty?"

It's a kind thing to say, but I badly don't want to speak about me. His eyes are looking at me sadly and his lips wear the ghost of a smile. He's trying to be nice, I know.

"I don't want to speak about me and ruin this beautiful night," I tell him bluntly, and I know my eyes are helpless and sad but I can't stop it.

"I know, but I truly do want to know you, and the only thing that would ruin this night is you not telling me about you and me not knowing how you lived," he says.

I'm thankful that the waitress breaks the silence again as she places a dish of steak in front of me and the same in front of Ben. "Enjoy" she says lightly, and glides away.

"I feel like your mom was powerful but her power drained off with every year," he continues. "Where is she now?"

"She died" I say. "He killed her." I look at Ben and his eyes are wide, shocked and angry.

"I'm so sorry babe. Sorry. Now I know why you don't like to talk about it."

I grab the fork and knife and start eating. He starts telling me when he first came here with his friend Aiden. He brought me here because he loves the place and would show me everything he loves. I'm so glad the topic isn't my pathetic past anymore. I fill myself with steak and wine, and it is exquisite. The waitress is back asking if we would like dessert and I shake my head and ask for more wine.

"No dessert?" Ben asks.

"No thanks. I couldn't eat another thing."

"Okay, just more wine then please," he tells the waitress and she glides away.

He sighs contentedly and fixes me with those eyes.

"Well, where would you like to go next?"

"I don't know. I don't get out a lot! Where would you like to go?" I joke, trying to lighten the mood.

"Well, if it's just about me I would like to walk. Just walk and talk."

"Let's just walk and talk then." I wink playfully.

After we finish our last glass of wine, and Ben settles the check, the waitress tells us to have a nice night and to visit again. I love everything. And I'll keep on saying that I loved everything.

I want to hold his hand again, so I just do it and he locks his fingers with mine, tight. His arm is warm but mine is freezing. Of course I'm freezing, I'm just wearing a short sleeveless dress, and the weather is getting colder.

"Hey, are you cold?" He stops walking and looks at me, I try to shake my head but he quickly removes his blazer. "Turn around," he says and he puts it on me.

It's big. I raise the arms and it is way too long. My fingers aren't even showing. He laughs and I thank him.

"You look better now you aren't freezing," he smirks, and holds my hand again. While we're walking we pass shops and restaurant and people walking and talking. We are getting close to where he parked the car.

"How did you get away from your dad?" he asks. We are switching the conversation back to me again.

"I didn't, he just gave me away to that horrible muscled guy." I shudder, even though I'm warmer now.

"And what did you do with that guy?" he says quizzically.

"Do you really want to know? I say.

"Yes. I do," he says firmly.

"He locked me down for seven years. He would let me go to school, but he wouldn't let me talk to anyone so that I wouldn't snitch on him. He paid a spy in the class, and if I talked to anyone, he would hear of it and beat the hell out of me when I got back."

I talk slowly and never raise my eyes to look at his.

"What a fucking douche!" He spits. "I want to take you to the lake front okay?" he says, and his voice is more angry than calm. I nod and we get into the car.

"Why are you angry?" I ask him quietly.

"I'm not. I hate the thought of anybody treating innocent girls like that." He hits the steering wheel and then holds it tight.

We drive to the lake, then get out and walk a little bit far away from the water. I can hear the splashes. I love how quiet it is at this time of night. There's a couple in front of us, the girl is all cuddled in the arm of the guy. Something inside me wants that so badly but I will settle for holding hands right now.

I remember my dad was nice to me only the once. He once gave me a book with just one hundred pages, with the rest torn away. I was so happy and thanked him five times until he said if I didn't shut the hell up he would beat me with what was left from the book. It was Christmas time.

I try to talk to Ben, who's been silent ever since I told him about my entrapment.

"I have a brother, he ran away when dad killed my mother, he was scared that they'd blame him. I have no clue if he is alive or dead. I'd be so happy to meet him if he survived."

Benjamin remains silent. So I continue.

"I stopped going to school when I became a senior because someone snitched on me. I talked to someone, just asked to borrow a pencil for drawing, but that was enough. He locked me down without food or water for three days. Then I heard his voice climbing the stairs to the locked room on the roof where he kept me. He always came at night. He kicked the door open, and I thought, "this is the day I'll be killed", and he was drunk. He was always drunk. He yelled at me to go to him but I didn't, so he called me a slut, a bitch, a filthy prostitute. But when I didn't come to him he ran over, hit me hard, and threw me on the bed with no mattress. I only had a sheet, even when the weather was freezing. A rock hard bed and one sheet."

I pause and stare at Ben who stops walking and pulls his hand away

Ben wants to know. He asked me to tell him. I can't stop now, even if I want to.

"He would slap me several times until I couldn't feel my face for the heat coming out from it. My tears were no relief because they were hot as well. He wrapped his big fingers around my neck until I ran out of air. Choking. Struggling to breathe. I try to kick out but my legs are kicking nothing. I cry and choke. I black out and don't know what happened next. When I opened my eyes I was always in the same place."

Benjamin is staring at me now, totally still and staring. Eyes wide and scared and angry. They are full of the deepest pity.

"You don't have to say anything," I whisper, and turn around to face the sea.

"What else did he do?" he asks, and his voice is faint.

"Over seven years he did a lot of things that you wouldn't like to know," I tell him, leaning against the sea wall.

"Maybe I want to know," he leans next to me.

"Can we please just enjoy the night and not talk anymore of my past? I beg.

"Okay. Whatever you want, sweetie."

He smiles and strokes my cheek, and I smile too.

Personally I don't know where our destination is, but if I'm with him I know it's some place beautiful. After a while he stops walking and stands in front of me, facing me. My heart is pounding and my stomach is refusing to stay still. His blue eyes are connecting with my green eyes.

Before I can catch another breath, his lips are on mine.

I pull away slowly and try to breathe. The tips of our noses are touching, he is kissing me slowly, and shiver goes down my back and we're still kissing, his hands moving to the sides of my face. When our lips part,

I open my eyes and he is smiling, a small reassuring smile. My heart is racing like I've been running away from someone.

I love it.

"Hey, it's late. Laura will be worried," he says slowly, and I nod. We walk back to the car and his hand is brushing mine all the time, until I make the move and grasp it.

We drive back and as we get out of the car and stand outside Laura's he tells me that this has been the best night of his life. I thank him, and tell him I'll see him on Monday. He says, "No. I will try to see you again tomorrow, if that's alright".

I smile, I wave goodbye, and then I go inside.

Laura is waiting. Of course she is.

"Well! How was it?" she asks excitedly, jumping from the couch.

"I can't describe it. I really can't." I place my hands on my chest.

"What happened?" she winces.

"Nothing. Except that he kissed me and it was the best most terrifying yet enjoyable thing I ever did," I say, and I can still feel his hands on my face and his lips on mine.

"Duh. Obviously. He forgot to take his blazer" Laura says pointing at me.

"Oh no," I say.

"Never mind. You obviously had a wonderful time," she says, and falls back into a chair.

I throw myself on the couch, and close my eyes trying to remember his face and every beautiful thing about him.

"Aw, I love you Eva. I'm so happy for you," Laura says playing with my hair.

"Me too," says Jacob, and when I hear his voice I jump from the couch and he is standing there holding a small suitcase. Laura screams with delight, and runs to him and kisses him. He hugs her and smiles at her. The way they look at each other is so beautiful and loving.

"You came home early," Laura says

"Yeah, the conference was cancelled, so I took the first flight home baby." He winks and kisses her, then makes his way towards me.

"How was it, was he good with you? " he asks, hugging me.

"He is the best. A gift from heaven to and sent right to me" I say, and Laura and Jacob laugh.

"Wonderful. Seeing you happy is all that matters to us," Jacob said.

"Thank you. So much. Now, if you don't mind, I'm exhausted and I'll just go to sleep, okay?" They smile, I yawn and walk to my room.

I throw myself on the bed and take off my heels. They're killing me. Then I remember the kiss. The restaurant.

Him.

I feel like my heart is dancing in heaven. I've never been this happy in my entire life and I'm grateful for this moment. Ben just showed me the beautiful side of love that I haven't seen before. And my life has changed forever because of that.

Chapter Nine

It's been a couple of weeks since my night out with Benjamin and we've been hanging out every day since we finished the semester.

Out of the blue, Laura calls me to her office, and I walk down to see her.

"Hey, need something?" I ask and sit on the chair next to her.

"Yes, well you know I am about to proceed with that case about your sexual and physical abuse. As you know, that asshole has two years in prison for vandalism and arson, but he is going to get even more if we win your case for rape and abuse."

"And?" I ask, trying to hide the fact that I'm suddenly really scared.

"Well, they are proposing a time to view the case and set a court date"

She looks hard at me.

"Okay, when is that?"

"We still don't know. It'll take a while"

I stay silent and I look at the photographs on the table, I find the one she took last week when we went out for a 'family day,' as Jacob called it. I love the picture, and the fact she has it there along with the other photographs that she says are the most beautiful things in her life. It makes me feel more loved and more precious. I see multiple photos of a small kid that seems like he hasn't taken his first step yet. I pick one up, and the kid looks so much like Laura I wonder if it actually is Laura, but he doesn't look old enough.

"That's my son," she says taking the photo from me and staring at it sadly.

"I didn't know you had a son." I raise my eyebrows in shock.

"I did. But he died six years ago." She clears her throat and places the photo back.

"What happened" I ask needing to know more. She is the one that always asks and listens to me. Well, now it's my turn.

"I used to be married to that guy, in the picture. I loved him so much we had a son together. We adored him. His name was Christopher, and he seemed the answer to all our prayers, but one day I was busy in the kitchen and my husband was out at the office working, and we didn't realize that Christopher had managed to get outside. And we had a pool with no fence."

Her voice trails off with the pain of remembering.

106

"After two hours I realized that hadn't seen him and began freaking out, he was only three. I began calling his name and he wasn't answering, but when I went outside I was literally broken when I saw him in the pool. He was just lying there."

She starts to sob.

"He was floating there, mouth and eyes open. Dead. I tried to pull him out and when I did I couldn't make him breathe again. I tried so hard, but later the emergency services told me he had drowned five hours before. While I was working and not paying attention."

She sobs even more, but continues.

"When my husband came back, all he saw was me crying and holding Christopher, his tiny body was dripping wet and my face was stained with tears. Then he started yelling at me for being a bad mother failing to take care of our child. He was screaming that I had only one job, to take care of our poor little kid, but I had failed."

"That is truly awful," I mutter, not knowing what to say.

"After that everyone stood by me and helped me through, but he never forgave me. He filed for divorce on the grounds of irresponsibility, and that damaged me even more. A year after that I began studying law and psychology, and I learned more just to forget my Chris. But no amount of learning could erase his beautiful smile, or his way of calling for his mommy every time he wanted me. Every time I sleep he pops up in my dreams, floating, mouth open, dead in the cold water, or he laughing and running away from me while we're playing. And every single time I wish that it was me who died. Not him."

Laura wipes her tears and looked at me, her eyes are red and hurt. I stand up and hug her, and when we separate, I tell her. "You've always listened to me and I'm always here to listen to you Laura. You helped me so much to be your daughter, and I will always be there for you and you can tell everyone that I am your daughter. Please. I don't mind."

"I know that honey. That's why I love you so much, and I don't think I can bear losing you too."

My heart aches for her, and I'm thankful that God sent Laura to make my life so much better.

And suddenly, it hits me.

I'm here to make her life better too.

Finally, I really matter.

I matter to someone.

She dries her tears and goes on.

"Sometimes it's hard to be a powerful and professional woman and cope at the same time with that level of loss. But whatever happens, you have to fight to survive. You have to be a fighter."

She looks at me again, a penetrating gaze. She wants me to remember this moment.

"Thanks for listening," she says.

I hear my phone ring and I run up the stairs, and it's Ben.

"Hey," I answer.

"Baby, where are you?"

"Home, why?" I'm trying to catch my breath.

"Can we go out for a walk in an hour or so?" His voice is unusually quiet.

"Um, sure why not?"

"Okay. I'll see you around seven."

"Cool. Bye." I hang up and walk back to Laura who is waiting for Jacob to come.

"Hey Laura, is it okay if I go out for a walk with Ben after dinner?" I ask her.

"Yes sure, but don't be late."

I sit down on my chair and Jacob arrives, we say prayers and over dinner, Jacob tells us how much progress his project is making and how he is so glad to be able to teach people who can't afford it.

I love that Jacob loves teaching so much. All my dad ever cared about was getting drunk and making our lives hell. Dad would tear away my books and stab my legs and hands with my pencils. It didn't stop me from going to school or reading, and writing. I must have been a fighter, like Laura says, even when the blonde guy bought me. His name was Ethan and he hated education too, although I was lucky in that he did allow me to continue school, as long as I obeyed him, and I did. I obeyed him and did whatever he wanted. I let him treat me like a toy. Like crap. I felt worthless, but going to school, in good shape or not, was the best thing. In school I was away from him. I didn't talk to people out there but I talked to my books, I didn't have friends but I had them in my books.

When we finish dinner the doorbell rings and Ben is standing there widely to me like a fool. I smile back and shout to Laura and Jacob that I'm leaving.

"So where are we going and why did you want to see me?" I tell him, zipping up my jacket.

"Just walking. Can't I see the most beautiful girl ever whenever I want?" he says, kissing my cheek.

"You can." I giggle.

"Anything new about that douche that locked you up and hurt you?" he says. I told him about the case being reopened.

"Good. Hopefully they'll keep him in prison forever," he says.

I have never told Ben the whole truth about what Ethan did. I have never explained that he raped me against my will.

I probably never will.

Ben notices my expression.

"Hey, don't keep worrying. I know some things. Jacob talked to me. And he also told me that if I ever hurt you he'll find me and skin me alive," he says fast, not giving me a second to respond.

I laugh at that, and so does he. Jacob has probably told Ben more than I have.

We walk for ages. His arm is around my waist and my head is on his chest. I feel more comfortable now, and I trust in him more. We've known each other over a month and I'm thankful to be loved by him.

"Can I ask you an honest question? Don't worry it's not about the bad stuff, " he says hurriedly, checking my expression which is blank and straight.

"You ask, and if I like the question I will answer" I tell him with a smirk.

"Did you ever fall in love before?" he says.

"To be honest, yes, but she left me and we didn't actually date. I mean I only saw her for one hour a day for one month." I roll my eyes at the thought of her.

"She?" His eyebrows frown.

"Well yes, she was my best friend. She was the one who dropped our relationship. I told you. I went to school just to see her and be with her, and then she did everything to keep me away. I didn't realize that until I saw her with someone else." I shrug.

"So you loved a girl." I can see he is shocked.

"Yes. I did love a girl" I tell him, staring at him while he tries to laugh but his expression is confused and his hand is covering his eyes.

"That's some fucked up life you have there."

And his cold sentence freezes my heart. I stop still. Shocked. Hurt.

Horrified that he just said that.

"Thanks for reminding me," I tell him and try to be strong. He just reminded me of all the bad feelings. How rough everything was, how they tore me like a piece of paper and tossed me in the trash. He comes closer to me without touching me, but he stares at my tears filled eyes.

"Don't." He whispers and wipes my tear away. "You know I didn't mean that," he continues. "I was just surprised"

I say nothing and he starts talking fast.

"Please don't cry. I didn't mean to make you cry." I can feel how sorry he is.

I try to walk past him, but he walks next to me. I start talking again.

"I used to have two hours after school, one to do my home work, and the other to sell cookies that my mom baked. My dad was good at stealing the money and buying himself some beer. I wonder how did he stay alive so long the amount that he drank," I say and my voice is emotionless and dead.

"If I ever see your dad, I'll kill him," he says through gritted teeth.

"You don't have to. I might do that myself," I tell him and try to smile.

We sit on a wooden seat next to a flower shop. A woman and her little child walked past us. The little girl is crying, while her mother, or whoever she is, is talking to a guy next to the shop. It is easy to see them but hard to listen, but what gets my attention is that the little girl is crying and this asshole woman is flirting with the guy.

I walk up to the little girl and say; "Hey what's wrong?" She points at akids shop across the road. It's closed. Nothing is open at this time, aside from the restaurants and cafes, and the flower shop.

"It's closed right now, don't cry! If you are good now, you could come here tomorrow and get whatever you want," I tell her and she nods and smiles a bit. "Good girl. Don't cry," I say and walk back to Ben who is just watching me carefully. The woman in charge of her hasn't even noticed that I've been over. The little girl is staring at me and smiling.

"What?' I look at Ben, and he is still staring at me.

"What did you say?"

"I told her to come here tomorrow and ask for anything she wants. But if she cries, she won't get it."

"She's still staring at you." He laughs.

Two lovers kiss on the other side of the street. I wonder how warm they feel in this cold weather. I move closer to Ben and he wraps his arm around my waist, and buries his nose in my hair. It all feels beautiful, like butterflies in my stomach flying everywhere in my body.

"I love you," he whispers in my ear along with a light kiss on my earlobe. My heart skips a couple of beats and my grin is wide and everything in me just flies to heaven. No boy has ever told me those three words. No boy ever told me he loved me.

I don't know if he means it, but I would love to listen to him saying it again and again.

I turn my face and our noses touch, our eyes connect, our lips aren't far apart, his hand is in my hair and the other on my thighs. We are close. Close to the point where I feel comfortable with him.

"What?" I whisper.

"I love you" He says it again, and I smile.

Our eyes are still connected, and our lips are not as far as they were. His lips touch mine but then he backs off.

"Don't move," he says, standing.

Motioning to me, he enters to the flower shop. I think of his words. These words mean everything. I've always read that if we have love, nothing else matters. Even if we have no shelter, love will shelter us. If there is love and trust everything will be perfect, and I just found it on a wooden chair next to an old flower shop. I just found love with a guy who accepts me even though he knows about my terrible past. I've found love with a kind and lovely soul. I can't believe it so I shut my eyes and cover my face with my hands. I love him too. It came out of his mouth warm, beautiful, and true.

"Why are you hiding your face?" he says, and when I peek out form behind my hands he is holding a red flower and grinning. "This is the only flower they had left, he said I was too late." He says it all with an innocent face, giving me the flower.

"It's beautiful" I say. He sits back next to me and kisses me like he is afraid to break me.

"I really do want to see you happy all the time," he says.

"Well, I've been happy all the time since I met you," I tell him.

He stands, checks the time on his phone.

"Come, it's getting late, I should take you home" He takes my hand and we walk back to Laura's condo. I feel like I am walking on air, or surfing on a wave of happiness.

When we get there he kisses me and hugs me goodbye. I enter and it is dark. I walk past Laura's office and Jacob is once again busy on his laptop.

"Hello? " I say and step inside.

"Eva, we missed you at movie night," he smiles, but he doesn't really see me, his eyes are focused on the screen.

"Goodnight, then," I say..

"Goodnight" he murmurs. He is really so busy.

I go to my room, place the flower on the table next to my head. Take off my clothes and put on my pajamas, brush my teeth and throw myself into the bed.

I want to have dream of him and his beautiful smile. I want to listen to him telling me he loves me over and over. I just want him.

I close my eyes and drift away and my thoughts are filled with love, his voice, and his sweet kisses.

Chapter Ten

I'm walking in the street barefoot, the sun is hot and the pavement is burning the skin of my feet. I cry and walk to houses knocking on their doors, sometimes they open the door and tell me to fuck off, and sometimes they throw trash at me. They call me the daughter of a slut and sometimes just ignore me. I go to the end of the neighborhood to the most luxurious house. I ring the bell and a voice emerges from the bell. I back off two steps when I hear a man say. "Who is it?"

I tell him I'm just selling cookies to stay alive.

"Come on in," he says, and the door opens automatically, but it's a woman, a tall blonde woman with a black eyes. "Hey," she says sweetly.

"Where are your shoes?" she says. "Why on earth do you look like this? This is awful." I wipe my tears and stared at her.

"I'm just here to sell cookies," I say, showing her the boxes.

"Alright. Give me two boxes," she says, and hurries away. In seconds she comes back with two hundred bucks in her hand, and a pair of socks. "Here you go," she says, giving me both. I shake my head because the two boxes only costs twenty bucks and this is way too much. And if my dad finds it, he'll take it all away.

"It's only twenty for two boxes," I plead.

"Well, I want to give you more. I'm the customer, and the customer is always right," she says, pushing the notes farther into my pocket.

"Thank you," I say with a big smile. I will try to hide the money from him so we can buy dinner, and I can buy a pair of shoes, and acceptable clothes. I sit in front of the door and wear the socks she gave me so I won't get burned on my way home. I walk back thinking of all the good things that will happen with my new fortune.

When I get back home, he is watching television with a beer bottle in his hand. I try to sneak in faster but I drop the last few cookies, and thismakes him turn his attention to me. He looks around, eyes red like fire, and shouts:

"Are you completely dumb?" he shouts. "Did you think I wouldn't see you, bitch?"

"I'm sorry" I sob but he is already on his feet, running to me, kicking the boxes away and pulling me until our faces meet, he smells bad. His breath smells like dead fish.

"Why didn't you sell all the fucking cookies?" he spits. My tears are rolling down my cheeks and my lips were quivering.

"Answer me, you fucking useless excuse of a child!"

He shakes me so hard I feel my brain move out of my skull. The money will falls from my pocket.

117

"No one wanted to buy," I say so he won't notice the money.

"I see you got something here," He says, dropping me and picking the notes up.

"Did you steal these?" he yells.

"No," I shake my head. "They were given to me."

"Liar!" he screams. "Well, however you got them, now they're mine."

He puts them in his pocket and slaps me hard. I curl into the ground and hug my knees sobbing as he kicks me time and again.

I hate my life. I hate him. I hate being poor. I hate the fact I was born into this fucked up family.

I wake and find it is another dream. Another memory.

Another world.

I dress and phone Laura to tell her I am spending the day with Ben.

"Yeah sure have fun!" she says. She is happy that I am happy.

I didn't tell Laura but I have decided that I badly need a summer job to contribute. I can't just take from them all the time. I need to address my own responsibilities. The doorbell rings and the woman that serves us food every day opens it. I think how bad it is that I have never asked her name or anything yet. The thought vanishes as Ben bursts through the door and kisses me on my cheek. I jump backwards.

"God, I thought you were someone else" I shriek.

"Chill!" He laughs. "You should've seen your face." He keeps laughing.

"Ha-ha, yes, very funny, good morning to you too," I laugh back.

"Well, here do you want to go today?" he asks, staring around the condo

"I don't know. Surprise me," I shrug.

"This is fancy," he says.

"Yes. It is. I'm very lucky." I smile.

I am.

He pulls me with him to the door, I shut it behind me and we walk down stairs.

"I thought we could go to my place and you could meet Aiden. I also have something for you, " he adds, mysteriously.

"Alright. Your wish is my command."

"Yeah. Right," he says.

It turns out his condo isn't that far away from Laura's. That's why he always arrives pretty quickly when I text him. It's only two blocks away. We climb the stairs, and he takes two at a time, but I only go with one because I'm still not that fit yet, even though we walk a lot. He opens the door and no one is there.

It's not big, but it's acceptable enough for two guys. I stand in the middle of the living room, waiting. He walks to one of the rooms in the end of the small corridor and motions to me not to move. When he comes back he says:

"Aiden isn't here, too bad he'll miss looking at this angel of mine."

I blush and push him away playfully.

"Turn around," he says.

"Alright. I trust you," I say turning around.

I turn around facing the half closed yellow curtain, he pushes my hair to the side and he moves his fingers on my neck down to the beginning of my back.

For the first time, I don't shudder, shake or move away from his touch. It seems like I really do trust him and feel comfortable with him. His fingers are still on the same spot, and I remembered that these are the spots where Ethan burned me the most. He would take the cigarette from his mouth and blow the smoke in my face, laughing as I tried not to breathe it. After that he'd press it on my neck. Hard. Painful. I would scream as loud as I could and my fist closed so hard on the sheet, my body pulsing from the pain.

I screamed so much I think that the entire people in this city could hear me, so would he kick me hard and tell me to shut up but I didn't.

"Fuck you," I yelled. And he laughed, saying that I have some balls to say that. Then he ripped my dress off, with me kicking and kicking, naked and begging for help as he bent me over.

But there was no one to help as he entered me from behind.

And if I cried out in the middle of being raped, he would burn me all over again.

It was a living hell.

"It doesn't hurt now," I say to Ben, getting away from Ethan and back into the present.

He turns me around and there are tears in his eyes. I place both my hands on his face and grabbed him to me, kissing him slowly, but he pushes away.

"If that filthy animal escapes from the court next week I promise I'll kill him with my bare hands," he snarls, and I hate seeing him so angry.

"I love you." I tell him. "I truly do."

He hugs me for a long time, and when we separate he shows me a necklace with a small crescent moon at the end.

"This is very special to me, but I would love you to have it," he whispers.

"It's pretty." Why would he give it to me?

He helps me with it and I turn around again to face him.

"Thank you so much," I tell him.

I throw myself on the couch and think of Ethan again. Ben notices.

"I would love to know what is worrying your brain so much" he says handing me a soda.

"Nothing, just thinking about my future." I mutter.

"Future? With me or without me," he says, winking.

"I don't know" I shrug sadly.

"No really, what's up?" he asks again.

"What if Ethan gets out, finds me and takes me back to that miserable life of mine?"

"He won't, okay? We all are here to protect you."

Before I think of answering, someone kicks the door open and I freeze in my place.

"Man, you could've knocked on the door," Ben yells.

"Well, my hands are full, but my leg isn't!"

A guy yells as crashes in. His face is masked by the huge amount of shopping bags he is carrying. I guess it's Aiden because Ben has been talking about him for two weeks, telling me I should meet him because he is such fun and so outgoing.

He kneels down, places the bags on the floor, tries to clean his shoes as they are dusty, and I really badly want to see his face now.

"Eva, this is Aiden. Aiden, meet Eva," Ben says introducing me to him when he finally stands up.

I know this guy from somewhere. He probably knows me too because his eyes are wide open with shock.

"I know she's beautiful man, but you can't look at her like that," Ben laughs pushing him but he doesn't move.

Suddenly, I remember him. Aiden is from old school, my English, chemistry and algebra classes. He studied with me for six years from primary through to high school and we only had brief conversations around four or five times.

"Guys, please, someone talk here," Ben says, confused. I drag myself back to reality and shake Aiden's hand.

"Nice to see you, Aiden" I tell him and stand next to Ben, smiling.

"Damn, I always wanted to ask you out," Aiden mutters.

"What the heck man?" Ben pushes him, and wraps his arm around my waist, hugging me closer to him.

"Man, Eva and I used to go to school together, for six or seven years she was in every English and chemistry class with me!" he says pointing at the couch so we can sit.

"And algebra for eight and ninth grade," I smile.

"True" He says. "Man, you've changed a lot."

"In a good way, I hope", I say, smiling.

"So, you were both are classmates," Ben's frowns.

I nod and Aiden continues. "You cut your hair, and your face isn't bruised."

"Yeah. Well, I'm free now. I escaped" I joke, trying to lighten the mood.

"You weren't there in the senior year, though," Aiden says, opening a beer.

"No, I didn't quite make it," I reply, glancing at Ben, who looks very uncomfortable.

Aiden was good to me in school. He didn't call me names and didn't fear sitting next to me during study periods. While everyone else whispered, he would be friendly. I would feel isolated from everyone and isolate myself, sitting alone for everything. During breaks, I would just sit in the library, read books or use the computers. I was pretty much self-taught. My teachers were the only one who respected me and knew who I really was, but they didn't know what was really going on with my domestic life, they didn't know that we had no computers and that books weren't allowed. My dad would pull books away from me and burn them in our ugly dirty back yard while I sniffed and sobbed and begged him not to do it. Once I told him to take all of my clothes away from me, but not to burn my books.

"Hey Aiden, how was that senior year?" I ask just to make conversation.

"It was cool! The prom was bad though. I only went for the dance, so I could show off my moves, " he laughs, and throws his bottle in the trash can. "Actually, I was this close to ask you to be my date for that prom, but you vanished and I kind of felt sad that you never came back."

"Hey, she's my girl now," Ben throws a small box at Aiden and I feel like giggling but I just smile. Ben really cares about me.

And it's not like I'm the queen of high school, or the prettiest girl in the neighborhood.

I rest my head on Ben's shoulder and remember when I was sitting in the back yard of our disgusting house, staring at the guys playing basketball beyond our fence. Whenever I felt like killing myself I would just go and stand behind the fence and look at these guys throwing the ball at each other. Sometimes I saw Luke playing with them and sometimes saw him sitting alone doing nothing. I would walk over to him and ask him if he would like to go for a walk but he just pushed me away, or told me to go and find a life.

I now know that Luke was depressed, I have since read books about mental disorders, and he showed all the symptoms of depression. He would sit for the entire day in his room, with the doors locked, and almost never eat. Mom would sometimes bring us something like small sandwiches, or water or whatever she could find when she went to work as a nurse for two days a week, but my dad would slap her and hit her with his bottles if he saw her giving us anything. I pitied her, when he would yell, saying it was her mistake that we were ever born, the worst thing ever in his life, our souls were like demons hunting him down and if she didn't feed us that we would die from starvation. What an animal he was. My heart is aching me and my breathing isn't normal.

"What's wrong?" Ben shakes me slowly.

"Just a bad thought, let's go for a walk," I say. We both stand, and I say "See you later, Aiden." I hug him and he hugs me back. Ben leads the way out into the fresh air.

"What happened back there?" Ben is really concerned.

"Well, when I get a bad memory from my past, I feel like someone is choking me. I can't even breathe, my heart hurts and my brain is aches. I don't know what do when that happens," I say, and tears roll down my cheeks, I cover my face with my hands and stop walking. Ben hugs me and I bury my face in his chest and sob. I know this is weird and awkward and it shouldn't happen in public but I can't help it.

"Hey, it's alright to cry, it's alright to talk about it," says Ben, stroking my face and wiping my tears.

125

"You know you look prettier with red eyes and red puffed lips," he says smiling, and I smile back but it doesn't reach my eyes.

"C'mon lets go sit somewhere more pleasant," he says, and we walk down the street to some cafes. Some are pretty crowded but we find an empty one and sit.

"Talk to me," he begs.

"I love talking to you. I'm writing everything down in a memory book or telling memories to Laura, but she freaking lost a kid Ben, she lost an entire family, and yet she still listens to me while I sob over being sexually and mentally abused. I can't wake up every day thinking of my dad finding and killing me, or even worse, Ethan who abused me so. I would kill myself and do you all a favor, but I think its weak to commit suicide and I think it's weak if I tell everyone about my horrible past. I feel like I can't win, Ben. I've never felt love, and here you are affording me love and it's way too much for me to handle," I tell him and he simply raises one finger to my mouth stop me talking.

"I have no clue what to say, and I'm no expert, but I will be there for you. Always. I love you, I will protect you and nothing can undo our love Eva," His voice is pleading for me to believe.

And I do.

Chapter Eleven

"Wait, I've never asked you when is your birthday?" 'Ben asks when we get back, just before I close the door to the condo, I looked at his eyes and smiled.

"I have no idea exactly when I was born but I know I turn nineteen soon."

"How can you not know when's your birthday?"

"My mom never told me and I never asked, because I'm not that interested."

"Well, I am. I'm interested in everything about you," he says, and my heart melts again.

"Guess so" I say and step out to kiss him. "Thank you," I whisper in his ear and he waves goodbye as I enter the condo and close the door. I still can see the look in his eyes. He truly does seem to love me.

I walk to the living room and no one is there, so I sit on the couch for a minute and recall that Laura sent me a text ages ago saying that she wanted to talk to me about going to the center. I go to her office and find her working. Alone.

"Hey, how's it going?" I sit on the chair in front of her and she takes her glasses off and gives me a small smile.

"Hello, Eva had fun today?" she asks nicely.

"Yeah, it was lovely," I sigh.

"Alright, Eva I have to tell you this before I forget. Tomorrow morning we have to go down to the care center. You have been called to testify about the entire Ethan situation from day one to the day that you escaped."

"What? How long will that take?" I blurt out, startled. "I mean, seven years worth of details?"

"I know," she replies, carefully. "That's why we'll take as much time as you need until you remember everything, if you want justice for yourself, and Ethan locked away in prison for life - or even executed - I'm afraid you have to testify." She wore her glasses again. "Now go and have some res. You have a long week in front of you"

"Alright," I tell her, and walk to my room. I take my phone out of my pocket and text Ben. I let him know that I can't hang with him tomorrow, that I have some testifying to do. I undress, shower and climb into bed. I check my phone and Ben has sent me a text saying me that he'll miss me and he wishes me luck. His text makes me smile. He is truly an angel sent from heaven to me.

The next thing I know the vibration of my phone wakes me up. I open one eye and answer it.

"Yello?" I say sleepily.

"Really Eva, yello? It's hello!" Ben laughs, I fake a laugh but my eyes are way too shut and it's to early for jokes. He shouts down the phone.

"Wake up! Its eight thirty, shouldn't you be in the center or something," he yells.

Suddenly, I remember the center. I've overslept! Ben is laughing at me, and my eyes are wide open now and my brain is buzzing. "God, how did I sleep until now?" I tell him, leaping out of bed.

"Well now I've woken you, I'll leave you to get ready. Talk to me when you finished testifying honey," he says, and hangs up. While my body is half asleep, I walk to the bathroom and my in five minutes flat I wash my face, brush my teeth, comb my hair and braid it. Big braids. I look much better. I don't look like I've been fighting with a monkey! I put on jeans and a shirt and go down to the kitchen where Laura is sitting on the stool eating and Jacob is nowhere to be seen.

"Ah, I was just about to come and get you," she says. "Let's roll!"

We walk to the center and it's just as bad as I remember it. Bright lights, dark halls, white walls, lost souls. We get to the room with the big chair in the middle to lie down on. I feel shivers down my spine.

"Can you please sit, Eva." Laura points at the chair.

I went to the chair and took a deep breath before I sit. I hear a familiar voice telling me to relax. I can't see anyone here but I can hear voices.

"Eva, tell us what happened when your dad gave you away to the man called Ethan," a male voice says.

I close my eyes and try to recall the early things that happened. I was eleven years old.

"I woke up in a dark place, it smelled disgusting. Nasty. Sickening. It smelled like someone had peed on every wall in there. I sat in the corner crying and sobbing to myself. I remember that my dad gave me away. I had no idea who to."

I swallow hard and continue.

"Suddenly, the door is kicked open, and a guy comes barging in. I ask him who he is and he tells me to shut up or he'll cut my tongue out. He also says that he loves little virgin girls like me. I don't even know what a virgin is. Every bit in me is terrified. He grabs my arm, andpulls me all the way up the stairs to the attic. I am moaning in pain the entire way. I want to be killed right now, and not go through anything I can't handle for the rest of my life."

I stop. Pause for breath.

"Good. Carry on Eva," continues the disembodied voice. I continue.

"He throws me roughly to the ground and he tells me to go to the bathroom and change. There is something for me on the sink, I can barely move because my legs feel like Jell-O, I can barely even see because everything is blurry. He kicks my ankle and tells me to move faster or he'll take my clothes off by himself. I run to the bathroom. The sink is dirty and smells so bad and there is a broken mirror in which you can hardly see your face properly. I catch my face, and there are bruises, under my eyes and on my cheeks. I look like I haven't slept in a year. My lips are cut and bleeding.

I take off my clothes and put on what he has put there. A dress, short and made of satin. At first I thought it was something that would make me feel comfortable and warm and clean, but it only made me feel exposed. I tried to pull it down as much as I can but it won't. My entire legs are revealed, up to my butt, and my hands my neck are on display.

He yells to me once, twice to get out of the bathroom and the third time he shouts if I don't get out he'll come and pull me on a leash as if I'm a dog. So I walk out trying my best to cover myself. He smiles lasciviously, licks his lips, then sweeps me up and carries me across the room. He holds me so tightly that I know his fingers will leave bruises on my arms, and then he tosses me hard on the bed like a piece of meat."

My voice trails off. The memories are too painful.

"Go on, Eva," murmurs Laura gently.

"Okay," I say. "I fall on my back, and he climbs on top of me, I try to push him away but he holds both of my small child's hands in his one hand. I cry and sob when his lips touch my neck, his face is unshaven and his breath stinks. His weight pins me down and his free hand is moving from my face to my neck to my breast to my belly to my private parts to my thighs and to my inner thighs and I cry out. Yell. Scream as he touches me in my most secret place. Violates me with his hand. Jams his other hand into my mouth. Licks my face with his disgusting tongue. I try to resist but I can't. I'm helpless.

He turns me over and spanks my buttocks hard until they are bruised and bleeding.

When he forces himself into me, I scream with pain. Somewhere in my head I know he should not do this. I am a minor. I am a child. I shut my eyes, tight shut, and make myself go to another world. I go to a world where I am dancing. I fly to a world where I am not being raped.

A world where I am chasing butterflies instead of screaming in pain as he thrusts himself in and out of me again and again and again.

I howl again and he covers my mouth with his free hand and yells at me to shut the fuck up. He pulls me by the hair to the bathroom, rips the dress off me completely and my entire body is exposed to him.

"You are a dirty little bitch now. Let's clean you up,' he growls.

He holds my arm tight while he opens the faucet and runs the bath, then after a few minutes he throws me in the cold water. I try to breathe but my lungs are shrinking and collapsing, the water freezing and stinging me everywhere. I squeal and he forces my head under the water.

This is it. I'm going to die for sure. I think I am bleeding between my legs, and I want to die anyway, after what he has done to me. But that is too easy. He pulls me out and my teeth are chattering and I am almost unconscious. He laughs a hollow, mirthless laugh. To him, torturing and raping a child is fun.

I cry and cry. He punches me hard. I pass out.

When I wake he is till leering at my naked body. There are now school clothes on the bed. He tells me to put them on tonight, as he is dropping me to school early in the morning. After everything he just did to me he still wants to take me to school? Like this?

When I try the jeans they fit perfectly but the shirt is too big. I had to roll the sleeves up. I slept on the hard bed that night, no cover or mattress.

In the morning I wake up freaking out, I think I have had a nightmare or something. But I soon realize it has all been real. The lights an empty room, there's nothing but the bed I'm sleeping on.

He enters the room and tells me he will take me to school but only if I stick to one condition. That I don't tell anyone about him, or reveal what he is doing to me. He has spies at the school, kids he has paid to inform on me.

I shouldn't talk to anyone if I want to stay alive.

My insides hurt, so I nod to him because I want to go to school and I busy my brain with anything except what he has done to me.

Then, whilst driving to and back from school, he hooded my eyes so I had no idea where he lived.

And he did it for six long years.

In school I didn't talk to anyone and I was so glad that my hair would cover my face so no one would see the bruises. He was careful to hit and burn me where it didn't easily show. I paid attention in all my classes, and when teachers tried talking to me and asked if everything was fine at home I said yes. I even lied to them and told them I had a fight with my brother and fell down the stairs. During breaks I would sit in the library and read books, or do my assignments because I knew Ethan wouldn't let me do them. When school finished, he was the first one standing outside. Waiting. In the car he would just cover my eyes again, and then throw me in that bedroom like I was his personal possession.

Sometimes he'd feed me cold green peas that tasted like shit, but I ate them anywaybecause starvation would kill me faster than he could. Once, when school ended, he didn't show up for a week, and I was sitting alone without food. All I had was water and a stubborn refusal to die.

One day he came to me, his eyes were red like his brain was boiling in his skull. He was literally shaking with anger. I was sleeping, I opened my eyes wide and he was sitting on my back. I was struggling to breathe, but he was smoking a cigarette and it smelled so bad I felt like I was running out of air. I knew he was high or drunk, but then I screamed as he took the cigarette and pressed it so hard into the back of my neck. The pain was astonishing, pulsing through my entire body. I think I was in so much pain and terror I wet myself.

I yelled as hard as I could so he punched the back of my head hard. My fist was taut on the sheet. And I yelled until he was off me, the pain didn't go away, it was the most painful thing I'd ever known, even more than the rape.

When I wake up the next morning he isn't there. I try to stand but I fall, I try again and I stagger to the broken mirror. My hair is long and disgusting. My poor dead mother used to trim my hair every two months, but not anymore. My body smells so bad because I haven't had a proper bath, so I scrub water all over me from the sink. It is the height of June, it's hot outside, and I will be twelve next birthday because New Year's Eve has been and gone, and my mom told me that every first of January was my birthday.

I am eleven years old, locked in an attic and raped by a maniac.

Some days he would come in, and belt me as hard as he could. Whip me like a cowering dog. I feel so sore that I think he has flayed me alive. I beg God to take my soul, then I can't be tortured again."

Suddenly, bright lights go on in the room. The chair is adjusted, and the male voice speaks.

"Thank you Eva. That will be enough for today.

I look for Laura and see her shaking in the corner of the treatment room.

She has been crying.

I am exhausted.

"May I rest a little? Before we go home?' I ask. "Of course you can, Eva,' says the male doctor's voice. Take as long as you like."

I drift away, exhausted.

When I wake up, I am in the same dark room, in the big chair. I look around for Laura but she isn't there. "Hello?" I shout. "Is anyone there?" I stand up and walk to the door, I attempt to open it, but its locked. I knock on the door and then scream for help but no one answers me. I try not to freak. I exhale and inhale a couple of times without moving, trying to think of a way out of here, Laura wouldn't leave me here. No way. "Laura!" I shout loudly and still no one answers.

"Well now. Look who it is," a deep voice hisses. It's not the doctor, Ben or Jacob. I turn around and a figure appears. My heart is beating so hard it is almost out of my chest, and when the man walks under the light, his face is clearly shown.

It's Ethan.

The man who tortured me for years

The man who burned me, belted me, and raped me.

I breathe deeply, and my eyelids are heavier now.

"You know my name now," he says walking closer to me. I back away from him.

"How did you?" I stop talking.

Terrified. Frozen to the spot in fear.

He comes closer to me, only inches away now. I can smell the same nasty breath. I'm taller now, so my face is closer to his.

"They told you my name. Didn't they?" he growls. "You never knew it before!"

"How did you find me?" I stutter.

He laughs the same hollow, evil laugh.

"Oh Eva. Don't you understand, you stupid little bitch? I never let you go."

"What?" I yell, and he moves his hand to my breasts. I try to step back but the wall is behind me. I am trapped.

"We will always be together." he says, his voice cold, and dead as the grave. "Always. I didn't leave you. I just ran away to keep myself safe."

"I don't understand," I murmur in sheer terror. Does he mean that I never left his side, and all these months I've been with him?

"No. NO!" I yell at him, and he vanishes like feathers in the air.

What is happening? Where am I?

Which world am I in?

I go back to the chair because everything is spinning around. I see Laura and Jacob and Ben and Luke and Mom and Ethan, all talking in words I cannot understand.

Then everything goes black, and as silent as the grave.

Chapter Twelve

" Eva, are you alright?" Laura is talking to me, and I open my eyes. She is standing right next to me and I'm lying on the same chair in the same room.

"What happened?" I ask her.

"You fainted, honey, but they want you to tell them more, if you can. Are you able to do that?" she says, concern clear in her voice.

"What time is it now?" I ask, trying to stand, but she pushes me gently back against the chair.

"It's nearly six," she says with a smile, and I wonder why I have a thumping headache and why I am so hungry.

"Alright. I can do this," I tell her and lay back on the chair. She walks to the door and blows me a kiss before leaving and shutting the door behind her.

"Eva, please start again when you're ready," a male voice that I don't recognize says.

"Nothing different happened for years. I guess between the ages of was thirteen, to sixteen. I suffered more years of rape and starvation. It was the same horrible routine. Then, just before I turned seventeen, he came back with food and a large sack over his shoulder. There was a slender arm dangling from it. He threw it on the ground, and a body crawled out, wincing in pain. It was a girl around seventeen. I backed away but he just threw a sandwich at me and told me to feed myself and be ready for him.

When he closed the door I crawled toward the girl and she gave me a whimper of protest. I told her it was okay, that I wasn't going to hurt her, but she scurried away and hugged her knees to her chest.

Her arms and legs were bruised and she had big purple circles around her eyes/ Her blonde hair was a total mess. I took half of the sandwich and gave her the other and she took it but didn't talk to me.

At that time, I felt that she wouldn't survive as long as I had, but she did, and she stayed with me for the rest of the time that I was there.

Suddenly, a thought occurs to me.

"Laura when they took me out of that house, did they take her out too?" I ask, knowing that Laura is listening to me.

"We didn't know there was anyone with you in that house," Laura replies.

I open my eyes and she's in the same room as me, staring in terror with her eyes wide.

"He took her one day, then me the next. He shared us and tortured us equally. Her name was Amelia and she's eighteen. She was a year older than me."

"Laura, can you please leave the room now?" the male voice says, and Laura leaves once more.

"Please keep talking Eva. Any more memories are vital at this stage," he continues.

"Well, one day when I was in the eleventh grade, I was sitting on the bed reading a novel that I had stolen from the school library before summer vacation. I had hidden it in my sweater so Ethan wouldn't find it. A strange man that I had never seen before came in with a pot and poured hot boiling water straight onto my back. I screamed loudly but he beat me on the head with pot and I almost passed out. He held my legs with both hands, Amelia was whimpering with fear as he pulled me all the way to downstairs to the kitchen.

He forced my head into the oven and turned all the burner knobs on.. I think I would have been gassed there and then, but God was on my side at that moment because, after a few seconds, he realized that the gas was out, so he grunted in anger and pulled me by my hair to another room, the one with the bed that Ethan would use when he raped me."

For a few moments, there was silence. I was so relieved when the disembodied voice said:

"Thank you, Eva. That will be all for today."

The entire drive back Jacob is talking to Laura, but I don't bother to listen because I can't stop thinking of Amelia. More important, I can't believe I've forgotten her these past few months. I've wiped it from my brain. She could be dead now. I feel selfish and worthless.

"Laura, we have to go back to that house," I say, interrupting their conversation.

"Eva, we can't. I will call the police station that found you, and tell them to go and check the place over again

"I want to go with them" I tell her, and she turns her face to look at me. It's the first time that I've ever seen her angry.

"No, Eva. Absolutely no. It's too dangerous. We can't afford to let anyone follow us, and find out where you are," she says.

And she means it.

I don't have anything to say. I stay totally silent, looking out of the window. Thinking of Amelia.

I can't eat dinner with Laura and Jacob, I feel like throwing up even though I haven't eaten since breakfast. I lie down on my bed and have flashbacks of Ethan holding the scissor threatening to cut my lashes off, but instead he just cuts my wrists to make me look suicidal.

The man with the boiling water came back quite a few times. Once with a woman called Bunny. She had the most annoying voice that used to ring in my ears.

She was abusive too. One day she forced me to take off all of my clothes and stand in front of her and Ethan, doing nothing. Naked. Then they threw water, beer, and trash on me. She laughed as he urinated on me.

Then she urinated on me too.

I thought that, as a female herself she would understand and maybe set me free, but she only told Ethan to keep going on doing whatever he was doing to me. She yelled at me, screaming that I was just a slut who got fucked by her own father.

I closed my eyes, and I tried to go away to my other world, where the butterflies flutter by.

Where Bunny and Ethan and the other guy never existed at all.

Chapter Thirteen

"You don't look so good," says Ben, hugging me.

"This past week has been hell. I haven't slept well since I started the testimony, it's like I'm re-living everything."

I throw my hands in the air and sigh. It's been a week since I last saw Ben or even talked to him, and I have missed him.

We go to Ben's apartment and Aiden is fast asleep on the couch, so Ben takes me to his room. I sit on the bed and he sits next to me.

"How did everything go?" he says, looking at me so kindly.

"Well, I think those people are sometimes so heartless. I know they are trying to gather evidence to convict Ethan, but I fainted a few times and they still took me back inside and told Laura not to listen or interrupt while I talked. In the end, they just kicked her out, saying that if she wanted to help me she has to leave me alone. I hate that place," I tell him, while looking out of the window. The view isn't as perfect as it is from Laura's condo.

"I had the worst week ever, they gave me injections and pills to keep me awake, and others to stop me from getting anxious. I stayed awake for days, it's just awful."

I lay on the bed and he lay next to me on his facing me while I'm staring at the ceiling.

"I'm sorry, I badly wanted to be with you but Laura didn't answer her phone and I asked Jacob about you and he just said you were fine, but you can't answer the phone." His voice is sad.

"What did you do for a whole week while I wasn't there?" I asked him, smiling again, trying to cheer him.

"Aiden and I watched a few movies, and some sport. You know, typical boy stuff. it wasn't as much fun as spending time with you," he sighed.

Then suddenly, he takes his shirt off, I try to turn away but I can't. He is beautiful on the outside as well as the inside. I lose my breath and get buried under the covers. I'm trying to look at his blue sparkling eyes but his naked chest is a bigger distraction. He closes the door and then gets under the sheets with me. His eyes tell me we are not going to leave this place once my lips touch his.

He tries to kiss me but I turn my face away, and the kiss lands on my cheek and I giggle.

"If we kiss now it will be difficult to leave your room," I whisper as his nose touches mine and butterflies gather in my stomach. "I don't mind, do you?" he says, and I shake my head.

His lips are moving in sync with mine. I feel loved, I feel confident, I feel myself with him, and his touch arouses my entire body every time.

His kiss makes me feel safe. I place my hands on his chest meaning to push him away, but he gets closer and I place both my hands around his neck and our kiss deepens. He breaks the kiss but his face is still close to mine,. I catch a breath before he once again places his lips on mine, moving down to my neck and I push him slowly away.

"I can't. I want to, but I just can't" I stammer, and I stand and leave the room.

"Eva," he says, pulling his shirt back on and running behind me. I'm sorry. What happened?"

"Nothing, it's just not right. I mean, it is right. But just not now, Ben" I tell him and he smiles, but it doesn't touch his eyes. He looks disappointed. A little crushed. I don't know if he feels like I'm a scared little girl, or if he regrets what he just did.

A few minutes later, we leave the apartment and walk to the mall. I interlock my fingers with his. He hasn't said a word since we left the bedroom.

"You know you are the only guy aside from Jacob that I feel safe with. I don't want to lose that," I say, looking anywhere but at him.

"Yeah I know. It's my fault anyway. I shouldn't move that quickly," he says gently, and wraps his hand around my waist and kisses me on my hair.

Suddenly, I catch a glimpse of someone I used to know. I turn around and it is definitely the same girl.

It is my best friend.

The one I loved so much. The one who cut me out of her life in a heart beat.

I stand there, staring at her. She stares back. My legs are like Jell-O.

She walks towards me, and then stops in front of me. I stare at her. Her face. Her eyes. They are a kind of pale green to brown. They are such lovely eyes.

My wounds open again.

She moves to hug me but I raise my hands so she can shake it. The secret handshake that we first invented when I thought we were in love. We perform it perfectly, as if it were only yesterday. She holds my hand tight. I can feel her regret. I can see it in her eyes.

I hold her even tighter.

"Hey, beautiful," I mumble.

"Hi there, Princess," she says.

All of my heartbreak comes back. I feel like crying. Like kicking her. Like hugging her. But I just stare at her.

Eyes locked. Memories flooding. She stares. I stare back. Pale green and brown eyes locked in memories. I bet my eyes reflect my own pain. I let go of her hand and she does the same. I turn around without any words.

I feel tears gather in my eyes.

Memories flash back in front of me.

I see memories of us laughing, hugging, and holding hands without anyone seeing. Staying up the entire night on the phone even though we weren't saying a word.

I see memories of us fighting and singing, or laughing and kissing.

144

Us. Us. Us.

No one ever knew what was it about us. But we did. It was special.

We were so full of love.

No one knew that we were so in love.

No one knew anything about her loving me.

No one had a clue that I was so in love with her.

Her eyes. Her hugs. Everything.

And she left me so easily, quite literally after kissing me for the first time.

She left me because she was scared.

Too scared of what society would think.

She broke my heart into little pieces, and I'm still trying my best to fix myself.

I will never talk about our love. My first unforgotten love.

A love that dare not speak its name.

"Come on, let's go," Ben said, pulling me with him, and we walk in a couple of shops and I'm not paying attention to him or anything else.

As we walk back to the condo he simply says:

"Who was she?"

"You wouldn't like to know," I murmur and try to climb the stairs, but he holds me back and points to the chair. We sit.

"Tell me," he says.

"I told you. She's the girl I fell in love with at school. That's the first time I've seen her since she dropped me for no reason," I say softly.

"Are you okay now?" he says.

"Yes. She just took me by surprise, that's all," I lie.

I didn't tell him how shocked I had been that I still had feelings for her.

"Alright," he says, but he isn't convinced. His brows are frowned and his jaw clenched.

"Benjamin, I haven't seen her in two years okay? Don't make a big scene out of this, please," I turn around to look at him and our faces are just inches away.

"You know what Eva, just go. Please. Just go." I can see he is trying to be as calm as he can.

"So this is how you solve things," I say, him and stand up, staring at him.

He is still not looking at me.

"No, Eva, you haven't seen yourself in the past couple of hours. Just daydreaming. I feel as if I have been walking and talking with myself.' He is almost yelling.

"I wasn't daydreaming," I say, and my voice is shaking. I just can't cry now.

"Yeah whatever, Eva just please leave," he says coldly. He has never spoken to me this way before I walk away to the condo. I feel the tears rolling down my face and my throat is like a rock. I run to my room because Laura and Jacob are watching TV and talking, and I sob into my pillow and hug it tight.

I don't love her anymore. I love him.

I don't want her anymore. I want him.

I don't want her hug. I want his.

Someone knocks at the door and I wipe my tears quickly, my red nose and eyes will not hide the fact that I've been crying.

"Did anything happen to you?" Laura says worriedly.

"No." I shake my head and hug her, my sobs get worse when she hugs me back, my crying is so loud that Jacob runs in thinking something really wrong has happened.

"He probably just hates me," I say in between sobs and whimpering.

"Who?" Jacob asks.

"Benjamin. I just didn't mean to drift away into my own thoughts. I'm so sorry." I say crying.

"Okay, calm down so we can understand," begs Laura.

"Do I need to call him?" Jacob says angrily, and I shake my head.

"I just saw a girl I used to date back in school. It wasn't like she wanted us to go public. She was ashamed of me, and of herself back then. Anyway I saw her for the first time in ages today, and Ben now knows everything about her because I told him. He thinks that I don't love him and I just want to be with her. That's wrong. I want him. Not her," I say and my sobbing ceases.

"Well, if he truly loves you he will never leave you, no matter how bad things are," Laura says. "You just need to give him some time to understand and apologize if he has been mean to you."

"What if he doesn't?" I tell her.

"He will. Trust me, if he loves you, he will," she says, stroking my back.

They tell me that they love me and it doesn't matter if Benjamin doesn't anymore, because family comes first and they are my family now. They leave the room and my head is buzzing and my eyes are burning.

I am so grateful for my new family right now.

Chapter Fourteen

I wake up late the next morning. I glance at the clock and its ten in the morning, I crawl to the bathroom and stare at the mirror my eyes are surrounded by black circles and I look pale and freaky. I wash my face and tie my hair in a ponytail. I fell asleep last night with my clothes on so I change into something warmer and more comfortable.

"Good morning frown face," Laura says with her best goofy smile.

"Morning," I murmur, and my stomach is still tied. I don't feel like eating anything.

"You feel alright?" she asks and her face is bashful.

"No," I snap.

"Can I help?" she mutters.

I shake my head and walk back to my room. I feel like reading and not talking to anyone. My phone starts vibrating and when I glance

149

at the watch its eleven thirty, I look at the phone and the number is unknown. I won't answer calls like that so I just ignore it and it starts ringing again.

I give in and answer.

"Eva?" The voice is familiar.

"Yeah? Who is it?" I ask, freaking.

"It's Aiden! Wassup?" His voice makes me feel better.

"Oh hi Aiden." I exhale, and lay down.

I thought it was Ethan.

"What are you up to?" he asks.

"Nothing much"

"Want to hang out?"

"Um, with who?" I ask warily.

"Oh, just us two," he says lightly.

A part of me wants Ben to be there. I would talk to him even though I'm pretty mad, and I don't want to lose him. Wonder if he feels the same.

"Oh yeah okay, if you want to," I say, and he says he'll be here at five because he has some things to do.

I hang up and keep on reading. A couple of hours go by and suddenly I feel starving. I walk down to the kitchen and make myself a sandwich. Laura is sitting in her office looking busy. I look at my phone and see a text from Aiden saying he is very excited to hang out. I text him a smiley face back.

I'm not sure what he wants, but it's great that I have started to make new friends already.

I wear my jacket and black shirt with jeans and go outside to find Aiden sitting on the same chair Ben was last sitting on. I shudder at that thought. But Aiden is smiling perfectly. I smile at him too.

"So, I actually wanted to talk to you a bit," Aiden says, scratching the back of his head. He's either confused or his words aren't getting out in a good way.

"About what?" I asked quizzically.

"Uh, what happened between you and Benjamin?"

We walk away.

I don't want to talk about this in front his best friend but I think telling him may help to fix things between Ben and I.

"Well, when Ben and I were in the mall, I saw an old friend that I used to have a thing with and he flipped out and yelled at me," I told him, looking desperate.

He nods and says:

"Yeah, I've never seen him smoke two cigarettes so fast at the same time. I knew there were something up but I didn't expect it was you until he got little bit drunk and started saying things," he sniffs.

"Things?" I echoed.

"Yeah."

"Like what?"

"Something about his family and about you leaving him soon, and things about studies and his hometown. You know, drunken stuff," Aiden says, lighting a cigarette and offering me one. I shake my head.

"I'm not leaving him, I just freaked out and got all emotional thinking he would leave me," I puff my cheeks out and roll my eyes.

"Well if he thinks you're leaving him and you think he is leaving you, both of you will leave each other pretty soon," he smiles. "Someone has to make a move and talk to the other. I'd help you and talk to him but I don't think he will be glad about us meeting Or you telling me about his condition last night." He puffs out smoke.

"Where is he right now?" I ask, sitting next to Aiden. He lights up another cigarette. I can't resist saying it.

"You do know that will kill you," I mumble, but he just smirks and carries on puffing out the smoke.

"He was doing things on the laptop when I left. Something about going to check on summer classes." Aiden's jaw is sharp and his blonde hair is bright yellow.

"I see. I'll just text him when I get back and ask him to meet so we can clear things up," I say, freeing my hair.

"You look much prettier when your hair is down," he says, and I flush.

"Thank you Aiden. That is a nice thing to say, " I tell him.

"I always thought you were beautiful and special. And I still do." He smiles.

"May I ask for your pardon?" I look at him and try to hide my smile.

"At school, I always wanted to be friends with you and stop everyone from hurting you and making you feel like you don't belong in this world. But you actually did belong. I never thought you'd survive high school. I was truly worried."

I find it strange that he is confessing his feelings to me even thought I am with his best friend. But he doesn't seem to care.

"What happened?" I frown, facing him.

"They all thought you died," he coughs. "We thought when you vanished that you had committed suicide."

I laughed, hard. I laughed because they all wanted me dead. I laughed because they never talked to me and got my side of the story, yet they still wanted me dead. I laughed because I got some of the highest marks in the class, and they all thought I was such a loser.

"What's so funny Eva?"

"They all wanted me dead, and I didn't harm anyone. I didn't even make eye contact with anyone

"Well, I think they were just jealous," he chuckles, and I tilt my head a bit and smile.

"You're right, but I still wish they had taken the trouble to ask me about why I wore shitty clothes or why am was bruised everywhere or why I looked like a monster."

I run my hand through my hair.

"You didn't look like a monster. You just looked tired on the outside. Even though your soul was just perfect. I could see it, if no ne else could." He winks at me.

"Thank you," I murmur.

We walk back toward Laura's condo because Aiden has a night shift at McDonalds and he can't be late.

"I really enjoyed talking to you" I told him and he hugs me and kisess me on the cheek. It doesn't feel like Ben's kiss but it shows me how much he cares about me.

"I enjoyed that too. Talk to Ben babe," he says, and walks away. I walk back to the condo and Jacob is sitting on the stool, reading a newspaper.

"You were with Ben?" he asks, confused.

"No, I was with Aiden. A friend of mine from high school," I say, sitting next to him.

"You and Ben still not talking?" he asks.

"I haven't talked to him," I confirm.

"Are you planning to?" he taps on the table.

"Yeah, actually" I smile to him and show him my phone.

"Good."

I realize that Jacob cares about Ben almost as much as me.

I stand and make my way to Laura's office. "Hey," I say. "Wassup mom?" Her eyes widen. "I mean Laura" I correct myself.

"No, it's okay to call me that, I love it." She motions her hand in front of her and I sat on the couch.

"Where did you go, I was looking for you?"

"I've been out with Aiden. He's a friend of mine from high school. He's also a friend of Ben's" I tell her, and she nods.

"So? How did it go?"

"Great. It went great," I say pulling my phone out of my pocket to text Ben.

"Alright," she says, returning to her work.

I text:

Hey Ben, still feeling like a storm of fury? Can we meet to talk? If you would like, please text me.

I send it to him and go to my room.

Half an hour later Ben texts me back. He is coming here in ten minutes which makes my heart beat as fast as a train. I close the book and run to Laura's office telling her I'll be gone for a bit.

"To where?" she yells as I run out.

"Ben is wanting to talk - I won't be long!"

I blow her a kiss and run out, down the stairs and into the street. I see him walking towards me. My heart feels like it will explode.

"Hi" I say my throat is dry.

"Hey," he says with a jaw set so sharp, I could cut my wrist with it. His hair is a mess and his eyes look tired

"I think we need to fix things up, " he says. We walk together to the park and by the time we get there, it's dark and there is no one out there.

He finally starts to talk.

"Eva, I know I shouldn't get this mad but I love you and I don't think I can handle you drifting away from me," His voice is desperate and his eyes are crying for help.

"I just don't understand why you got so angry, it's not like I hugged her or anything. I just said hi," I say.

"Yes, you say that, but you should've seen your expression, it was all about regret and love. I wish you'd look at me the same way. After you saw her, you were so distracted it was like you weren't with me, and the thought of losing you is like losing my family all over again. I couldn't bear that." He stops walking and wrings his hands in a gesture of regret.

The light above illuminates us, and I can see his hair, his eyes are desperate and his lips aren't even smiling. I feel a pinch of guilt and pain.

"No way could I leave you for her. She broke my heart. I only felt regret when I saw her. I regretted kissing her, I regretted hugging her.

I regretted allowing myself to love her. Love is powerful, Ben, you can't just control it. I'm in love with you now and there's no way I would drop you for her, no way I'd love her back now," I tell him and tears swim in my eyes. There aremere inches between Ben and I, yet we aren't touching. My body would die for his touch right now. Just for his hug.

"Believe me you are the best thing that has ever happened to me," I whisper to him and he is just staring at me without moving or saying anything.

Seconds later he moves his hands and places them on the side of my face.

"I love you too," he says, pulling me to him, and carrying me from the ground. I bury my face in his neck and he smells so good that I can't describe it. We seem to hug forever, before his phone rings and he lets go of me. I didn't want to let go of him. I wish I had never met her, I wish I had never fallen in love with her.

He is talking German I guess because I don't understand what he is saying.

He hangs up and places both of his hands on the sides of my face and kisses me. We separate and he says we have to go because it's getting late. We walk hand by hand and I smile widely like a fool. Before I go back into the condo he says:

"There's something I haven't told you."

And my stomach is tied in one hundred knots.

"About?" I say, clearing my throat.

"I have a sister, and she's visiting me tomorrow for a week," he says, running his hand through his hair haven't told me about her.

"You never mentioned her," I say.

"Well, that's because I hate talking about her. You'll know why soon," he shrugs.

I nod and smile. "Tomorrow?" I ask him.

"Yes, and I'll come get you before I get her," he smiles.

"Sure. Until tomorrow then," and I kiss him goodnight.

And it is the sweetest kiss in a lifetime.

Chapter Fifteen

I wake up to the sound of talking I walk out to the top of the stairs and I hear Laura talking to Jacob.

"I'm worried that she has fallen in love whilst she is still under the watch of doctors at the center, even though she hates the place," I hear her say. I can't let her get even more damaged by him," Laura says, and her voice is tired.

"I understand, but if Ben makes her happy there's nothing we can do. As long as she's happy, we should be happy,"

What are they talking about? I don't understand.

"I'll give her some time then," Laura sighs.

I sneak back into the room, closing the door quietly. Surely she can't be thinking of taking Ben away from me, and she sure as hell can't take me back to the center. I press my face into the pillow and feel like choking myself but I soon calm down, I am learning to cope with negative thoughts. I glance at the watch and its only two in the morning. I text Ben and tell him that I can't sleep. Fifteen minutes later while I'm stretched out on the floor he calls and the vibration causes me to jump up and hit my head on the table next to the bed.

"What?" I hiss softly down the phone.

"Hey, its' Ben." he says.

"My head just hit the table, while I was on the ground" I tell him, rubbing my head.

"What are you even doing on the freaking ground?" He laughs and I smile.

"I'm bored."

"Well I couldn't sleep too, I'm just trying to look for a place where my sister can stay for a week." He sounds angry again.

"Are you really that angry that she'll be visiting?" I asked getting back into the bed.

"Not really. I haven't seen her in like five years. She didn't even attend my parents funeral," he says.

"Not nice" is all I can say.

"Actually she's my twin sister. She ran away on our seventeenth birthday, our parents got really angry and worried. I'm not sure they ever forgave her."

"Hey, I never even knew you were a twin. If she's like you she can't be all bad," I say, trying to calm him down.

"Yeah. I'm not so sure. She's been living in Las Vegas since than. I received some emails from apologizing for not attending the funeral. She said I could come and live with her, but to be honest, I prefer being by myself. Anyway, just reading between the lines, I sometimes wonder whether she is on something." His voice is deep with pain.

"Who knows? We'll get to know about it when you meet her", I say.

"But I don't want to meet her. She betrayed my family and practically destroyed it!"

His voice is furious again..

"Ben, will you ever leave me?" I ask him, and I can hear him breathing.

"No. I will not. What brought that up?"

"Just wanted to make sure," I say quietly. I want to trust him. I want to prove to Laura that he will never hurt me, or do me wrong.

"Hey, Ben, do you like brownies?" I say, trying to change the subject and distract him.

"Yes. I love brownies." I can hear him relaxing again.

"We should bake some together, I can bake them perfectly," I tell him, bringing back bitter memories of selling them on the streets. Knocking on doors, barefoot. I push it away.

"Yes, we should, I'll be your assistant," he says and his voice makes me need him here with me.

"I wish you were here right now," I whisper, and I hear him sigh.

"I wish I were too. Maybe you should spend the night with me we could watch a Disney movie and cuddle."

"Maybe. Who knows?"

"What are you doing?" he asks.

"Just in bed, reading, why?"

"I just want to know, is that weird?"

"No," I giggle.

I fall asleep with the phone still on, and the sound of him chattering away to me.

I wake up to Laura opening the curtain and allowing the sun to flood the room. I groan and she says: "Wake up lazy head!" I raise my head and my phone is still under my face. I remember that I was talking to Ben, and wonder when he hung up. I get dressed and go downstairs wearing my new Converse and my cool purse and its fifteen minutes past eleven

"Good morning, Jacob" I kiss his cheek and sit on the stool next to him.

"Good morning Eva."

"You look great, going somewhere?" he asks, not looking at me but at his newspaper.

"Yeah, I'm going out with Ben and his sister,"

"I didn't know he had a sister," he says, surprised.

"He has a twin sister. He hates her but she insists on visiting him."

His mouth is an O and I giggle at his expression.

"I never knew he was a twin," he says.

"Anyway, Laura and I are going to a conference about Laura's new book," Jacob says, and I frown and stare at Laura. She hasn't said anything about a book.

"It's not out yet, it'll be out next month," she corrects Jacob. "We are only going to answer some questions. You can come if you want to," she asks me and I shake my head.

I'm a little annoyed, I've been living with her for four months now and she didn't even tell me about it. But then why would she? I finish eating and listen to Jacob saying something about going to Europe on a tour to promote the book.

"That's a great idea" I add up.

"Yeah, I was thinking of it but,"

"But what?" I interrupt her.

"What about you? I can't leave you here alone," she says hurriedly.

"I'm not a child, Laura. I can manage myself pretty well. I was actually looking for a job did I tell you?" I'm trying to stay calm but my tone betrays me.

"You guys are always so worried about me, like if I fall from your hands I'll break. Laura I've been broken badly and you have helped to tape me back together but I'm still living, and I love you but you have to know, I am nearly nineteen. I'm an adult now." I smile at her and tears swim in her eyes. I feel so bad.

"I know Eva, but seeing you getting hurt again would destroy me," she mumbles.

I shake my head. "I'm good. I'm safe here. Trust me," I say, and hug her.

"Anyway, that's news!" she says. "What kind of jobs are you looking for?"

"I don't know. Anything respectable and easy," I tell her and she grins.

I feel good that I have told her about this. She needs to understand that I am responsible for myself now. I am a survivor. And I am powerful. Not like a year ago.

"I have to go" I tell them, 'I'm meeting Ben." They smile, and I leave quickly.

On my way there, my old paranoia starts to surface.

I think everyone is staring at me. I walk faster, taking no time to get to Ben's building. I can't even breathe normally so I just sit on the stairs, tilt my head back and close my eyes trying to get some air into my lungs.

"Oh Eva!" Aiden's voice frightened me I knock my head on the stairs. What's up with my head getting knocked everywhere?

"Ouch!" I say loudly.

"Sorry" He sits next to me. "Let me see that." He pulls my head and fondles it. Kisses my hair and says:

"It's all fine don't worry"

"Thanks, where are you going in such a hurry? " I ask him.

"Well, I thought of walking around to see you, because Ben is not here.

"Where is he?" I ask, confused.

"I think he went to Target. Where he works," he shrugged.

"I didn't know that he had a job," I say, irritated. Why didn't he tell me? I kept him up the entire night on the phone.

"We both do! How else would we pay for this shitty apartment!" he smiles.

"Oh okay, well I think I'll wait here if that's okay," I inform him.

"Do you want me to stay here with you?" He sits next to me, lighting a cigarette.

"If you insist." I wave my hand. I hate that smell.

We sit there in silence. I find it awkward at first but then I realize that he is thinking deeply about something. Or someone.

"Are you alright?" I elbow him lightly.

"Hum, yeah I'm great," he smirked. "Just thinking of visiting my mother"

"Do it" I encourage him.

"Yeah she lives in Atlanta" he shakes his head, puffing out the smoke.

"That's like eleven hours away from Chicago, in a car it's like three states or four away." I try to remember the states.

"You've been to it?" he asked surprised.

"Nope, never left Chicago," I smile, covering my face from the sun.

"You are a smart kid," he laughs.

"Yup. I get this a lot."

He laughs, and so do I.

We chat and joke around until Ben arrives fifteen minutes later. He looks at me quizzically.

"I've been here for nearly half an hour," I say. "Luckily, Aiden is keeping me company," I explain, and he looks surprised that I'm here at all.

"I thought you were still asleep, that's why it took me awhile to come back. I did call, " says Ben.

"Oh, I didn't notice. Sorry."

I take my phone out of my purse and there are several missed calls from him.

"Sorry, it was on silent" I mutter and he kisses my cheek.

"I'll be right back, I'll just change my shirt."

He runs up the stairs and Aiden yells after him;

"Sure, that's okay! I'll keep your girlfriend company."

"Shut up!" he yells back, and I giggle because they are both so stupid.

"How did you guysmeet?" I ask Aiden.

"Well we went to the same classes a year ago, and I was working at Target too, he was new there, and I was his guide," he says, smiling.

Ben walks down the stairs wearing a black stretch shirt showing all the details of his body.

"Okay. See you guys later." Aiden waves at us and walks away. I'm staring at Ben and he looks like a model, why does he even date me or love me?

He kisses me and I smile. We walk to his car.

"How are you today honey?" he says, kissing my hand.

"I'm happy, how are you?" I reply.

"I'm happy because I'm here with you," he murmurs, and I blush.

I don't ask him where are we going, I just guess we are going to get his sister.

"Is she flying here today?"

"Yes, her flight lands in like thirty minutes and we have thirty-five or forty minutes to make it to the airport."

He runs his hand through his hair and I can see he is nervous or stressed about something. I place my hand on top of his and he holds my hand.

"Are you alright?" Ben drags me from my thoughts.

"Yeah" I say. "You never told me you had a job"

"Nothing brought it up, besides, I just started working again, I had half a shift today because I told them I have my sister visiting," he said, squeezing my hand.

We drive in silence. His eyes are on the street but his mind is far away, I stare at his perfect face, his jaw is sharp and his lips are soft and his blue eyes dark now. When his eyes are dark it means there's something up with him.

"Is there something wrong with my face babe?" he says, as he checks himself out in the rear-view mirror. I shake my head.

"Just admiring the view," I laugh.

He doesn't.

"Ben, what's wrong?" I ask and he shakes his head.

"Ben, I need to know."

He puffs his cheek out and sighs.

"Well, I don't know how I will react with her, it's frustrating me."

"Just act normal, like the way you act around me." I elbow him lightly.

"The problem is I don't actually feel like seeing her, but I also want to make sure for myself that she is doing fine and that she is safe."

He grips the steering wheel with both hands and continues.

"I know she did a lot of horrible things but she is still my sister after all is said and done.""

Family, I tell myself. Love and care and respect - all the things I didn't have until now.

"Babe, that means you really do care about her, so just act normal and make her feel as if she is missed. Don't make her feel like she has done something wrong," I tell him and he doesn't reply

And then it occurs to me. What if Luke is still out there looking for me, his own sister, wondering if I survived and still breathing? What if he still cares about me and wants to protect me from dad, even though I am capable of protecting myself now?

Even worse, what if Dad killed Luke so he won't snitch on him for killing mom and abusing us,?

The very thought of Luke being killed made me tremble and Ben turned his face slightly to look at me.

"Eva?" His eyes are fixed on me.

"I'm fine," I tell him. He's still looking. "Ben, the road!" I motion ahead, and his eyes fix on the road again.

"We have like fifteen more minutes, are you tired?" He places his hand on my thigh, squeezing lightly.

"No, I'm fine

He turns on the radio and a song booms from the speakers, I have no idea what it is, but Ben starts singing along. I smile at him and stare at him. He is so goofy. He hits the steering wheel and starts singing out loud.

"This is my song" he tells me, turning the volume up. I laugh, really laugh, and he just keeps on singing.

Chapter Sixteen

Forty more minutes of listening to Ben sing and we finally get to the airport and park.

Ben holds my hand and we walk inside, it's crowded and people are pulling bags or crying or hugging or kissing or saying hello and goodbye. People holding flowers just standing there, people with the biggest smiles and the most tearful eyes I've ever seen in my entire life. I smile at the ones who are smiling and look at the ground when I see people crying. Ben stops walking when we get to 'Arrivals,' and I can see how nervous he is.

After five minutes of silence and watching people coming through the arrivals exit, Ben walks a step towards the door when he sees a girl with red long hair, and white skin turning to pink, wearing a black shirt. The shirt reveals her ripped abs, and her navel is pierced. She wears black skinny ripped jeans. She is just gorgeous. If I were a guy I would probably date her. When she takes off her glasses, the blue eyes are the same as Ben's. She wraps her arms around Ben and he does the same. I feel jealous but then, it is his sister. I can see her saying things to him but I don't understand what. They separate and Ben points at me, I tilt my head a bit and smile when she smiles, her white teeth shining.

"Hello there, Eva" she says shaking my hand. "Hi," I say smiling at her and I shake her hand back.

"Ben, she's so hot," she smiles, and Ben's jaw drops. "Thank you so much," I tell her and Ben pulls me to his side from my waist.

We walk back to the car and I move to sit in the back seat but she tells me to sit next to my boyfriend. She is really nice but her look contradicts that. She looks like a rebel, one of those Goth types who celebrate Halloween all dressed in black.

"How did you both meet?" She asks, and Ben rolls his eyes.

"We take classes together" I tell her and she says, "sure you do!" She makes a clicking noise from her mouth.

"By the way my name is Charli. With an I" she says. "I know my brother didn't tell you that"

"Nice name," I say, smiling at her and Ben stares at me with a don't-be-friends-with-my-devil-sister look.

"Thank you," she coughs and we both giggle while Ben goes red as if he will explode.

The entire drive back to the apartment, Charli tells us about her friends at Vegas and her boyfriend here in Chicago. Ben just answers her coldly or makes her feel bad every time she says anything, and eventually she curses at him in German. In truth, they're talking German most of the time, and I feel like some kind of dumb statue between them.

Ben parks his car, andwe get out and start walking to Ben's apartment, with Charli pulling her bag behind her. Ben still looks mad, but then I glance at Charli and she has a wide grin across her face and I wonder why she is this happy.

We get into the apartment, and she tosses her bag on the ground and wanders around. Ben is straight out on to the balcony, and before I go to him Aiden gets out of the room wearing only pants and talking on his phone. Charli looks at him, kind of shocked. I roll my eyes at Aiden and I go to Ben. He is smoking a cigarette.

"I didn't know you smoked" I joke, leaning my body on the wall so I can see his face.

"I try not to in front of you," he snaps, sarcastically.

"You look so annoyed, Ben," I frown and I realize that his brows are even more knotted.

"Yeah, I am." He tosses the cigarette and steps on it.

He stands there sulking, and my eyes drift inside to Charli and Aiden. It seems like she's all over him or he is all over her. She's very close to him and they are giggling. His smile is wide and confident, and so is hers. I sigh and shake my head.

"Um, I think I'll go back home," I say and he doesn't look at me.

"Why?" His voice is hoarse.

"Because you obviously don't want to talk to anyone and I don't feel like hanging with your sister and his new best friend," I shoot back.

"We can all go out for lunch if you want to." His eyes are on me now.

"It's not what I want, it's what you want. All I want is for to be less angry and annoyed." I move my hand to his face, and his eyes fix on mine, clean blue to brown. He doesn't blink and I wish I had the ability to read minds and see what's bothering him.

"Just stay with me, please, I need your company" he whispers, and I lean down to kiss me, but he pulls away. I smile and pull him inside. I take a quick glance at his face and he looks so confused, so pretty and so young.

"Guys, lunch is on me!" I say loudly and Aiden cheers calling me his new best friend. Charli just smiles and I notice that her eyes are on Ben. Maybe she knows he's not fine with her being here. Or there's something they both know that I don't.

They all want pizza, so we walk to a pizza restaurant. When we get inside, I sit next to Ben, and Charli sits next to Aiden, facing us.

"How long are you staying here," Aiden asks Charli.

"About a week," she answers immediately looking at Ben.

There is a moment of silence. Ben says nothing. I try to break the awkward atmosphere.

"You know, Laura and Jacob might go on a tour to Europe soon," I mutter.

"Are you going with them?" asks Ben, who is now looking freaked.

"I don't know. I might" I look down at my knotted fingers.

"When?"

"I really don't know," I shrug.

"Don't leave me for months, I don't think I could bear it" he says quietly.

"I might not go though. I don't know." I feel stupid for telling him, it's just made his mood worse.

The waitress placed two large sized pizzas on the table, with fries and drinks. Suddenly, I feel famished.

Before eating Ben holds my chin and locks his eyes with mine. "You look so beautiful," he says and Aiden yells:

"Please! Get a room!"

The mood lightens during pizza and Ben gradually starts to relax with Charli around. Maybe this won't be so bad after all. However, I know that they both need time to themselves to talk, so when they visit the rest rooms I hatch a plan with Aiden.

Eventually, we all finish up and I grab my purse and place the money on the table. "My treat," I say emphatically. As we leave the building, I motion Ben and Charli to sit in the shade.

"Now," I say, suddenly getting all bossy. "You two are going to have to wait here for the rest of my treat. Aiden and I will go and fetch it."

I wink at Aiden and he smirks back at me.

Ben goes to protest but I motion him to sit back down.

"Hey, Ben. You are always treating me. Now it's my turn."

And with that, Aiden and I race off and leave them to it.

Aidenand I walk together and Charli and Ben are far behind us.

"Well, that worked surprisingly well. You can be quite forceful when you need to be!" he smiles, and then proceeds to tell me terrible jokes all the way to the ice cream parlor. I laugh, even though they aren't funny.

I laugh because Aiden is so full of happiness. I've never seen him sad. He is always cheerful, smiling and making jokes, and to be honest, he cheers me up almost all the time.

We get in the line to buy. It's not crowded. Ben and Charli have followed, and they stand outside, deep in conversation.

Suddenly, I inhale sharply and reach out for the counter. Aiden looks at me.

"Are you okay? Do you want to have a seat," he says, grabbing my hand to steady me. I shake my head.

"Its fine. I just feel a bit tired," I sigh.

We only order for two, because whenever we look outside the window, Ben looks angry, waving his hands around and pointing.

"It doesn't look like it's going great between them," Aiden says, looking at me, and I nod in assent.

"I don't know what's going on but Ben acts so angry around her" I say.

"It's a long story" Aiden mutters. "You should hear it from him"

Is it that bad? Is there something Ben hasn't told me? It reminds me of the last time someone didn't want me to know a secret.

As we sit and eat our ice cream and Aiden fools around, I remember back when my mother was alive. When I saw her and dad talking bluntly, and sneaked up behind them to hear all the conversation.

When he told her that he doesn't want us anymore and that it was not his responsibility to look after someone else's kids.

That was the day I suddenly realized, to my horror, that we weren't his kids.

And if that was true, who the hell was our father?

Worse, what if she's not even our mother?

And in that case, who the hell is our mom?

I fight the urge to curse. I shake it off and Aiden is looking at me anxiously.

"You don't seem good, Eva," he says, eyeing me carefully.

"I'm not." I agree with him. "I feel bloated," I lie, and his expression softens.

Aiden stars talking about senior year again, and how my English teacher gave a talk about helping others and mentioned my name.

"She really was so proud of you, you know? I think she was heartbroken when you left school," he said.

"One day, I hope you will tell me why you left, Eva," he says softly, but Ben walks in looking furious and Charli isn't anywhere to be seen.

"What's wrong bro," says Aiden standing, up and I stand too.

"I think we should go back," Ben mutters and walks out quickly. Aiden lights up another cigarette and gestures to me to go with Ben.

I have to jog to catch him.

"Ben," I say trying to catch a breath.

"If I talk now, you'll regret knowing me," he hisses, and points at me.

"Fine," I say walking slowly, and he storms past me.

I cross my arms and begin to wonder.

I am starting to wonder why I fell in love with him. He is almost like two people in one - stressed and angry, or happy and smiling. I am trying to love him, and it would take a long time to forget about him, but I'm full of doubt now.

I'm not sad, I'm just angry because he is being such a dumb fool to himself, his sister, and to me.

And then I suddenly realize that it is Ben's recent behavior recently that is making me ill. Negative. Unhappy.

He has left behind without looking back, and I don't think that is a very loving thing to do. I inhale and it hurts to breathe, my heart is beating as fast as ever, and my blood is rushing around my body. I feel it pulsing in my temples.

I feel hot, sweaty, what on earth is happening to me?

Another panic attack, I think. I sit and hold my head tight like I'm able to get drive out the demon that's inside me, tormenting me whenever I'm alone in the street.

"Eva, hey Eva." Aiden is shaking me and I look at him, lost, wondering where I am.

"I knew there was something wrong with you" he says, really worried, and he sweeps me up in his arms and carries me, I can feel him walking but I can't open my eyes to see him, its black, all black.

I hear voices, noises. And I hear Aiden's breath in my ears, warm and concerned.

"Aiden I can walk," I whisper. "Trust me"

He lets go of me, places me gently on the ground, and I hold his hand fast to balance myself.

"Thank you. Please link my arm, Aiden," I plead.

Aiden helps me up the stairs to their apartment. My vision is blurry and my head is spinning. I sit on the couch next to Charli.

"Charli," I say slowly and she doesn't answer me. "Ben loves you, but he don't know how to express it, he's just little bit mad."

I feel her eyes on me, Aiden hands me a glass of water, and I take a sip of it.

"He is being so hard to talk to, I understand why is he angry it's just," blurts Charli, and then she cries.

Aiden takes the glass and sits on the stool, looking at his phone.

I place my hand on her back and rub it, I have no idea how to comfort her properly, but I know crying helps.

"Do you need to rest?" I say glancing at the time on my phone. I shut my eyes and open them again.

"I think you need to rest, Eva, not me. Maybe he will be better in the morning. I'm sure of it," she says.

"Hey Charli, come on, I'll show you your room," Aiden calls and she smiles at me with a small, sad smile, wipes her tears, and follows Aiden.

I dial Laura's number, she doesn't pick up quickly. "Hello, Eva?" she says, her voice worried.

"Yeah, hey Laura" I say walking to Ben's room.

"Are you alright?" she breathes

"Yes I'm great." I try to sound unconcerned.

"Oh okay, so, what do you want honey?"

"Um, I was wondering if it's okay to sleepover at Ben's tonight?"

I close my eyes tightly, praying for a yes.

She hums and it feels like a no, but then she says, "Are you sure?"

"We won't do anything," I reassure her.

"Alright, fine. But you had better call me or Jacob tomorrow morning, or I will file you as a missing person." She sounds serious and I laugh. I hear Jacob laughing.

"Thank you so much. Can I talk to Jacob?" I ask, and she hands him the phone.

"Yes, sweet heart" he says and my heart warms.

"You trust me and know that we won't do anything, right? And you know that I will come back home on time, yeah?" I tell him, and my voice is small.

"We trust you. Just be careful," he says, and I nod as if he can see me. "Good night, and take care," he says, and I wish him a good night before he hangs up.

I call Ben but he doesn't answer. I throw myself on his bed and stare at the ceiling. My brain is too painful to be awake right now. I close my eyes, to rest them, and wait for Ben.

I open my eyes and darkness overwhelming me. I'm not in my room and everything is different, it takes me awhile to remember that I'm in Ben's bed. I turn over and he is lying on his side, we're facing each other. He looks so peaceful and beautiful.

"I didn't want to wake you up," he whispers, and I stay still. He moves his hand to my face, and caresses my cheek. Sweet.

"I don't remember falling asleep," I whisper.

"Hey, I know. I cannot believe that you're actually in my bed," he says sweetly and I giggle.

"I need to get out of this dress." I climb out of bed and shrug my jacket off. I turn around and he is staring at me. I blush.

"Well I only have my shirts, but they will look like a night dress on you. Only if you want," he adds hastily.

"That would be more comfortable to sleep in," I say softly.

He gets out of bed, takes his shirt off handing it to me, I raise my eyebrows at him and he says. "What?"

"Nothing, just give it to me!" I grab the shirt from his hand, and hear him getting back into bed. I turn my face to look at him and he is busy with his phone so he doesn't stare.

I take my dress off and I thank God that Laura bought me the fancy black underwear. I take off my bra as well, only because they told us to do that in the shelter, just to prevent breast cancer. I pull on his shirt and it smells of him, I can't resist it, it's literally the best, and I climb back into bed and snuggle next to him. His eyes are open wide.

"What?" I tell him, making myself comfortable next to him.

"To be honest, I never thought you were this brave, " he whispers.

"You were looking at me!" I hit him lightly.

"Well, who could resist?" he says, and I blush wrapping my arms around him. He kisses my forehead repeatedly. "Stop," I whisper, even though I love it. "We need to sleep"

"Alright," he groans, and we lay there next to each other, warm and cozy.

Suddenly, he smiles.

"It's so distracting knowing you aren't wearing anything under my shirt" He mumbles and I move until our faces are on the same level then push my lips against his. His lips move with mine, my tongue is exploring his mouth, his exploring mine, he moves on top of me and deepens the kiss.

I never hesitate. I thought of sleeping with him first, and I love him so much, I just want us to be together forever. I am in no doubt that he is the man I will stay with as long as I'm alive.

He rests his forehead on mine, and our eyes lock. How perfect he looks right now. I move my eyes down to his naked chest, and he is perfection indeed.

"I don't think I've ever seen anyone as perfect as you, Benjamin," I smile and he kisses my smile.

"And so are you," he murmurs into my neck. "I would literally lay like this with you forever," I say and I look at him until I sleep sweet dreams.

Forever dreams.

Chapter Seventeen

I 'm lying in the bed and Ben is not by my side but Ethan and Luke and my dad are standing at the end of the bed staring at me angrily.

I try to move my hands but they're tied.

"Dad," I whisper but he doesn't answer me. "Luke" I say, and he doesn't speak, but they all move closer to me, not even blinking.

Luke is mumbling something but I can't fathom what it is. Ethan pulls my hair and I yell with pain, my dad doesn't say anything, but there's a ghost of a smile on his face. "Help me!" I cry, but he doesn't move.

Ethan takes the belt that is hanged on the side of the bed, and starts whipping my back. I shut my eyes to forget the searing pain.

I struggle to breath and open my eyes. I have had another nightmare. I turn to look at Ben and he is sleeping like an angel.

I clamber out of bed and open the door slowly. I realize that I'm only wearing Ben's shirt and my panties. It would be so awkward if I ran into Aiden. I go to the kitchen and open the fridge, there's some food and bottles of beer.

I take a bottle of beer and walk out on to the balcony. No voices No noise at all. It's like I am alone in the world, alone with a misty moon that doesn't shine much. I take a sip of the beer and it tastes weird.

"Babe?" Ben's voice startles me in my reverie. I turn around. His hair is a mess, and he is shirtless.

"Hey there, " I say quietly.

"Are you okay?" he asks, eyeing me carefully, and I nod.

"Just a nightmare," I tap on my head and he nods back.

"Come on, come back to bed," he says and I place the beer on the table before climbing back in. I give him my back but he wraps his arms around me, pulling me to his body. I feel his face in my hair. "I don't think you are allowed to drink beer, especially not right now," he murmurs and I don't respond.

I wake with Ben facing me. I smile and move my hand to his face and stroke his cheek lightly. He opens his sweet blue eyes and mumbles, "Good morning" with a small smile.

"Good morning pumpkin pie," I say, and it sounds so weird. Laura says it better.

"What?" He frowns a bit. I giggle and in one move he is on top of me.

His hands are on my waist and his tongue is entwined with mine and he is searching and exploring. My hands move to his hair, it is so amazing, it feels like silk. He pulls away trying to breathe and I do too. His eyes are so beautiful, asking me for permission, and I nod. I trust him. Enough. His lips move to my neck and his hand travels up my body, moving the shirt up, and I feel my body exposed, but in a good way, to a good man that I trust.

Suddenly, Ethan is there. I try to push away those memories. Ben's lips are back on mine. I shudder and Ben stops kissing me. He freezes.

"Fuck you Ethan. Fuck you for ruining me," I think, and Ben is waiting patiently for me to say something but instead I just cover my face. "It's okay?" he says, and I shake my head.

"No. Sorry. It's not okay."

I feel terrible. I know how badly he wants this, and so do I.

"I'm so sorry," he whispers, moving my hands away.

"It's not your fault, Ben. It's his. Everything reminds me of that filthy asshole. His mouth on my body." I wave my hand rapidly in front of me, trying to wave the memory away.

"I do want you Ben. I want you so badly, but it's so hard to forget what happened."

He keeps on telling me its fine and we will try again someday soon, we can try every day until I forget Ethan.

"I'm going to shower," he says walking to the bathroom. "You can join me if you like!" he jokes, but the mood is broken. I shake my head and take off his shirt, and then put my bra back on.

Ben walks back out of the bathroom, one towel wrapped around his waist, water dripping from his hair. My mouth goes dry and he smirks at me devilishly. He looks at me like it's the first time he has ever seen a girl wearing fancy black underwear. I don't know, maybe it is.

I walk closer to him. I pull him closer and place my lips on his. He kissesme passionately, and his hands are on the end of my back and moving down to my butt. And I kiss him back forcefully. He moves down to my neck just from where he stopped, his lips and hands on my body. I fall backwards on to the bed, and I wrap my legs around him. He pulls back and his nose touches mine, and his eyes are deep and wanting. I feel my heart racing, and I see him trying to breathe. I move my hands through his hair and its wet and perfect. "You are so beautiful, " he says softly.

I kiss him deeply, and I just want him, everything about him, and only him.

I want him to make love to me, I know he won't hurt me and I know he won't make me cry.

"Whoa, not now, Aiden will probably crash in" he says kissing my neck and letting me back down on to the bed. I pout to him and he kisses me again.

"Go, get ready," he says, slapping my behind.

I take my dress, walk to the bathroom and look at myself in the mirror.

For the first time in forever, I feel beautiful.

When I am washed and dressed, I walk back in and Ben is sitting on the bed looking at his phone. I suddenly remember that Jacob said to call them in the morning. "Shit" I say loudly.

I look for my phone in my purse, and check if there are any missed calls, but there are none. There's a text from Laura saying that she wishes me a good morning and breakfast is weird without me being there. I laugh and dial Jacob's number. Ben is staring at me, but I ignore him and sit next to him.

"Eva, hi. You okay?" Jacob answers, coughing.

"No, I just thought I'd better tell you that I'm still alive and I will head home shortly to change my clothes. But I may leave again." Ben'sexpression is priceless. I smile to him and Jacob says joins in the joke. "Well, I'm glad you are still alive," he laughs. "Make sure you spare us some time in your busy schedule, hey?" he jokes back, and then ends the call. He is still coughing.

We go back into the living room and Charli is reading, sitting next to Aiden while he works on his laptop.

"Good morning" I mumble, and they both greet me at the same time. Aiden is looking at me with a how did you get permission to sleep here look and I wink at him.

"Good morning," Ben's chirps, with a wide smile.

"Hey Charli? I thought of going shopping later, is it your thing at all?" I ask and she nods. It's not my thing at all, but I want to make friends with her.

"Sure. Later?" she says.

"Yeah, that will be great" I look at Ben and his smile has vanished.

Ben opens the door and motions to me with his head to go with him.

"See you later, guys," I say and we leave.

"Why did you do that?" Ben asks immediately, and once again, he looks mad.

"Do what?" I snap at him.

"Ask Charli out?"

"Because I can, Ben. Please give her a chance to prove something to you. Anything," I argue, and he looks away from me.

"You don't know her, Eva. She's a fucking snake. Trust me," he hisses.

I shake my head and ignore him because I've had such a great morning and I don't want to ruin it. We walk in silence for a while before he places his hand in mine.

When we get to Laura's place I un-lock the door and Ben walks in after me. I go to my room and he follows.

"Is this your room?" he asks, astonished.

"Yup. It's too much, right?" I raise my eyebrows.

"Well, you deserve it," he smiles sitting on the bed. "I used to have a room as fancy as this back in my hometown. I should fly you there someday," he says and he has his stupid grin back.

"Someday," I tell him and walk in to the closet. I pull on a fresh black top and clean white jeans.

I undo my hair and let it fall down my back. "Alright, lets go" I tell him and we walk out.

Ben leaves to go to work, and I text Charli to arrange a meet at a nearby mall. She is perfectly on time, and runs towards me when she sees me. Hugs me. I laugh.

"You don't like shopping at all, do you" I say, and she laughs.

"I really don't, do you?" she replies and I shake my head at her.

"Nope. Me neither. I just wanted to have time with you to prove to Ben that I think you are a lovely person," I smile, and she smiles back.

But suddenly, get the feeling it is a fake smile.

It is a smile to shut me up.

"You don't know me," she says, shaking her head.

"You can tell me, I will understand," I say, and she looks uncomfortable.

"Ben should've told you," she says.

"Look Charli, I don't care what you've done in the past, we all make mistakes. It's not like you killed anyone," I say, and instantly regret it. She stares at me coldly. Her face is a mask. "Have you?" I ask, terrified now. She just laughs, and changes the subject.

"You know, my boyfriend looks like you, but with sharper features. There's something that reminds me of him when I see you. It's so weird," she says, sitting on one of the benches.

"He's arriving tomorrow to meet Ben. Maybe you should meet him too. We could double date." Her smile is real now.

"Why not? I can't wait to see him if he looks like me! I mean, I've never seen a man that looks like me".

We go to a coffee shop, buy some cakes and drinks and talk. She asks me if I live with my parents and I tell her no, my mom is dead and my dad ran out on us. It's a lie but a white one. I don't know her well enough to reveal my old awful past.

"How about you?" I ask, curious to get her side of the story.

"Well, I always loved my parents but they didn't allow me to do things I wanted to. They always compared me badly to Ben. As you know, he is a bit of a nerd sometimes and loves studying, but he liked to sneak around and make out with the girls that lived outsidehis school. My parents didn't notice that, and eventually I got tired of being ignored. I got tired of being the bad sister, and tired of being a disappointment to them, so I just ran away with a couple of friends. We lived rough for a year, working in coffee houses and bars, just like this one, until we turned eighteen and could flee to America."

She paused, sipped her coffee and tossed cake in her mouth.

"After Ben graduated and came to the USA, our parents died. But there was no way I could afford to go back for their funeral. I was practically living on the streets by then, and I cried and blamed myself a lot, but I had to move on and survive. I got a job in a bar in a strip joint in Las Vegas, and got back in touch with Ben, but I don't think he's ever truly forgiven me."

"How is the job?" I ask, now curious.

"Well, Ben wouldn't like that either. Some of the men in those joints can be, shall we say, a little rough."

"Have they done anything bad to you, Charli?"

"No, Eva, they wouldn't dare! Especially as the manager was in love with me, so he did whatever I told him. Even more so when I gave him sex whenever he wanted. He loved a good blow job!"

I must look shocked because she continues:

"Hey, he was hot so I didn't mind! Then I met my boyfriend and went to work in the lingerie store. That's where I am right now." She lit a cigarette.

"How did you run away?" she asked, staring at me. Hard.

"I didn't. The care home I was placed in was burned down and they rescued me. I woke up at the hospital," I lie, and she rolls her eyes.

"Trust me, Eva. Take it from one who knows. I know when someone is lying to me. What really happened?"

"I'm a victim of abuse," I mutter and looking down at the table.

"What do you mean?" She is genuinely shocked and I can see that in her eyes.

"Sexual, mental and physical abuse," I say, and she looks at me in awe.

"I'm so sorry," she says and I shake my head.

"How sick are people to do that to a child? Oh my god I feel like hugging you so much," she says, so quickly and sincerely that I start to like her despite all the things she did. Someone like me has no right to hate her.

"It's alright. Ben is helping me a lot," I say, and she smiles.

"Well, I've never seen him this happy with a girl since he was thirteen. I'm telling you. He loves you," she says.

"And I love him too," I say.

Later that day, Ben walks me back to Laura's, and I wish him a goodnight. He walks away. He hasn't mentioned my meeting with Charli, much to my surprise. I don't think he is angry anymore. I wave him goodbye and when he turns his face to look back at me, I think "Wow. He is such a cutie."

I'm walking on air when I get in but Laura sits straight and looks at me anxiously. I look at Jacob and look back at her.

"What?" I say. "Have I done something wrong?"

Laura places her hand on my knee and tightens her grip.

"No sweetie, not you. You could never do us wrong".

"What then Laura? What is it?"

"Well, Eva, it's Amelia."

A part of me freezes.

"Well, yesterday I filed a report to try and find out what has happened to her. I just got the results back."

"And?" I say. "What happened to her?"

"The report said that she's been missing for years." Laura closes her eyes slowly, and re-opens them. "But yesterday, I got a call from the police, and they told me that they found her."

My eyes widened and I began to smile

"I knew it! I knew she would be alright!" I start to say, but Laura raised her hand to my lips. She hasn't finished.

"I'm sorry Eva. They found her body yesterday evening."

My world spins.

The black page turns again.

"They said they found a half burned body in the ruins of the house you were rescued from."

I sit in stunned silence.

"I'm so sorry, Eva."

Suddenly a thought occurs to me.

"It might not be her!" I shout in desperation.

"Oh, I'm afraid it is, Eva. That's why you were questioned so closely. They ran tests on the body and it matches the age, shape and height of the girl you described perfectly. She's gone, Eva. I'm terribly sorry, but she's gone."

I scream and run up the stairs. I throw myself on the bed. And I cry my heart out.

Amelia is dead. My mother is dead.

My soul is dead.

Whenever I feel like things are getting better, death simply laughs, and comes knocking on my door.

Chapter Eighteen

I stand next to mommy while she's baking my favorite cookies and brownies, the only thing she can do good is bake. I try to steal one, but she hits my hand playfully and smile wide, motioning no with her finger. Mommy is nice to us but dad always makes her cry and cry. I hate him because he is rude. After she finishes baking, she gives me the boxes so I could sell them to the neighborhood.

I walk out in the hot burning sun and start selling, but no one buys. The sun hits my head so hard I can't walk, and my eyes dizzy and close.

I open my eyes scared, with drops of sweat on my forehead, in bed at Laura's. I wait until my breathing is normal, and see the sun is hiding behind the curtains. I look at my phone and there's a text from Ben.

Pick you up at two? Going out for dinner. Double date. Love you

I recall that we are going to see Charli's boyfriend. Which is weird. I walk lazily to the bathroom and take my clothes off to take a shower.

God bless mother fucking nature, hooray my period. At least I'm not pregnant.

Actually, it would be a miracle if I were pregnant.

My eyes are black and swollen from lack of sleep. The shock of Amelia kept me awake all night. My lips look normal, if a little bit red. I hear Dad's voice again:

"The lips of your mother, and the tongue of a slut. I see you working in those ugly club's some day. Swallowing those dicks. Licking those balls like a whore."

The memory of his words hit me hard and his voice is loud in my ears. I shudder and push the wordsaway, not allowing them to haunt me, hoping so much that they aren't even true.

I know they are lies. I just know they are.

I wear shorts and Ben's hoodie that I found with my clothes. It's big and warm and smells like him. It smells like Benjamin Eisenberg.

I look at myself in the mirror and it's the first time I wear something so revealing ever since Ethan forced me to do. I feel so comfortable in my own skin now, and I have no idea why.

Laura looks at me without talking and Jacob is having a phone call outside on the balcony. I hear his voice. Tense, I would say. I sit on the couch and Laura is still looking at me, probably thinking I'm mad with her, but I'm not.

"Laura" I cough, clearing my squeaky voice.

"Yes, honey." Her eyes light up.

"Do you think I can have something to eat served to me while I'm sitting here" I smile innocently.

"Alright why not, my lady!" Laura calls our maid, and gets her to bring me a tray with everything I love on it. How does she even know that I need these things? Laura woman is amazing, and i am so lucky..I know this too.

"Thanks" I mouth to her and she winks.

Jacob enters looking extremely angry.

We just wait for him to speak and it doesn't take long for him to say:

"They are really thinking of blowing up this opportunity for me, Laura, and it's like a bad dream," he says, almost yelling. Laura tries to reassure him but he just storms out of the apartment.

"He's just mad because of work. He'll calm down," she says and I return to my book.

I hate endings. Every book shouldn't end. I text Ben.

"Can we go grab a brownie from the café later on, I'm craving one."'

Almost immediately he texts back.'

"Why later? Ten minutes, and I'll be there."

I thought he was working?

I kiss Laura, thank her for being so kind, run from the condo and there he is. Wearing a red shirt with a company logo on it. I jump and wrap my legs around his waist.

"Whoa, didn't know you'd be this happy to see me," he says ears.

"I'm always happy to see you, and this is for you," he says, pulling a box from his shirt and sitting down on a bench. I pat on the bench for him to sit, but he shakes his head saying,

"I have to go, sweetie, I'm on my shift."

"But you only just came," I pout, and Laura walks by.

"I came because my babe craved a brownie. Which is weird this early in the morning. But her wish is my command."

He kisses me quickly on the lips, and whispers,

"See you later, enjoy it."

"Did you ask him to bring this?" Laura laughs, sitting next to me.

I frown and pout.

"He really is so nice" she says. "Maybe you should invite him around for dinner?"

I should be happy. But my entire face is sad.

"Why are you sad?" she asks softly,

"I don't deserve him, " I reply. My voice is small and shaky.

"Oh, you do deserve him. You really do." She pats my shoulder.

She runs to leave, and blows me a kiss over her shoulder.

I have a really lazy day, watching movies and eating treats. It was so sweet of Ben to get the brownie. I don't notice the time passing, until suddenly I remember our date, so I dash to change into my favorite outfit I get dressed just in time, as the door bell rings and it is Ben.

As we walk to the restaurant he looks fearful. Apprehensive.

"What's wrong?" I ask.

"Oh, nothing."

He tries to sound normal but his voice fails him, I give him a look and he runs his hands through his hair and puffs his cheeks out.

"Sit" I recommend, and I sit on the chair next to him.

"What's wrong Ben?

He speaks slowly and deliberately.

"Well, I am afraid you are not the only one with a past. I had some trouble with my heart when I was a child."

"What kind of trouble?" I say, trying to sound brave.

"Rheumatic heart disease, have you ever heard of it?" he asks, and I shake my head. "Well it's a condition I've had since I was seven." He clears his throat and continues. "I'm just worried it may have returned," he says.

He hugs me hard and tight.

"There really is nothing to worry about, I was just thinking about it because I have visited the doctor again in the past few days and he changed my medication." His eyes lock with mine, blue as the sky and perfect as the stars.

"I love you" I say, and he answers, "I know."

We walk toward the restaurant Charli said that we are going to, but they are late so we just stand waiting for them, I'm leaning against the wall and Ben is looking at me like I'm the only person left on the planet.

"What was with the lazy mood today, anyway. Demanding brownies, etc?" He smirks at me.

"I'm on my period, and I hate periods" I mumble, and he laughs. "Too much information," he grins. Walking two steps to me until we are close enough, he leans down and kisses me, and I kiss him back, sweetly and gently.

We hear the voice of an old man screaming.

"Hey! You two! Move away from my shop. Stupid teenagers blocking my shop!"

Ben pulls away and we both look at him, his face is turning red and he is staring at us angrily, I giggle, and Ben takes us away from his shop.

"We weren't blocking anything were we?" I ask, still laughing at the man.

"Nope. He just doesn't like to se young love I guess," he laughs, smiling his one thousand watt smile.

I don't hear his phone ringing but he answers it, it might be on silent, which reminds me. I check my phone and there's a text from Laura saying,

"Bring Ben to dinner tomorrow."

I text back:

"Excellent. If he's not working."

Ben turns around while talking on the phone and I see he is frustrated. He tosses the phone in his pocket, and his eyes are dark and angry. "She's not coming," he says through gritted teeth.

"Well, you and I can go for a drink instead, and then we can watch a movie," I smile, walking past him to a nearby bar.

After a few drinks and a long chat, I suddenly feel a little dizzy. 'Oh no, I forgot about you and drink,' Ben teases me, and I know I'm not drunk but I feel like the world is spinning faster than usual. I take a look at the time and it is nearly nine. "Shit" I say it's really very late we stayed here a lot. No time for a movie now."

"Come on, we can back to go my place and watch a movie."

He takes my hand and leads the way, until we arrive at his place. He takes off his shirt and turns on the plasma TV in his room. "Great," I mutter and he smirks. Before I climb into the bed I take off my jeans because I am so uncomfortable. I climb in and pull the quilt over me. Ben goes out of the room to fetch drinks,

"You know what, I hate this," I say to myself, and take off my shirt as well, making myself really comfortable. Minutes later he walks in carrying DVD's. "Shut up!" he yells over his shoulder, laughing.

"Aiden is acting very dumb tonight," he smiles and inserts one of the discs. I text Laura to say that I'm staying one more night and that I will see them at dinner tomorrow.

I wait for him to get in the bed next to me, and his eyes widen but he acts like its normal that I'm almost naked in his bed.

"Laura insisted that I ask you to come to dinner tomorrow," I tell him watching his face in the light of the TV.

"Well, do you want me to be there?" he asks artfully.

"Sure I do," I smile.

"Excellent. Now. Let's watch a movie," I say, wrapping my arms around him.

We don't speak. The Disney movie is a children's film, but it is superb, I have never ever seen one. He tells me he used to watch them as a child, because they comforted him when he was ill. I don't want to think of illness, so I hold him even closer and the sound of our hearts beating together is enough to comfort us both to blissful sleep.

Chapter Nineteen

Ben is standing at the end of the bed holding a sharp tool I can't recognize, I try to ask what's happening, but my mouth is taped up and my hands are tied upon my head. Ben is walking closer to me and it's a big knife, blood dripping from his hands. I feel trapped and he is sitting next to me now, looking at me without any words, and I think I can hear his heartbeat. I feel his eyes on me and his hands on my body, but I'm unable to move or do anything.

This is exactly what Ethan used to do to me.

"Get ready to be raped, little bitch," says the horrid voice.

I scream in terror. "No. NO!" I yell.

I awake and Ben is shaking me.

"What happened," he says, and I sob.

"Eva, what happened?" He is yelling now.

"A nightmare" I say through sobs, and he pulls me close to him.

"God, you scared me to death," he says. "Its fine, you are safe with me."

I shake my head and hug him tight, even though he was there in the nightmare. He wipes my tears and tells me to go back to sleep. I close my eyes and drift away.

I feel kisses on my face, cheeks, eyes, head, hair and finally lips. I open my eyes and the sunlight is so shiny. I close them and re-open them slowly.

"Good morning honey," Ben says, smiling and he smells so fresh.

"Morning," I murmur, turning around and covering my head with the pillow. "You lazy thing, wake up I want to show you something." He slaps my behind and walks away from the bed.

I pull myself out of bed and stretch. I have a terrible headache - did I do something while being asleep?

I dress and shower then walk into the living room. Charli is sitting on the couch busy with her phone and says, "Morning, love birds."

I smile at her and wish her a great day, but Ben just ignores her. Not a great start.

We walk to a cafe for breakfast, and over our pancakes, Ben asks:

"What time is dinner?"

"Dinner? It's only breakfast time," I say, and he laughs.

"I mean tonight, you clown. Dinner. At Laura's."

"Oh yes, six o'clock, I guess," I catch up, and he laughs.

"Speaking of clowns, I would really love to take you there," he says, enthusiastically pointing at a big poster of some kind of carnival. I turn and look.

And there really is all the fun of the fair.

"It does look fun," I say.

"It is, trust me, so much fun! I always go with Aiden but now I want to take you."

He is full of joy, just like a little kid, and it's all because of a carnival. I shake my head and smile.

"Sure, but when?" I ask.

"I will check and tell you later." He hugs me and gives me a quick kiss. I love seeing him like this. Really love it. We sit on the chair, staring out at the lake. It's so quiet and peaceful here. There is so much room to breathe.

I think heaven must be an open vista. A wide open plain filled with flowers and joy and lakes just like this.

"Ben," I say in the tiniest voice I can manage.

"Eva," he says and the sun on his face makes everything about him shine. His hair is lighter, his eyes are lighter, his mood is lighter, everything. He looks like he was sent from heaven to this place, and doesn't deserve his heart disease, or any pain, or all the things he is going through with his sister.

I drink in his face, and the way his eyes sparkle when I tell him something.

"I think if I just spend my entire life telling you I love you, it won't be enough. You have pulled me through so much in these past months, and I just wanted to say how I appreciate your existence so much."

There. I said it. I just wanted him to know that I love him to the point I'd sacrifice my soul for his. I know that it's important to let the people who we love know of our love, for time is short and life is fleeting. A blink of an eye, and we can be gone.

I know this in my heart and soul. I know this because of my mum. And Amelia.

"I love you too. You know that Eva."

He smiles widely, placing his hand on my cheek.

"I don't think I will ever be able to live a day without you."

We go back to Laura's because the weather is getting hot and we really have no plans. No one is in the condo. We go to my room and climb on the bed, hugging and kissing.

Suddenly, I freeze. My throat is being choked. My brain is shutting down. My body is paralyzed on top of him.

I try to tell my awful brain it's only a nightmare before he notices but it's too late.

"What the hell, Eva?, he says, worried and almost angry. "What's happening? Tell me!"

I clear my throat nervously. "Sorry. I had a nightmare earlier. And you were in it."

"What was I doing?" His eyes are dark now, and he looks sad, nervous and a little angry.

"I don't know, but you were holding a knife or something sharp and there was blood all over you. I was tied to the bed and I couldn't even speak," I stammer and I see him trying to hide a smile. "Do you find this funny?" I scold him.

"No, not at all" He shakes his head and his smile is wider. "I just love the way you talk when you are scared, and it was just a nightmare baby. Don't worry." He kisses my forehead and grabs the book on the table next to the bed.

"What is this?" he asks, fanning the papers.

"It's about some guy that went to rehab for addiction," I tell him and he puts it down then leans back.

"What do you think of it?" he says dreamily.

"I love it," I say,

"Well then, tell me all about it."

"It's boring," I reply, staring at his beautiful face.

"I want to be bored then."

I admire his show of interest, even if he is pretending. "But you don't love books," I tell him.

"Who said that?" he frowned. "I sure do!"

"Well, this one is about a guy who found himself passed out on a floor or something. I don't remember where. Neither did he, as a matter of fact."

He laughs at my joke and I laugh with him. "So, this dude went to rehab to try to fix himself and falls in love with a girl who, sadly, is a prostitute and a crack addict."

"Keep going," he says.

"Well, I found her character to be tragic but beautiful. The trouble is, the book doesn't have a happy ending."

"In what way?" asks Ben, who is suddenly interested.

"Well, the author goes on to have her commit suicide."

"Not good,' jokes Ben.

"Not funny!" I chide him, hitting him with a pillow.

"To be honest, I would ask that author a question."

"And what is that question?" He bites his lip and it distracts me with lust for him, but I look away.

"I would ask why does he kill her? How does his heart allow him to kill a character who is so sweet and fascinating, and then, to make matters worse, why does he go on to kill everyone else in the book?

"Well, strictly speaking, that's three questions babe," Ben says trying to sound serious.

"Shut up," I say laughing, and he laughs too.

Ben goes home with an hour to go to get ready for dinner with Laura and Jacob. I choose a skinny yellow dress, to the knee. Laura curls my hair and helps me with makeup. I look odd, but I am so happy about this night. Laura chooses high white heels for me.

When I walk downstairs Ben is already there, shaking hands with Jacob, wearing a suit and looking formal. Jacob laughs at something Ben just said.

Ben's eyes lock with mine and I give him a brief smile, he smiles back and runs a hand in his hair. Why are you running your hand through your hair like this, Benjamin?

I walk to him and he slips his hand around my waist.

"You look as beautiful as the sky tonight," he whispers in my ear.

"And you look so handsome," I tell him, and the bell rings and I move away from him reluctantly to open the door.

When I do, I see a couple standing there, with wide and friendly faces. The woman smiles and says.

"You must be Eva! We have heard so much about you, it's lovely to finally meet you!"

"It's a pleasure to meet you too," I say. I should invite them in, but I am still a little awkward in social situations. Luckily, as ever, Laura saves the day.

"Hi, Franklin and Mellissa, my dear friends, come on in," Laura says happily, welcoming them inside.

Mellissa hugs Laura like they are little girls back at school and Franklin nods to me. I introduce Ben to them.

"Is there anyone else coming that I don't know about?" I whisper in Laura's ear while she's placing glasses on the table. She laughs.

Laura looks like a super model. She is wearing a short azure blue dress, and her long hair is falling down her back.

Lucky Jacob.

I turn around and Ben is in deep conversation with Jacob and the guy Franklin. Mellissa comes to give us a hand with the table.

"I never imagined that you were so beautiful," Mellissa says and her voice is like a little girl.

"Thank you," I say, blushing. She isvery much ablonde, but her eyes are auburn. She would look great wearing dark colors, but she is wearing white. She is so bright she shines.

"Dinner's ready" Laura calls, and the guys stand up and walk towards us. Mellissa sits next to her husband and Laura next to Jacob. Ben pulls the chair out for me like a true gentleman, and I flush. I bet my color is more pink than the flowers all around the apartment at the moment, and everyone is looking at us like it's the first time ever they see something like this. Grace, our maid, brings in the food and we start eating, they are engaged in conversations and Ben is talking to Franklin and Jacob, and Mellissa and Laura are discussing work. At the dinner table!

"Baby what's wrong?" Ben whispers and his hand moves to my thighs. My breathing hitches.

"Nothing," I smile broadly at him.

"Eat, I have something to show you after dinner." He turns his attention back to Jacob who is asking him about his knowledge of solar power. I never knew that Ben was this smart. I know he is clear minded, but not as clear as it seems right now. He should study at a higher level. I make a note to ask him why he isn't studying at university.

We all pass a few hours discussing all kinds of topics - politics, religion, the economy and culture. I am pleased with myself for being able to cope with this new situation, and incredibly impressed with Ben. He seems born for these occasions.

My angel.

The party is a great success, and after Mellissa and Franklin leave, Ben asks me out to walk because the weather is so nice.

We walk in a new direction, to a poorer part of town. Passing by homeless people lying in the corners. Passing by guys smoking hash, drinking, and even, in dark corners, couples screwing up against walls. I hear the grunts of passion and cries of pain, and it offends me. With its stench of unclean drains and graffiti clad walls, it looks just like the place where I was raised. It looks like the place I used to walk through every day on the way to school when I was a little kid. I shudder. Ben holds me close to him, I hear guys shouting and someone is crying.

"Don't make eye contact with anyone," he says, holding me firmly.

We make it to the other side of the road and there are buildings that look old and closed shops with broken windows and barred doors.

"Where are we? Why have you brought me here?"

"I want to show you something." His voice has turned bitter again.

I don't say a word and just walk. It is colder now and my teeth chatter from the wind. "Are you okay? You cold?" he asks, and our eyes lock for the first time since we started walking. All I can see is fury. He shrugs off his jacket and helps me wear it.

He stops, and his eyes are almost popping out of his face as he stares at a large group of guys and girls who must be aged around twenty.

"Look. I knew it," he says angrily, pointing to the group, and when I look more carefully, I see Charli. She is with a guy, who is drinking from a bottle and ostentatiously smoking a very large cannabis joint.

Okay. This is not good news.

"Maybe it's her boyfriend?" I plead, holding his shoulder and standing in front of him. I try to make eye contact with him but Ben is just ignoring me.

"Ben, let's leave. Tonight was great, but don't ruin it," I beg, but he doesn't move or speak.

"Say something," I shake him and he is still mad, looking straight ahead, I pull my phone out of my purse and dial Charli. Ben literally freezes. It takes her seconds to answer and when she does she sounds worried.

"Hi Eva, are you okay?"

"Yes, Charli. Look behind you," I try to sound like I am making sense and she turns around and I wave to her.

"Shit!" she cries. She hangs up and runs toward us. The guy she was kissing runs after her. Even in the dark and from a distance, I can see he is larger then Ben.

"Eva, Ben," she says, trying to get her breath. "What are you doing here?" She is looking at Ben with his jaw clenched and I remember his heart problem and I hug him. Hug him as tight and as long until he hugs me back whispering that it's okay in my ear.

We separate and he gives the guy with Eva an angry stare.

"Ben, this is Luke. My boyfriend" Charli tries to explain.

"Hey, I heard a lot about you," Luke says and I turn to look at him.

Luke stares at me, his face finally illuminated from the light in the street. His greenish blue eyes lock on to mine, and I forget about everyone else in that split second.

Because all I care about is my long lost brother, who is looking straight back at me.

It's Luke. My Luke.

And he's alive.

"Eva?" he says in a small voice filled with heartache. I throw myself at him, wrapping my arms around his neck and holding him to me. His hug is strong. "Oh, little Eva," he whispers and I sob into his neck, all of my memories flooding back to me.

Memories of the times he sacrificed himself to save me, before the abuse and depression overwhelmed him.

"Luke, how are you?" I sob through a flood of tears.

Ben pulls me away from him, looking angry and confused. I pull back.

"Ben, this is my brother. Luke. The one I told you about!" I shout, and he lets go of me.

"Eva, I can't believe you are alive. And you look so well," Luke says, shaking his head in disbelief.

"Yes I am. I'm safe now. What about you?" I splutter, wiping my tears.

"I'm still running away," he says, and Charli and Ben are staring at us, confused.

"From who?" I ask, fearful of the answer.

"Anderson," he mumbles.

"Who is he?"

"The one we called Dad all our lives. Except, get this. He is not our dad. And he is looking for us."

Luke holds me. He checks Ben's expression briefly and his eyes are on mine again. "To be more honest, he is looking for you Eva"

"What? Are you serious?" Ben yells, grabbing me and backing me away.

"Please, please hide, Eva!" Luke begs and I know that he is really scared.

"No, no, this can't be happening," I stammer.

"And another thing," Luke continues.

"I think you've said enough for one night, Luke," says Ben angrily, but Luke ignores him.

"I'm sorry, my friend, but this is too important not to say. Eva?" says Luke.

"What, Luke?" I mutter, not wishing to hear the answer.

"I also found out that Mom was never our mom."

Luke is shaking now, and I feel the earth is turning fast.

I look at Ben and his face is as dark as thunder

"Ben?" is all I can I say, just before I black out.

Chapter Twenty

I wake up in Ben's bed, wearing his shirt and my. Ben is sleeping next to me. I think I dreamt of Luke. Or was it real.

"Babe," Ben murmurs raising his head and getting closer to me. "I was so worried," he whispers, and I shake my head and hug him. He rubs my back and hugs me tight.

"Come, your brother is still outside"

"How long have I been sleeping?" I told him.

"About an hour, I guess."

We get up and enter the room, and Luke is sitting on the couch. Charli isn't there, but Aiden is on the stool looking at his laptop.

So it wasn't a dream. I am filled with joy.

My brother really is alive.

"Hi," I say and smile broadly.

"Hey there sis." Luke stands and hugs me for seconds and let go. "Are you okay now? You fainted, you know?" he asks, his eyes searching mine.

"I feel fine, and you? How did you get here? What were those things you were saying? How?"

"Try and calm down, Eva," says Ben, stroking my head.

Luke continues.

"Well, when I turned eighteen, the bastard that kept us and sold you told me that he was not our father. He also said that our mother wasn't even our mother, and we were the reason his life had been so fucked up. That's why he hated us so much, Eva. He threw me out with a second glance to fend for myself. Just gave me the fare and told me to get the hell out of his house. I made it to Los Angeles, and that's how I met Charli. I've been looking for our real parents ever since, but I must warn you. I found some more stuff out that I have to tell you. You are in terrible danger!"

"Why? How? I'm in a completely different state!"

"Listen to me Eva. He is here. He's here in this state and he even knows you are in Chicago!" Luke's voice is louder now.

"Does he know exactly where I am?" I shout, trying not to panic.

"He knows that you're in Chicago,' he says flatly. "But not exactly where."

"I felt like someone was chasing me the other day. Didn't I Aiden? You were there! Has this bastard found me or not?"

"No, Eva, surely not," replies Aiden.

"This can't be true," I say, shaking my head in disbelief.

"You need to rest," Ben says, but I shrug away from him and shake my head.

"I don't need rest!' I scream, panicking. "I need to get out of here. Now!" I narrow my eyes, and Luke looks down, embarrassed, scratching his neck.

"You don't Eva. Trust me. You need to lie down, and rest," says Ben. He holds me tight and carries me to his bedroom, lying down next to me and holding me tight.

How can I rest? My brain is working overtime. What will happen if he captures me? Will he torture me? Will he kill me?

Why did Luke have to come back into my life right now? Why did he tell me about him? When everything was so perfect?

And then I realize something. If the bastard really isn't my father, he has no legal rights over me.

This means that I can go and tell the police about him.

That I'm in danger of kidnap and torture.

With this slightly more comforting thought, I fall asleep. It's a fitful sleep, but at least I close my eyes.

When I awake, Luke has gone. It's a beautiful day, so Ben offers to walk me to the park. I love the park. Most of my new happy memories have already been forged here with my beautiful Ben.

Luke's revelation that he has been looking for our real parents enters my mind, and I am unsure whether I want to bother at all. To be honest, why did they give us away in the first place? Were they so ashamed of us that they didn't want us in their life? And if we do find them, will they be poor? Or will they be wealthy? Will Laura let me live with her forever?

Questions. I have so many questions.

I look at Ben and wonder the same about him. Will we be together in ten years? What about his weak heart - even if he loves me forever, will he be around forever? That thought kicks me so hard in the stomach that I feel guilty for even thinking it.

"If your heart ever fails, I would gladly give you mine," I say out loud.

"What?" Ben says. I'm not sure if he thinks I've gone totally mad now.

"If anything should happen to you. You deserve to live. To fall in love with a girl that will live with you forever"

"But you are that girl!" he shouts.

"I might not be here forever If that murdering asshole catches me."

He looks at me patiently, with such love in his eyes.

"He won't, not with Laura and Jacob and me around," he says kindly. 'And even if yours was the last beating heart on earth, I wouldn't take it. I don't want you tolive in me, I want you to live with me. I don't want to lose you. I fall in love with you more and more every day. I want to be the one that will save you, and cherish you forever. If you are going to live in hiding, I will hide with you."

"You are my everything" I manage to say, and he hugs me tighter to him.

Later that evening, we go to the carnival he spoke about a few weeks ago. It's s amazing, everything is full of light and it is crowded with kids, old people, parents, guys, girls. Everyone is so full of joy. We get on the ferris wheel, and although you can see way over the city rooftops, all Ben ever looked at was me. It's like I'm the perfect view for him.

After we get off the big wheel, Ben sits down on a box next to a red big tent, and he looks out of air. "Hey are you alright?" I worry, sitting on the floor in front of him.

"Yeah I'm just little bit tired, it's alright." He fakes a smile that doesn't touch his eyes and inhales deeply.

"Do you want to leave?" I ask and he looks at me, I can see he wants to, but he still desperately wants to show me around.

"No," he says, tilting his head a bit.

"I think we will. I'm so tired and starving," I tell him a little white lie, and give him my hand so he can stand. He shakes his head and walks with me outside, to the bus station. We in silence but he places his hand on my thigh.

"Thank you, I really enjoyed today so much," I smile widely to him.

He smiles and kisses me as the bus arrives. We get on, show the driver our tickets, and sit on the last two chairs. It's almost empty, which reminds me to look at the time. "Oh God, its two in the morning," I say in horror, and Ben smiles.

There's a man sitting on the front seat who looks really drunk, and he turns around and rests back on the window with his profile to us.

My jaw clenches, my heart beats out of my chest, and my hands are squeezing Ben so hard that my nails is digging into his skin. Everything around me spins.

I know my heart will actually stop if he turns around and looks at me.

"What the? " Ben says.

I whisper slowly in Ben's ear.

"That's Anderson. That's the man who said he was my dad."

Ben freezes for a second, but he remains calm.

"Listen to me. Be quiet. Put your head in my neck and he won't recognize you,' he says calmly, and I immediately do just that.

The journey is a nightmare. It seems like the longest bus ride of my life, but the drunken man doesn't look at us and as our stop approaches, Ben tells me to walk fast and shields me with his body as we pass the man.

When we are finally off the bus, I can see that the man is now unconscious.

I grab Ben and look him straight in the eye.

"Okay, Ben. First Luke. Now Anderson? Who next? Ethan?" I can't take it anymore. I have to talk to Laura. We have to do something."

When we get back, Laura opens the door for us. She looks really tired. "Are you okay?" I say, concerned. She nods and motions to us to get inside. It's nearly three in the morning and she is still awake.

"Probably a touch of flu," she says. She produces coffee glasses.

"Let me help you," I say and she shakes her head, pointing at the chairs, I sit down and Ben sit on the chair on the other side facing me, looking worried. She hands us the cups and sits down in the chair between us. I wrap my fingers around the cup and she is looking at me quizzically, waiting for me to speak.

"Eva what is it?"

I remain silent. I can't find the words.

"Eva! Talk to Laura, please," says Ben and my eyes flicker.

"Laura," I begin, "I think I need to go back to the center and get some extra help from them." I clear my throat so that I won't cry or my voice shakes. "I've talked to my brother Luke again."

Laura looks shocked to the core, but she tries to hide it.

"What? Where?"

"Over at Ben's. His sister introduced us to this guy she's dating. Turns out to be Luke. He's been in the States for a few years now."

"Luke? Eva, I can't believe you haven't told me this!" she says, looking really worried.

"Well, there's a reason for that, but you won't like it," I reply nervously, summoning the courage to tell her.

"What? Eva, what is it?" she says, panicking now.

"Well, Luke told me that my dad - or the person I thought was my dad - is here in Chicago."

"What? No, no, Eva, that's impossible," she cried.

"No it isn't, Laura. We've just seen him."

It is a good job Laura is sitting down, as she almost faints with this news. For a few seconds she opens and closes her mouth to speak, but no words come out. She looks at Ben as if for confirmation.

"I'm sorry Laura. It's true. We saw him,' he says slowly. "Luke was with Charli, and we just saw Eva's dad on the bus coming back from the carnival," he finishes, and she shakes her head in disbelief.

"Well, our records show that your dad isn't in this country. Eva, it can't be him."

"Well, I'm telling you, it was! I would recognize that bastard anywhere. His face is burned unto my brain!"

"Eva!' Ben yells, shocked at my language. "Calm down!"

I jump to my feet.

"I don't want to fucking calm down! Have you any idea how frightened I am right now?"

"Oh, Eva," Laura rises to hug me, but I back away.

"I don't want to be here anymore!" I shout.

Laura looks devastated, and Ben just looks lost.

"I'm sorry, but I'm living in constant fear now" I whisper.

"That doesn't mean you should give away everyone who loves you Eva," Ben says pleadingly.

"He's right, Eva. Why leave this life? The one where you have been so loved? The one where you are getting better every day? Why trade diamonds for sand rocks?"

"Because I'm tired of it all, can't you see? I can't walk out in the streets without feeling like someone is going to push me into a corner and do something awful to me. I can't sleep because when I do, I have nightmares of being belted, burned, or tortured! I love you guys but I don't love my life. Not like this. Not in constant terror like this!" I shout, and Laura's eyes pool with tears. Ben looks like he has been slapped, and I sob. I start to cry and run to my room.

I look in the mirror hoping to see the happy girl form a few weeks ago, but she has gone now. I'm left with that fearful girl.

"Babe." I turn around and Ben is standing there looking at me. I throw myself at him and sob into his chest.

"I feel so weak," I say through sobs.

He doesn't say anything. He just strokes my hair and hugs me.

"I've started seeing things, Ben. I feel like I'm getting delusional," I sob.

He doesn't say a word but holds me tight. Just holding me as I break into a thousand pieces. I hate crying, I hate being weak. We stand there as I cry, and when I can't cry anymore he holds me at arm's length, looking at me steadily

"You need to rest, Eva. It's late. Things will look better tomorrow," he whispers, and kisses me lightly on my lips. He carries me and tucks me in bed. I see a stain on his chest and I realize it's from my tears.

"I love you" he whispers, and it's the last thing I hear as my eyes close.

Chapter Twenty-One

I wake up on the ground, feeling cold and nasty. I look around and I think that this place is familiar. I have been here for days and months and years what is this place? I look around and I find Amelia lying next to me, her pale skin ghostly against my brown. I look down at myself and my nails are blue and my hand is paralyzed. I am cold. I probably gave Amelia my blanket because she looked like she was going to freeze.

I am back in Ethan's and we are both trapped here. We haven't eaten in four days, we ran out of water, and I can hear the thunder and feel the lighting outside. I've never heard a storm as fierce as this. Amelia is shuddering and I have nothing more to keep her warm. I'm worried something will happen to her. She has stopped talking ever since Ethan threw her back in here a few hours ago. I don't know exactly what he did to her but I hope it isn't as awful as what he does to me. I sit next to her and she reaches for my hand and squeezes it. I would say she wants to smile, but why would she when we are in such a hellhole.

I hear footsteps and Amelia pushes herself to me and I hug her tight. one got to be strong.

"Okay, you little, sluts where are you?" I hear Bunny's voice. It is so high. So annoying. She pushes the door open and my eyes locks with hers. She is a filthy evil spirit with no humanity.

"Come here," she hisses, motioning to me. I stand and walk to her slowly until we are so close that I can smell her awful liquor breath She slaps me hard on the face, and I lose sensation on that side. I place my hand on my cheek and rub it as my eyes water. I will not cry because tears are for weak people. I am strong, and I have to be strong for Amelia too. My face feels hot and pulsing.

She laughs loudly and her voice rings in my ears so much they hurt. I want to kick her and run down the stairs away from this damned place.

She grabs my hand and her nails sink in my skin. I bite my tongue to stop myself from yelling but she does it even harder, and with her other hand she holds my neck, sinking her nails into that too. I yell. I yell because it hurts. I yell because she doesn't have a heart.

I stop yelling as she punches me in the stomach I fall down hard, hitting my head on the ground.

I open my eyes, breathing fast and the beat of my heart is loud in my ears.

Why is it dark here?

I turn over and there's a guy sleeping next to me.

"Who are you?" I scream, and his eyes open fast, looking at me, fearful, worried.

His eyes are blue and clear and shining in the dark.

"It's Ben, Eva," he says confused.

"I don't know you," I say and get out of the bed. This place is fancy. Rich. Who the hell brought me here?

"Where am I?" I scream.

I see a young man. He isstaring at me, terrified. He jumps out of bed and puts on his shirt hurriedly.

"Who brought me here?" I shout, and he is trying to come closer but I step back. Every step he makes, I step back.

I have seen him before but I have no idea where or when. I'm sure I know his handsome face, but I can't recall how.

"What have you been doing to me?" I scream, and back into the glass door of the bedroom. It sends shivers down my spine.

A woman with auburn hair and blue eyes walks in wearing only a shirt. She looks scared. A man enters behind her and my heart beats so loud that I can't concentrate. She is talking to the guy who called himself Ben.

"What happened to her?" she asks.

And he shakes his head.

"I woke up to her yelling," he run both his hands through his hair.

"Eva. Calm down and come here," she says, and I shake my head.

"I don't know you, leave me alone!" I cry out and she comes closer to me. I try to run away but I can't get past them. She turns around and whispers something, to the other guy.

"Where is Amelia?" I whisper and she turns around and her eyes soften like she has the secret solution to the hardest question ever.

"Amelia is in the other room, sleeping" she smiles. This woman seems so nice. "You are both safe now," she says walking closer to me.

They are all moving closer to me. Closer. In one movement they are all holding me and I'm not capable of moving. I pass out.

When I open my eyes again and look around, I'm still in the fancy place. I try to move my hands but they're tied to the sides of the bed. "Help!" I cry to the guy sleeping on the chair next to me, and he raises his head slowly. His eyes are a beautiful blue, but red as if he has been crying.

"Eva," he says, and I gasp.

"How do you know my name, who are you? What are you doing to me?" I say, crying. Crying quietly.

"I'm Benjamin, we-" He clear his throat. "We are f-friends" His tone is sorrowful.

"I don't have any friends," I close my eyes and shake my head.

The woman with auburn hair comes in.

"Okay, so she fell or was hit hard on the head a year ago, and I guess the pressure of remembering her past has triggered the injury again," she says clinically. "I would suggest that the blow took her right back into her past, and she is suffering from a type of stress induced amnesia. She recognizes us, but doesn't remember us." Her voice is terribly morose as she stares at the floor.

Ben looks at me and his eyes are pooled with tears.

"So she doesn't remember anything? Anything between us?" he says, and starts to sob. The woman shakes her head, and he runs his hands through his hair while I stare at them in silence.

I feel heavy and I can't move but I can still hear them. "Fuck!" He yells and I hear the sound of breaking glass, and I shudder and shut my eyes tight.

"Benjamin, please go back to home and I'll call you if anything changes okay?" The familiar voice of an older man speaks too, but I can't tell who it is.

Later, I awake in the same fancy room and I look around. I am alone. Relief floods through my veins. I climb out of bed and walk out of the room, and I feel like I know this place,

I take a few quiet steps down the stairs until I'm in a large lounge. From the furnishings alone, I realize that these people are really wealthy.

Amelia is in the other room, sleeping.

Her words return, and I open every door in this place looking and for her.

I open the final door and the older man is sitting there.

"Hi Eva, " he says cheerfully, "How do you feel now? " he asks, and his smile is friendly.

"I feel fine. Where is Amelia?" I ask and further into the office. There are a lot of photographs on the tables, all in classy frames, and I look at every single one of them. They are so heart warming.

"Eva, do you remember me?" His tone is full of hope, but I have to tell him the truth.

"No. I have no idea. Who are you?" I say, sitting on the big couch.

He smiles at me and removes his glasses.

"I'm Jacob, I was your teacher for a few months, and I'm also the boyfriend of your psychiatrist," he says gently.

I shake my head. "I'm so sorry. I don't remember you" I say, and he sighs.

"Where are the people who were here?" I ask and he raises his eyebrows.

"You mean Laura and Benjamin? Well I don't know at the moment, but I can call them if you want to see them?" he says calmly. I like this guy. He seems kind.

"No, it's okay. I just want to go back to home" I murmur.

"This is your home, Eva," he says softly.

"Since when?" I say.

"For almost a year now," he says, and my eyes widen. I honestly can't remember.

"Eva?"

A voice behind me sends shivers through my body and suddenly, I feel safe. I turn around and it's the guy with the smiling blue eyes that I saw earlier.

"Hey there pumpkin, how are you?"

It is so familiar.

But it is far away from my memory.

"Who are you?" I ask coldly, and the look in his eyes changes back to sadness. "Do I know you?"

"No, you don't know me" he clears his throat, and blinks at the floor and his eyes are back on mine. "But I sure do know you."

"How come?" I whisper.

"Would you like to go out for an ice-cream? I will pay," he smiles and I don't know if I should trust him but the older man nods, we walk outside. The weather is sunny. I feel kind of calmer.

"May I hold your hand?" he asks and it would seems rude not to, so he moves his hand to mine and our fingers interlock. His touch is soft and nice. His hands are warm and familiar.

We enter a busy, colorful ice-cream shop,

"Hello sir how can I help you today?" the girl cashier says.

"Can we please have two cups of vanilla and chocolate?" he asks, and after a minute or two of scooping, she hands one to him and he gives me one.

"I've been here before haven't I?" I say, and his smile becomes as big as the sun.

"Yes. Yes you have."

"With you?" I try to smile.

"Quite a few times," he points at the window.

"What happened then?"

"To what?" he asks, confused.

"To us" I mutter, and his eyes widen.

He sighs.

"Eva, you woke up the other day and you didn't remember any of the people who love you. Including me," he says softly, as if his heart is breaking.

"Did I love you?" I say.

"Yes you did. I hope you still do," he says.

After finishing our ice cream we return to the fancy place again.

"Eva, did you have a nice time?" the woman with auburn hair asks.

I say that I have, and I go back to the same room again,. I have no idea what to say to her.

I lay on the bed and I fall asleep.

When I wake, the guy with blue eyes is sitting next to me.

"Who are you?"

"I am Benjamin. And I love you so much, " he says gently.

And all of a sudden I see us walking in a park, holding hands. Kissing. Hugging. Falling in love.

Ben is everything to me.

And I am to him.

His blue eyes are like the clean ocean letting me drown in his love. "I love you, Eva."

His words echo in my head over and over

And suddenly, I remember.

He is the guy that showed me the beautiful places, Dinner. Movies. Ice cream. Home. His home. Bed. Park. The carnival. The lake.

And suddenly I remember. Benjamin Eisenberg. I know him because I love him. He is my safe place, the guy that I would sacrifice my soul for.

I would give my whole body for.

And then, he is gone.

I must have passed out again, because suddenly, I know that I am awake, and that I am in Laura's fancy condo.

Laura! That is her name!

And she loves me and takes care of me.

I run to Laura's room and she wakes up, scared.

"What's wrong, Eva? " Her eyes are wide with fear.

"I had a nightmare Laura. That's your name, right?" I babble, and she smiles so widely it would blind the moon.

"I had a nightmare that I forgot Benjamin and you and Jacob, and it was bad, so bad" I stammer.

"It wasn't a nightmare, Eva," she says and it feels like I've been slapped in the face. Hard.

"What do you mean?" I whisper.

"Sit down," she says and I sit next to her.

"You've has a brain injury, Eva. We think it was when a nasty woman, Bunny was her name, actually assaulted," she says, but I interrupt.

"Yes. I remember Bunny," I sigh. "She pushed me over and I hit my head. I passed out for an entire day."

"That's right, Eva." She breathes heavily, as if relieved that we are making progress. She goes on, looking serious.

"Well, your brain has recently made you completely forget what has recently happened in your life. You've been like this for a couple of days. It is brought on by stress, and we think recent events, especially meeting Luke again and seeing the man you thought was your dad took you right back to the moment you suffered the major head injury. It's called dissociative amnesia."

She pauses and searches my eyes for my reaction.

"Is it dangerous?" I ask.

"Well, no, it's not life threatening, but it can make you a danger to yourself and others, as you often wake up not knowing the people who love and care for you."

"Is that what just happened?" I say nervously.

"Yes. I'm afraid it is."

"Am I, am I back? Am I in the present?"

"Yes. We think Ben was the reason. When he took you to the ice cream parlor, like the first day he took you out, it made you remember him and then us. His love for you is very strong." She smiles.

"Where is he?" I ask her.

"Home" she smiles.

"I need to see him. Can you call him?" I beg, and she nods. She dials his number and he answers immediately.

"Benjamin?" she says putting it on speaker.

"Laura." His voice is sleepy. "Is everything alright with Eva?" He says immediately and my heart sinks.

"I'm fine" I mutter. "I just need you."

"I will be right there, hold on" He hangs up the phone and Laura is still smiling. Jacob is covering his face with his arm behind her.

"I'm sorry Jacob, if I caused any sorrow" I murmur and he shakes his head.

"No problem. Laura and I have to go out for a little while. Will you be okay here with Ben?"

"Oh yes. I will. I really will," I answer, smiling, and they rise and leave.

I go and get a shower and wrap a towel around my body, I go to brush my teeth and when I turn around Ben is looking at me almost not believing that it's me there. "Eva,"

His blue eyes are full of love and promise and I know that I feel the same. I run to him and he carries me as he hugs me. Hugs me so tight.

"I thought I lost you. You were so ill," he says. He holds me at arm's length and eyes me, as checking if anything is missing.

"I have no idea what happened but I know I never want to lose you again," I tell him and he kisses me. My entire body softens and leans in to him.

If there's one thing I want right now, it's for him to make love to me. Our kiss deepens and he carries me to the bed. He backs off, asking for permission and I nod to him. If I'm sure about only one thing now, it is that I want to lose myself in his love.

Chapter Twenty-Two

I open my eyes and the sun cheers me awake again, I blink a couple of times before opening them. Ben is facing me, I touch his entire face from forehead to nose to lips and before his eyes open, I place my lips on the corner of his and kiss him. "I love you," I whisper against his lips, and it twitches to a grin, and I kiss him fast and get out of bed grabbing a towel to cover my body.

I wash and dress and while Ben is in the bathroom I go down stairs. Jacob was reading his newspaper like every day. "Morning," I smile to him and kiss him on the cheek.

"Good morning honey, uh finally got to see you. I want to talk to you," Jacob says sipping his coffee, and the smell is awaking every sleeping organ in me. I feel full of energy.

"Yeah what is it?" I ask, and at that moment Ben walks in.

Jacob clears his throat before locking his eyes with mine.

"I want to propose to Laura," he says, and I yell with surprise.

"Yaaaaaaaaaaaaaaaaaaaaasssssssssss, " I scream, and I start jumping around. I glance at Ben, and he looks so pleased.

"This is the best gift a girl could ever have!' I say. "This is worth getting better for!"

"I'm going to pick the ring up this afternoon. I want you guys to bring Laura to that restaurant by the lake at seven. I'll surprise her then, is that okay

"We can manage that. Don't worry, " I say lightly.

I've never been happier than I am right now.

"Alright. I will see you guys later," Jacob says, walking upstairs to his office.

I turn around to Ben who is staring at me with a small smile, and immediately I remember last night and blush.

"I didn't even say a word, " he laughs.

"You don't have to. Your eyes are saying enough," I tell him and lean closer to kiss him.

An hour or so later, after eating some breakfast, Ben is out on the balcony. He is smoking and it kills me to see him smoking because he only does it now when he is stressing over something.

"Hey, you" I say stepping out and my hair flies backwards in the breeze. I feel so pretty.

He doesn't say a word and just gives me a worried stare. "What's wrong?" I ask, moving my hand down his back.

He shakes his head and blows the smoke out. "Jacob is really nice," he says and I know whatever is in his mind it isn't about Jacob at all.

"He is." I nod. "So, what is it?"

He really is hopeless at lying. His hair is getting longer, and I like it.

"I was just thinking." He takes a drag of his cigarette.

"Yes. What is it?" I say impatiently.

"I think I might go back to Germany."

He exhales more smoke, and as he does the air goes out of my lungs too like I've been punched. Why is he leaving? Why now?"

He turns around to face me and pulls me to him but I back away from him.

"Why would you?" I say my voice is small, and my throat is aching.

"Because I have a lot of things to do. I have to like complete my studies," he says, and his tone is cold.

"When would you go?" I say, not really taking the news in.

"Well, I still have a month in the States, but then it's decision time. I've been thinking about it for a while, but I couldn't say anything. Not the way...."

"Not the way what?" I stammer, knowing the answer.

"Not the way you were. How ill you were getting."

I want to slap him but I also want to hug him and tell him not to leave me, but I do nothing as my mind is racing.

A month. So short a time, but at least I have time. I can figure something out in thirty days to persuade him to stay.

Or I could just go to Germany with him.

"Thirty days?" I ask.

"Thirty, including today. I'm so sorry, Eva. I always had to face this one day," he murmurs and walks closer to me. I wrap my arms around him and he does the same.

"Can we not count the days and just enjoy them?" I say.

He laughs loudly and I tilt my head a bit. The wind gets stronger, and colder. Winter cannot be far away.

"Yeah. Let's not count them," he says softly, and we stand silently, staring at the view.

Chapter Twenty-Three

I sit with Aiden, who is working on his school stuff, whilst waiting for Ben to get changed for dinner. There's an hour until seven and we have to go and pick Laura up. I've told her a little white lie about us meeting for some girly talk.

Ben is appears, wearing a dark blue suit and his hair is parted at the side. My dress is dark blue and it is kind of cute that we match. He walk to the car, and he opens the door for me and I get in, but I notice his jaw is clenched and I won't ask him what's wrong because it looks like he is going to explode.

I dial Laura's number when we reach the apartment, and she walks out of the door wearing a white knee length dress. Her auburn hair is done in waves, her makeup is perfect, and she looks so gorgeous. She gets in the car smiling.

"Okay people, let's go" She says and Ben drives away. Laura keeps on talking about how long it took her to get ready and all she the new patients she has to deal with. "I apologize that Jacob is not coming," she says sadly, and I stare at Ben from the corner of my eye and his jaw softens.

"It's alright Laura, he is busy" Ben says, smiling at her.

We reach the restaurant, and Ben parks and turn around to open the door for me, I stand out and he holds my hand and kisses it. Whoa, that's a change in mood!

We sit at the table. Ben is facing me and Laura's facing an empty chair. She doesn't look completely happy, but tries just for me.

And then she sees Jacob, walking towards us, and her face lights up.

Jacob is wearing a black suit walking to us, smiling wide.

"Hey, my love, " he says kissing Laura and sitting on the empty chair next to Ben. She gasps and he grins. "Did you guys order yet?" he asks.

"No, we were just about to. Where did you come from?" she giggles, and Jacob just winks and doesn't reply.

The meal is fabulous and as it draws to an end, Jacob takes both Laura's hands.

"Okay I have something to show you," Jacob says, and guides her to the end of the bridge where we can see the lake. It is dark now but the lights illuminate it beautifully. It's so romantic I feel like crying. We stand next to each other but a little bit far away from Laura and Jacob.

Jacob goes down on one knee and Laura is staring at him quizzically. "What are you doing?" she says, in total surprise.

"Laura Ely Allen, I have shared the best days of my life with you. You have led me from darkness into the light," Jacob's voice is shaking. "Will you be my partner in life forever?"

Laura is absolutely blown away.

"What?"

He looks up at her in adoration.

"Laura Ely Allen. Will you marry me?"

Laura gasps and covers her mouth. She looks at me and then looks back to Jacob and starts sobbing quietly.

"Yes! Yes, of course I will!", she says softly, and he places the ring in her finger and stands to hug her, but they end up kissing, and I turn around away from them.

"This is too much" I whisper and wipe my tears away, looking at the lake.

I'm so happy for them, and when I turn around again there's a guy holding some big silver balloons that read 'I love you, L.'

I walk over to Laura and she hugs me so hard sobbing in my shoulder. "Congratulations, Mom" I murmur and she hugs me tighter, sobbing even more. I know she is so happy and she wasn't expecting any of this.

We separate and Ben kisses both of their cheeks and congratulates her as I hug Jacob, who is grinning like a happy cat.

"Hey do you think I've finished with all the surprises?" Jacob says to Laura.

"There's more?" She yells with excitement, like a little kid.

"I booked four tickets to travel to Dubai," he smiles widely at her, pulling travel papers from his pocket.

"Four?" we both say, at the same time.

"Yes, Laura, You, Eva and Ben, and I" Jacob hands her the papers and I glance at Ben who looks happy like he already knows about this.

"Did you know about this?" I ask him and he doesn't answer me. "No," he says, and walks over to Jacob shaking his hand and whispering something in his ear. I really want to cry because of Ben's attitude has been off all evening. Maybe he is just angry because he is going back to Germany. I don't know.

Laura and Jacob leave together and

Ben and I drive back in silence. I really don't know what is bothering him, but I'm not going to let it spoil such a perfect evening.

We arrive back at Ben's place and it's completely dark. Aidenand Charli are not here. I'm about to ask him where are they but he pushes me to the wall and presses his lips to mine, hard and hungry. Kissing me hard, so hard, and his body is pushing into mine hard and wanting. He carries me and I wrap my legs around his waist as he walks to his room closing the door behind us. Our lips don't break the connection and I deepen it, I want him as much as he wants me right now. He takes off his blazer and shirt and I open my dress and toss it on the ground, after last night I don't fear him or his love anymore.

His lips are on my neck kissing and licking. My body arches as his strong hands skim down my waist and I feel him enter me, and it is perfect, and right.

I close my eyes as he makes love to me, slowly and gently. It's not like it was with Ethan. It's all about love and pleasure and mutual satisfaction. He begins moves in me faster and faster and his lips are so close to mine I can feel his breath and my manicured nails graze his back and he shouts "Love me, Eva!" and I beg him to do it.

"Yes! Yes!"

He moves faster and I give myself completely to him, his body, his sex and the sweet, sensual moment.

When we are both spent, he falls next to me and I hear his heart beating so fast. I place my ears to his chest and raise my eyes to look at him and he is looking at me.

"You okay?" he asks kissing my forehead.

"Yeah, that was fabulous. What's wrong? You've been a little off all evening," I ask, running my fingers through his hair.

"I don't want to leave you" He whispers.

"Then don't." I say, lovingly.

"You don't understand," he sighs.

"Try me," I tell him, and he shakes his head, getting out of bed and covering me with the quilt.

Something is definitely wrong. And I don't know if he will tell me anytime soon. But I forget my confusion as sleep claims me.

Chapter Twenty-Four

We emerge from our cocoon and go over to Laura's place.

My place.

My home.

Jacob and Laura are sitting on the couch all cuddly and loving.

"Finally, " Jacob says, sitting up straight, Laura smiles at me and I smile back. "Our flight is at noon tomorrow', he says, 'and pack for six days."

"Yes, it's very hot and humid at the moment," Laura says, smiling and we both know that all we are both going to pack are shorts and summer tops.

"That will be so cool." Ben hugs me to him. "Jacob, I don't know how to thank you enough."

"No worries, young man. I think we all deserve it, don't you Eva?"

"I don't know. Maybe," I blush, and they all laugh. But Laura eyes me suspiciously.

A little later, she approaches me in the kitchen while Ben and Jacob are making plans for our trip.

"Eva, are you okay? Is everything alright with you and Ben?" she asks, concerned.

I shake my head and look at the photographs. I never tire of the happiness on display in them.

"Yes, it's wonderful. But, but.."

I hesitate, as the tears fill my eyes,

"What? But what?" she says.

"He is leaving in less than a month. And I'm not even sure he will come back, Laura."

And the first sob comes out.

"He is going to leave me alone," I cry and she hugs me to her chest, where I can sob and cry.

When I finish, she says,

"Eva, I'm sure for such a big move, he must have his reasons. And if you truly love someone, you will sacrifice your own feelings to let them live their life and be happy. Do you know why is he going back?" she asks.

"He said something about finishing studies" I tell her wiping my tears.

"We'll see. Want my advice? Let him make his own decisions and live his life and if he loves you, he will come back for you."

And it suddenly occurs to me that she is absolutely right. I'm being selfish. What future is there for him if he doesn't finish his education? Will he want to work in a supermarket all his life?

Suddenly, I understand what true love is.

Letting go.

We walk back to the living room and they both stand when they see us. Ben hugs me, and I hug him back, burying my face in his neck. I try not to cry.

"This is hard for me to deal with," I say. "Please be patient. It will take me time to get used to you leaving."

He whispers in my ear, "I love you."

And I love him too.

Ben goes home to pack, his things, and I reflect that I have never done this before. I have never gone to somewhere else with someone I love. The thought makes me smile. I lie on my bed with my phone looking where place we are going to visit and it seems beautiful.

I would love to see such places with Ben and give him some priceless memories to take back to Germany.

After my evening meal, I bid Laura and Jacob goodnight.

"Big day tomorrow," Jacob winks.

It feels weird to be in bed alone. I haven't slept here alone since I started dating Ben.

But I can't wait to see what tomorrow brings.

❧

Chapter Twenty-Five

I wake, shower, change, and grab my phone and my backpack. I make it out to the living room where Laura is talking on the phone and Jacob is nowhere to be seen.

"Eva did you call Ben? We should be going now" Laura says as she hangs up.

"I'll call him," I say, tell her making my way outside. He doesn't answer but I see his text saying he will be here at nine sharp. Another five minutes. "Hey Jacob," I wave at him and he waves back smiling. I stand on the steps staring at the cars passing by,

It is a great day to be leaving Chicago.

I feel a tap on my shoulder,

"Eva."

I turn and Luke is standing there.

He pulls me down the side of the apartment building, where the garbage cans stand. I gasp loudly.

"Hey, calm down. I'm your brother, remember."

"What are you doing here?" I say stepping back away from him. "Where's Charli?" I add.

"Charli and I broke up. She went back to Germany."

"But, Ben never said..."

"That's not important. Can I talk to you for a second?" He looks desperate. Lost.

"You really do have just got one minute, I'm leaving for the airport, " I say, crossing my arms against my

"Listen Eva, there is something you have to understand." Luke breathes deeply and his eyes stare at something behind me.

"Talk! I have to go!" I snap at him again.

"Eva, I've been doing some searching in the local archives and county records, and I just discovered that we are registered as the kids of Henry Wilson." I arch my brows at the name. I've never heard of it. "Henry Wilson is our biological dad, and Destiny Wilson is our mom."

Ben shows up. That is all I need.

"Hey, is he bothering you?"

Luke scowls but I tell him to go on.

"Eva, we are the kids of Henry and Destiny Wilson, but I am not the child of Henry Wilson you are

"So Henry is my dad and not yours, but we have a shared mom?"

"Yes. Where are you going?" Luke asks.

"Out of town," Ben growls, and I hear Laura calling us. "I have to go." I point behind me and Luke backs away.

"Eva, keep in touch. There's more I need to tell you much more." he says.

"Well, Skype me when we get back," I say, and give him my cell number.

Ben looks as angry as hell and sits in silence. I know he is mad at me but Luke is still my brother.

"Eva who was that?" Laura asks, and I ignored her, I swear if she knows anything about this I will be so angry.

I'm also pissed that Ben never mentioned Charli leaving.

Not such a good start to the day.

Rage hits me so hard to the point I don't realize I'm digging my nails in Ben's arms.

"Hey, Eva?" Ben pushes me lightly and I'm back to reality. "What are you doing?" He moves my arms to him and his eyes are full of worry.

"Why did you lie to me? About Charli?" I ask, and Laura turns around to look at us. I ignore her once more and she frowns.

"Well, I didn't know Charli was actually going back to Germany. She told me that she and Luke were going to Vegas. Obviously, she lied to me as well. Once again," he says, and his voice is calm but his eyes are full of disappointment.

I remember Laura's advice, and slowly inhale and exhale to calm myself down.

We arrive at the airport, and my eyes drift from Ben who is busy with his phone, to Laura who is daydreaming about something, to Jacob who is deep in conversation with a guy helping him with our luggage, to a woman wiping her tears, an old man sleeping on the chair, and teenager with his loud music.

To the man in a suit typing on his laptop, the little girl pulling on her dad shirt while he is talking to the woman next to him.

Suddenly I'm calmer.

A voice booms from the speaker calling the passengers to get on the flight

When we get on the plane, Ben and I are seated next to each other, with Laura and Jacob behind us.

The plane roars into the sky, and slowly the clouds gather under us like a soft blanket. I hold Ben's hand, and I hopethathe will fly back to me from Germany.

The rest of the flight passes like a dream. I guess I slept a little, though what Luke told me still runs around my head.

We arrive and our first step outside and even though it's late at night, my top sticks to my body. Jacob was right this humidity is the highest I have ever experienced.

"Is it like this all the time?" I ask Ben and he shrugs.

Its dark here but I sure as hell know from the pretty lights that this place is beautiful. We take a cab to the hotel and I cannot stop gazing at the buildings, lit up like Christmas trees.

The hotel we are in is so fancy.

"I will wake up early and explore this place," I mumble and Ben nods. Jacob and Ben check in, and we to my joy, Ben and are not only in the same room, we are sharing the same bed.

And as we fall asleep in each other's arms, I forget Luke, his news, and all the stress.

I think I am in paradise

Chapter Twenty-Six

I walk out on to the balcony and the hot waves of air hit me hard. I look at the amazing view from up here, and most of it is palm trees and water

I put on my orange bikini and the white sundress Laura bought me, and I love how my body is so much more fit and shapely since Laura began to take care of me.

Ben is asleep. Deeply. I don't want to wake him up because he seemed so tired from the flight, so I will let him rest. I wear my sunglasses and walk out of the room, taking the stairs down as I am only on the second floor.

When I get outside, people are lying under the sun, sipping drinks in the pool and chattering happily.

I sit down and the bartender asks me if I want anything to drink. "Yes please, something cold," I smile to him and he walks away.

I turn around to face the people and the weather is pretty much amazing to dip myself in ice. I tie my hair in a bun, and the guy places my drink next to me. "Thank you" I tell him.

I sip my drink and stare at people. I already love this place. It is so comforting and quiet. There's a group of people gathered on the other side of the place listening to a guy ranting on about something, so I grab my drink and walk over to them. I pull out a chair and sat near to him. He gives me a nod, and keeps talking.

"My culture is so fucked up. A woman wears shorts and tops showing most of her skin and they say she is the one seeking attention. That she deserves to be raped. They make stupid dumb people famous. They've stopped loving themselves and think suicide by bomb is a noble career choice." He shakes his head and when he stops talking for seconds the people listening ask him to carry on, and I look at him with his swarthy features, and his dark eyes, and a fierce flame burns within him.

"If there's one thing you guys should do, stop being judgmental and love people for who they are, not for what they look like. Love the people who spread love in the world, not the dumb ass who posts videos making fun of someone else. Stop making dumb people famous!"

He sips his drink, and the people listening to him gradually walk away.

I stay there staring at him. I want to know him. I want to listen to his philosophy. I like people who speak with dignity and hope for the future.

I like this guy.

"Hi, I'm Eva," I smile to him, and we shake hands.

"Hi there Eva," he says kindly.

"No name?" I ask, and he shakes his head.

"No name. I walk into your life, make an impact, and leave in a flash," he says, and I frown, confused

"How come?" I ask him.

"You will know one day," he says, sipping his drink.

"Anyway, I like what you said. It was so full of life."

"How old are you?" he asks, and smiles to himself.

"Turning nineteen soon," I say trying to suppress my excitement.

"Happy early birthday," he whistles.

"Thanks," I say, smiling.

"You are young, but your soul is old," he says, and stands, glancing at his watch.

"Uh I have to go, see you around Eva?" He smiles and I nod to him.

"Sure," I smile back to him and see him walk away.

"Want some?" A blonde girl moves a cigarette pack towards me and I look around to see if she's talking to someone else. "Yup. Talking to you, girlfriend."

Her voice is deep and freaky for a girl.

"I don't smoke" I mumble and shake my head.

"Strict parents?" she smirks, blowing smoke towards me.

"No, I just don't," I snap at her.

"What are you doing?" she asks, and I turn around and look at her.

"Just checking out the place," I say. "I'm on vacation."

"That's cool. I work down there in the town." She exhales and sips from her cocktail. "I've been here for five years now, I was twenty when I first landed."

"Alone?" I ask.

"Yeah, totally" She raises her eyebrows when she talks.

There's silence between us for long seconds before she says, "You are not much of a talker, aren't you?"

"No, not really," I shake my head at her.

"You should come to town. I will show you around," she smiles and I have to say no, because Jacob has the holiday planned like a military campaign. I'm surprised they haven't come looking for me already.

"Well, that would be amazing, but I'm here with my friends and I don't think they'll go for that," I shrug, drinking my glass of coke.

"Too bad, get you access to some cool places," she winks.

"Well, if you give me your number, I can call you or something. Or I can just find you here," I say.

"How long are you staying here?"

"Six days I think"

"Only six? A vacation should be longer," she laughs

I roll my eyes at her, laughing too.

A cold hand touches my shoulder and I tense, unable to move.

"Hey there." The voice sends shivers through me and when I turn around it is only freaking Ben, goofing around.

"Holy cow you almost made me shit myself" I tell him and he laughed.

"Who's your friend?" he asks and they shake hands. I frown because I have no idea..

"I'm EL," she smiles, and suddenly i feel a little jealous.

"I'm Benjamin," he smiles back, with that megawatt grin of his.

"Eva, Benjamin nice to meet you," she smiles. "See ya, wouldn't wanna be ya!" she laughs, and lopes away.

I sit in the sun by the pool and Ben tries to tempt me in, but he's splashing me like some goofy teenager, and I don't want to get wet.

"Eva!" I hear his voice and he is splashing water on me, I sit up.

"What?"

"Come here" he motion to me.

"No way," I shake my head.

"Why?" he asks confused.

"I fear water."

"Ah. Understood," he says, and swims away like a young German God.

His eyes match the color of the water and my heart skips a beat at his light hair and his amazing figure. He deserves someone as beautiful as him but he chose me. He goes back under the water and I sit waiting for him to re-appear. How come he's mine? I don't care. I love him.

I drowse off until I hear him calling me again.

"Eva, your phone," Ben shouts from the pool.

I answer.

"Hello?" I say.

"Eva?" It is Luke. Freaks me out. What now?

"Yes, Luke."

"Can you talk right now" I can't tell anything from his tone.

"It's okay, talk" Ben is narrowing his eyes at me but I ignore him

"Eva, I went to the station last night," he coughs,"– I know some people there. Well, I asked them about Destiny Wilson."

"And?"

"She was arrested for stealing in the year 1996. The year you were born."

I feel even worse now. My real mother was in jail.

"Well, not only stealing, but drug addiction too."

It just gets worse.

Ben gets out of the pool.

"What else?" I ask, as if that's not news enough,

"Eva, I don't know how to say this, but you have a twin."

"What?' I almost yell.

Ben moves towards me, looking really worried.

"Eva, hang up on him. You're on vacation. Don't let him spoil it."

"It's too late now," I say. "Go on," I say to Luke, still in shock.

"She stayed with Destiny. But you and I were given away. To Anderson and his wife."

My heart can't handle this.

She gave me away and kept someone else.

"I talk to you later, Luke" I cry, and shut the phone.

Ben opens his arms for me, and I throw myself on him and he wraps his arm tight around me.

He is rubbing his hand on my back. "It is all right, calm down. Let's go back to the room.

Once we shower and change we sit on the bed, just looking at each other. Then Ben just says:

'You never told me about your fear of water."

"Well, that's from when Ethan used drown me in the bath with cold or hot water," I tell him, avoiding eye contact. "He would hold my head in the water until my legs stopped splashing water, and it felt like my soul had nearly left my body."

'What a bastard,' Ben says. He never likes to hear of my pain. What human being would?

"I just saw death millions of times with him, and never died."

I weep, and he holds me so, so tight.

Chapter Twenty-Seven

Laura and I go wedding shopping. She sees some dresses that she likes, and is hesitating to buy them.

"If you love them, buy them," I tell her, like I've been shopping all my life, and she laughs.

I throw myself on a couch. We've been walking all morning and my legs are in so much pain. I'm still kind of angry.

I am angry with Laura for lying to me. I am angry that she didn't tell me the whole truth concerning my family.

That is if she knows the whole truth.

I see a girl choosing a wedding dress with her mother and it throws me.

I wonder if I will ever marry Benjamin Eisenberg. And I would want my mother next to me.

Except that she wasn't my mother.

And she's dead.

And my real mother gave me away and kept my twin.

It's so fucked up it's almost funny.

But I'm not laughing.

"Eva. Eva?" Laura is calling me, I turn around to look at her and she is wearing a long white dress.

She looks like an angel.

My heart stops beating and my eyes are crying and my soul is praying for a break from all these beautiful, awful moments.

"So how is it?" She turns around.

"Jacob wouldn't want you to get out of it," I whisper and she clutches her hands on her chest looking at me with tears in her eyes. "Laura you look as perfect as ever, this is so beautiful on you," I tell her, and my anger vanishes. I focus on her happy day. Trying not to be selfish and wanting answers all the time.

"Really? Should I?" she asks and I nod.

"Yes, definitely." I nod quickly to her.

"Alright. I will!" she says like an excited schoolgirl.

"So did you choose one?" she asks, placing her arms on my shoulders and I shake my head. "Why not?"

"Nothing would ever suit me," I mumble.

"Everything would be perfect on you Eva, what are you saying?" She waves her hands around and walks to the long dresses there, but my eyes are fixed on the black long dress at the very end of the shop. I point at the dress and her jaw drops. "That one?"

"Yeah."

"Try it," she demands and the woman brings it to me. I take it from her and walk to the fitting room, I stare at it for a whole minute, it's too pretty for me I can't wear this. I strip out of my clothes, avoid looking at myself in the mirror, put it on, and walk out. My head is down and my hair is covering my face.

"Oh. My. Jesus," gasps Laura, and I raise my head staring at her, shocked.

The sales woman is covering her mouth and I really think that I have made the dress look worse.

"You look so pretty," the woman whispers, and I stare at her, puzzled.

"Eva, we are so buying this for you, get out of it," Laura is fanning her face with the paper as if she is going to cry.

We walk to the nearest café.

"I just want water and a brownie, please, " I tell Laura and we order and chat about the wedding, and the honeymoon, and whether I will be okay home alone if they go away.

Her wedding will be held in her parents' house in Missouri, exactly fifteen days from today. That's why she bought her dress here. "We will stay in the same apartment until Jacob get his project finalized and then will move to a house somewhere in Seattle. And you can have your own place nearby, if you want."

"I will be fine, wherever I stay" I tell her.

"Are you sure" She reaches for my hands.

"Yes, if I get a job my own apartment would be excellent. I think I'm coping now,"

Just shows how wrong a girl can be.

Chapter Twenty-Eight

"Maybe we should overcome your fear of water," says Ben, as we sit by the pool. He sits straight and I do the same.

"No"

"Yes, come" He stands and walks to the water. Holds my hand like I am a little kid.

"No Ben, I can't do it, I plead.

"Oh yeah. You so can." He laughs, and leads me down the steps to the pool. He walks in the pool and order me to sit on the edge of it, I do what he says and my legs are in the cool water. His entire body is in the water, and he holds my hand and pulls me to him. I fall in the water and gasp so loud but he holds my waist. His hands are on my bare waist, and it makes my entire body want him.

"Trust me. You are okay. Open your eyes."

I open my eyes and he is looking at me, his blue eyes are light and matching the water. I wrap my arms around his neck and hug him to me. I can feel his heart beating aggressively.

Slowly he moves his hand from my waist to the end of my back pulling my body to his. The water is pushing me towards him. I love it. There are some other people in the pool with but we ignore them as he holds me firmly afraid, of letting go.

I'm afraid of drowning and he is afraid of letting me drown. Just like Jack and Rose in the film Titanic. I laugh at the thought, but I know deep down that he would sacrifice his life for me, just like Jack did for Rose.

I love trusting him so much. He is helping me conquer my fear.

I move my face to face him and his nose is touching mine now, he smiles a small smile but his eyes are shut. "It's not scary isn't it?" he whispers and I shake my head slowly.

"Not with you, my love," and his eyes open, looking deeply into mine.

"Do you want us to go farther in?" he asks, and I shake my head.

"We are just fine here," I tell him and he laughs.

"Who taught you to swim?"

"My dad. He used to be a high school swimmer so he taught Charli and me. I almost drowned in the sea twice, and I told him I would never swim again but he ignored me and just said 'a tough man isn't tough if he isn't scared.'"

"So you never gave up on it?" I say, and he shakes his head.

He carries me out of the pool. I stand and he wraps the towel around my body, and places one around his neck.

He is such a gentleman.

He is a truly gentle man.

Later, we walk to the beach, and Ben starts talking to a guy wearing shorts and a black top.

"You might want to take this off," he points at my towel and I place it on a nearby bench. We walk on the sand towards the sea, and it tickles my feet. I look at the people and for a second and fell in love with the view of everyone enjoying themselves - the little kids enjoying the sand and the little castles they have built, and the girls chasing each other.

I suddenly realize that Ben is waiting for the man to bring a jet ski to him.

"Wait! I am not riding that, no way Benjamin," I shake my head and he turns around staring at me. "What if we crash and drown?"

"Well when we drown, we will die in love with each other!" He flashes his smile at me and I roll my eyes, he forces me to wear the life vest and tightens the straps on me. He does not wear one.

We get on the machine and I sit behind him, wrapping my hands tight around him, my cheek is in his back. In seconds, we take off out to sea and I yell out, I can feel him laughing but I gasp for air and I feel like I am flying.

Flying into love.

Chapter Twenty-Nine

I'm lying on a lounger while Ben swimming in the sea. I recall Luke's last call. Birth mother went to jail. Father is nowhere to be seen. I HAVE A TWIN SISTER. I have been raised by a monster and ignored by the poor weak woman that he murdered. Shit, I forgot to ask Luke if he know any thing about who she really was.

"Eva?" A hoarse voice surprises me, and I open my eyes and sit up.

"Eva right?"

"Ah, yes, the philosophical guy," I smile broadly at him.

"You alone here?" For the first time, I notice his poor British accent.

"No. Are you British?" I ask him and he shakes his head

"No, but I recently studied in the UK," he replies.

"Did you study philosophy or something?" i ask

Again, he shakes his head.

"No, I didn't study philosophy but books and the internet can teach a great deal, but actually seeing things and witnessing them in real life made me start talking about them."

"Your society?" I state.

"Exactly, in the past years I've learned a lot about the people I have to live with." He shakes his head and I feel like he is rolling his eyes behind the sunglasses he is wearing.

"Like what?"

"Let's just say that I learned the heard way. I lost people I cared about, and I learned."

He is as mysterious as ever.

Ben walks towards us, water dripping from his shorts.

"Hey, Ben this is the guy I told you about the other day. I call him the philosopher."

The stranger smiles and then shakes Ben's hand.

"I'm her boyfriend," Ben says, and I detect a hint of jealousy.

"And I'm just a guy," he smiles, and his answer makes me giggle and he laughed with me.

"So how long you staying here?" I ask taking of my glasses and looking at him. He looks shocked, as if he knows me.

"Um, just today," he says, shaking his head slightly. "Leaving tomorrow morning."

"Oh, so no more wisdom from you?"

"Too bad! No more." He winks, taking his glasses off.

Ben is just staring at the sea without speaking, when the philosopher rises to leave, then offers his hand in a parting gesture.

"You know what," he says, as I place mine in his.

"What?" I ask.

"Most of us are confused. Most of us don't know why we are working, or studying. Most of us don't even know what we they doing with their lives. Eva, have a goal and spread positivity. Happiness is something you should work hard to achieve,"

Our hands are still touching and I can see in his eyes that he is only trying to bring joy to this sad world.

"We are excessively lost, and we must find ourselves again. You must find yourself again."

And with that he lets go of my hand, makes a sweet little bow, and walks away.

"Who the heck was he?" Ben asks, getting dressed.

"Oh just a guy I met that day, I love the way he talks though," I say, putting on my sundress.

"Yeah. Right, " Ben mutters, and I definitely think he's jealous!

Chapter Thirty

The flight back was uneventful, and memories of our wonderful vacation have barely faded when Luke asks to meet me in the Starbucks café.

He briefly asks me about my vacation, then wastes no time in getting back to the subject of our real parents.

"So, I've discovered that Destiny Wilson worked in a bakers shop for six years."

"Wait" I say, "what bakers shop? We could call or visit them," I tell him and his eyes widen.

"Why didn't I think of that? But there must be hundreds in Chicago."

"We could borrow a phone directory from Ben or Aiden, and call them all," I say.

"Good idea. Hey, Eva, You do know that I'm sorry I let you go. Anderson gave me no choice. Said he would kill me if he caught me looking for you. You must know how much I cared about you. I still care, Eva," he says softly, his voice is full regret.

"I know that," I check the time on my phone and its already two in the evening. "Let's go to Benjamin's, I only have nineteen days left to spend with him." I roll my eyes and grab my purse and we walk out of the café.

"Why? I don't understand?" Luke asks, standing and pulling on his beanie.

"Because he is going back to Germany." My voice is shaking, but I don't want to cry. Not in front of my brother.

Luke doesn't say a word but I feel like he knows what I'm going through.

"Did you love her?" I ask him as we leave the building.

"Who?"

"Charli Eisenberg"

"I was ready to sell my soul for her," he says sadly.

When we get to the door of Ben's apartment, Aiden opens the door and smiles, but Ben scowls when he sees Luke.

What is he doing here?" he says, his voice cold with anger.

"Luke is with me," I say briskly, and walk past Ben.

"Aiden, can we use your copy of the phone directory for Chicago?" I say, sitting on the couch next to him.

"The Yellow Pages, you mean?" he says curiously.

"Yes please. Luke and I have had an idea."

"Okay, just a second" he says, and goes to his room

"What do you need that for?" Ben asks cautiously.

"Um well we are going to call every bakery shop in Chicago and ask about Destiny Wilson"

"Every bakery shop?" Aiden gasps, returning with a large yellow book. "Do you know how many bake shops there are in here?"

"Um no" I raise one eyebrow.

Most of them will be on the internet," says Ben.

"Yeah I know," I reply, "but I want to call ones from a long time ago. And this copy of the Yellow Pages is, as I thought, quite old," I say, thumbing through the curled pages.

It took us hours to call every bakery shop. Many had gone out of business, and were disconnected. Many had never heard of Destiny Wilson. Aiden and Luke go out to bring us some food and I simply carry on dialing.

"You alright?" Ben whispers.

"Just tired of calling," I mumble.

"Why are you even looking for her?"

"Because I need answers. Ben. Answers about my life."

Chapter Thirty-One

Laura's wedding is at her mom's old house in Missouri, which is six hours away from us in a car. Benjamin and I go together in his car, and Jacob and Laura go in theirs. The wedding is going to be small, just friends and family. I'm so glad that she finally found her soul mate, and I have never seen her this happy.

After what seems like a forever drive through the empty American landscape, we arrive at Laura's parents place. "Come on babe, Jacob and Laura already arrived, " Ben says, waking me up. "Come on sleepy head."

We walk inside and Laura is sitting with another woman on the chair and they look alike.

"Here she is!" Laura runs towards me and clasps me in a huge warm hug. "Eva this is Lauren my sister. Lauren, Eva."

I didn't know she had a sister.

"Hi there Eva,' she says in a cute girly voice. You are even prettier than I thought."

She is almost prettier than Laura. Does this entire family look like angels?

"Thank you so much, " I say happily, Ben walks in and Laura introduces him to Lauren, they shake hands and Lauren shows us to our room. The house is old, but and big and beautiful.

"Well, you guys, it's late, so I guess you will have to meet the other members of the family tomorrow," giggles Laura, and closes the door behind us. There are two separate beds. It will be kind of fun sleeping in a bed alone but in the same room as Ben. I shrug myself out of my jacket and shoes and clamber into bed. The bed is comfy and warm but I don't feel comfortable alone.

"Ben," I whine.

"What's wrong?" He asks.

"Can you sleep next to me?" I sound like a little kid

"Okay" He gets in with me and I snuggle under him, breathing him in, and he hugs me close until I drift away to sleep.

Dawn arrives. It is the day of the wedding. I wake up and head right to the bathroom at the end of the corridor. I can hear noises outside and I know that the rest of the family has arrived.

"Look at this place, everything is amazing," Ben whistles as he looks out of the window.

"Yeah, I think it'll be great," I say. Lauren walks in, all smiley with her blonde hair done in a bun.

"Morning guys. The rest of the family should be here in a couple of hours," she says.

"Great! I can't wait to meet everyone else!" I shout, clapping my hands in glee.

Someone shouts for Laura and she disappears, leaving Ben and I alone again. Sixteen days left, and I have no idea what am I going to do when there are only six. Laura and Jacob go on honeymoon to Morocco in two days for over a month. All the people I love will leaveme all of a sudden!

And I have no idea what I will do when that happens.

Saddened, I suddenly kiss Ben. He pulls me to him and makes the kiss deeper, then lays me out on the bed and gets on top of me. "This is a great morning".

"Good morning to you too," I giggle and he kisses me more, moving his hand up my thighs and I wrap my hands around his neck. It's been a long time since we last did this and I miss the closeness when we make love,

"I'd love to not let go of you, but this would be wrong,' I say. "We really do need to get ready." He smiles. Kisses me. Gets out of bed and I pout at him. "Well, you said it!' he laughs. "So get your clothes and get ready."

I climb out of bed and put on some black lingerie that I haven't worn before. Laura told me 'this will make whoever you will fall in love with, never let you go' and just the thought makes me laugh. I don an oversized shirt with and shorts, grab the dress that I will wear later, and walk up stairs to the room Laura is getting ready in. I enter and there's Lauren and two others. She introduces Sophie, who is my age, and Camilla, who at twenty-two is one of the most beautiful girls that I've ever seen.

I smile to them and hang my dress with the other dresses.

"We were actually discussing the wedding" Laura says, pulling a chair for me to sit with them. "We were thinking if you and Ben could walk first down the aisle, then myself and Jacob's brother John, then Sophie and Brad, and finally Camilla. She'll be carrying the flowers. Since there are no bridesmaids or anything I want us to all look alike. I mean we all are wearing black dresses, right?" I look at the other girls and they seem to agree.

Laura's mom appears outside, and Lauren sighs. "Oh, shoot, I forgot about my mom! She will be walking in with her friend Christopher."

We all laugh, then sit there for a couple of hours talking about Laura when she was younger. She was an intelligent little girl, her mother says, and Laura's mom's eyes match mine so much, Lauren says that I look just like her mom when she was younger.

Then the time comes for dresses and put on some makeup. Camilla helps me out, applying eyeliner, blush and a red lipstick. I look at myself in the mirror and I love the difference. My hair is waved and moved to one side, my makeup is amazing. My dress is just the way I wanted to be at the prom I never attended.

Sophie's dress is short and black with a V-neck, her blonde hair is done in big waves and she looks lovely. Camilla's hair is straightened, it's a light brown just like Laura's, her blue eyes are wide and her makeup is breathtaking on her. Honestly, I'm jealous she looks so perfect, her dress without sleeves just like mine, long but tight on her body.

Lauren's dress is a long, black wraparound. I love how we all look.

"The red lipstick squad," Lauren yells and we all laugh.

The guests start arriving and we walk down the stairs before Laura. The boys are waiting, I see Ben busy doing up his jacket. He raises his face and our eyes lock, blue to brown, and I blush. He is wearing a beautiful black suit and he looks like a model. I wait for Lauren and Sophie to hold to their men's hands and it's finally my turn. Ben is staring at me, astonished, and I smile wide enough to light the room.

"What?" I giggle.

He covers his mouth, for once, speechless, and I take his hand.

"Come," I tell him and we walk slowly outside, on to the grass and there are chairs full with people. They all turn around to look at us, and I hold Ben's arm tight because I know my anxiety is trying to kick in.

We walk down the aisle and I'm smiling at Ben because I have always wanted this. It's happening, and as we arrive at the end, I walk to the left and he walks to the right. Sophie is behind us, and after they all walk in we stand next to each other waiting for Laura to walk down.

It breaks my heart to know that she will be walking alone and not with her dad. Her mom is in tears as the slow music starts playing and here she comes, gliding slowly like a beautiful angel come down to this world, and when she gets to Jacob he kisses her hands. He too is speechless with wonderment and joy. He takes her hand gently and leads her to the pastor, a smiling, happy guy who begins his speech.

"On behalf of Jacob and Laura let me just express their gratitude for all of you, their family and friends. As you can imagine, this is an amazing day in their life and it means a lot for them that you are here to celebrate it with them. Let us all take a minute right now to pause and reflect upon the beauty of this moment," he says.

I cannot stop smiling.

"Now, let us start with a prayer. I invite you to pray with me,' he says, and everyone bows their heads.

"Let us pray. God, we ask for your blessings upon this man and woman, as we celebrate this momentous occasion in their lives. Grant them happiness and contentment as they establish their new home, create a new family and explore the depths of their love for one another, and for you, Bless their families and friends and the relationships which have supported, strengthened and sustained them throughout their lives. Bless their home as a place of love and of peace. And if times grow hard and tempers grow short, help them to look into their hearts and remember the love that brought them here today. Amen."

I think it's the most wonderful wedding prayer I have ever heard, and I cannot help smiling across at Ben, who is smiling back.

The pastor continues:

"Personally, I want to thank you both for inviting me to marry you, I have known you Jacob for a long time. I've Laura since you were a child, and to witness Jacob loving Laura this much you bless me," I blink and try not to cry. I'm not a religious person, but the pastor's words make me believe in something. He continues:

"I don't just want you guys to have a biography. I want you to have a legacy too. The children you will have together will that legacy - a testimony of the love you feel towards each other. Now. I know that you guys have written down your vows," he says, hands Jacob the microphone, and he begins.

"Laura I know that I'm not perfect, but I vow that I will cherish and respect you, comfort and encourage you, be open with you and stay with you as long as we shall live,"

Laura wipes away tears and murmurs, "Yes you are. Perfect to me."

Jacob hands her the mike, and now it's Laura's turn. She smiles prettily, clears her throat and begins. She looks so radiant that I think she will explode with happiness.

"Dearest Jacob, I always wanted a fairytale love life, and had given up on the idea until the day I walked into your office and our eyes met for the first time. I instantly knew you were the one, and when you dropped down on one knee next to the lake that day and asked me to be your wife, I couldn't believe this was happening to me! You are my best friend, my hero and the love of my life and I vow to stick by your side through thick and thin no matter how hard things get. I promise to communicate with you about my needs and feelings and to listen when you need it, and I will never give up on you. I give my heart to you and vow to love you until God calls me home," she says, and I wipe my tears. We are all crying now, even Ben as a tear in his eye.

They exchange rings, kiss, and walk back down the aisle, Laura starts dancing as she walks. We all laugh but this is beautiful. The girls start dancing down the aisle as we walk out, and I hold Ben and we start dancing like fools.

We spend time with the family, chatting and joking and the music strikes up.

"May I ask you for a dance?" Ben says, pulling me on to the dance floor. "I don't know how to dance" I whisper shyly to him and he smiles, shaking his head as if telling me not to worry.

We start moving, his hand on my waist. I move with him. We are dancing! I love it. "I love you," I whisper, resting my cheek on his shoulder.

"I love you, Eva," he says, and I don't think that I could ever be happier than I am right now.

Chapter Thirty-Two

I miss Laura already, I feel like crying remembering her happiness yesterday. She was truly adorable.

When we arrive back, Aiden greets us with a smile.

"I trust you had a great time. I'm so glad you arrived back safely because I need help with my calculus" he jokes, and I walk after him, not waiting for Benjamin.

"I am going to stay here for fifteen days until my man leaves" I murmur, and Aiden gives me a pitiful look.

"Yep, I will miss that dumb head" Aiden whispers. "Hold on and be strong," he says, patting my back and hugging me.

That evening, Ben takes me for a walk and we sit on a bridge by the lake. The moon is full and it looks huge. I have never seen the moon this pretty before.

The reflection of the skyscrapers and the moon in the lake is captivating.

"I have no clue how will I survive after you leave," I say, and he sighs. I recall the words of the philosopher we met on vacation. He told me to share happiness and positivity among those who may have none, and suddenly an idea comes to me.

"Ben, let's go and hug people in the street," I tell him excitedly.

"What?" he frowns "have you gone quite mad" he jokes, but then he sees my expression and knows that I am serious.

"Come on, Ben" I plead, "lets spread some happiness and love." I beg and pout until he exhales and looks at me with a weary smile.

"Eva, you drive me crazy," he shakes his head. "But in a good way."

"Benjamin Eisenberg, I have been through hell and I am crawling slowly towards heaven. Lets help get them to heaven too. With smiles plastered on their faces," I joke.

"Alright," he says, rolling his eyes and I turn around pulling him with me toward the city.

I take him to the nearest store, which happens to be Target, and he asks, "What are we doing here?"

"I just need some things. By the way, Aiden told me you stopped working here. Why was that?" I ask, and he shakes his head, "My contract finished," he says, and I pout.

"Well, get your memory in order, because we need to find papers and crayons or markers, you know, like the ones we used to do projects with at school," I say, and he points directly ahead of us. We go for paper, markers afterward and tapes, the perfect stuff for kindergarten teachers. I pay the cashier and we walk outside. Ben stays inside talking to someone so I sit outside on the ground. I write 'Free Hugs' on the papers, and draw small hearts all over them. I make four papers, so we can stick them on our backs and our fronts. I stick them on me first and wait for Ben to finish his conversation.

After five minutes of me standing outside staring at people, he finally comes out. "Put these on, " I order him, and he does, smiling.

We walk and walk and ironically, don't encounter a single human being. It's like we are all alone in this world. "Um, Eva," Ben says, sitting on a bench, let's go back home. This idea is a flop."

I frown, refusing to give up so easily, and suddenly I see an old man sitting with a newspaper in his hand. "There," I yell, making Ben jump, but I ignore him and run to the old man. "Hey!" I shout, smiling like a lunatic. "My name is Eva, and I'm here to spread love." The old man looks startled, and then notices the papers.

"Oh hahaha come here," he laughs, then stands and holds me tight. "This is such a sweet thing you are doing." He hugs Ben as well and we thank him and walk away.

I am so glad that we didn't give up because as we walk on people start appearing and I know that all we needed was enthusiasm and excitement. We hug people and they smile at us, hugging us back We hug women who look tired walking home, men who are drained and sweaty from their work, groups of girls and guys we find sitting and chatting. They, of course, thought it weird at first, but when I explained my motives they told us to keep on spreading love and happiness.

We hugged everyone we saw, until we made it back home. I didn't mind hugging the sweaty bodies, with the nasty smells, I didn't mind being touched by them at all. I didn't mind because their touch was gentle and full of love. Silently, to myself, I thanked Giovanni for teaching me how to help others and spread such amazing positivity.

My philosopher. The gentle friend I will never forget. The one I will always love and miss deep down in my heart, having him as a friend for couple of months opened my eyes to a lot of things, basically he lead me from the darkness to the light.

A lot of things he did to me, but one of the most important words he ever told me, "stay strong and never be a coward, think about the people who care about you before doing anything stupid that would crash them all into pieces"

Chapter Thirty-Three

Wearing Ben's shirt is so comfortable. If only we were allowed to leave home like this. I move slowly out of bed not to wake him up, grabbing my annoying vibrating phone. The caller ID shows it is Luke.

"Hey, brother," I answer sleepily.

"Sorry. I didn't mean to wake you, it's nearly eleven."

"Yeah, no it's okay." I get out of bed and sit on the stool. "What's up?"

"Well, you know that day at Ben's when we got some promising addresses from the Yellow Pages? I thought if you weren't busy we could go and check some of them out."

Suddenly, I feel more awake.

"Yes, sure! When do we have to go?"

"I can be there in an hour," he says, and I check the time even though I know its ten fifty.

"Yes, alright. I'm at Ben's, okay?"

"See you then. Bye." He hangs up and I tie my hair in a messy bun. I had prepared a little breakfast for the boys, as they are still in bed. I haven't done this since I was in the shelter. I push away memories of the shelter, because I was such a mess at the time.

I cook some eggs and place them on the table with orange juice and coffee just like the way Ben likes it. I leave a note for Ben. "Gone with Luke to hunt down some old bakeries." I know Ben doesn't like the idea, but I have to find my birth mother. I have so many things to ask her. Especially why she just left me with a stranger. There must be an answer

I catch a local train a few stops to where I have arranged to meet Luke and we begin our slow quest. The first three bakery shops we enter are new, and no one remembers her or has ever heard of her. Slowly, we get closer to the old town, and the neighborhood where Luke and I used to live. I feel like my legs are heavy and struggling to move. We are very near the neighborhood where I used to walk barefoot, selling tray bakes. I can feel the ugly spirits. I have a terrible premonition that Anderson will see us

"Hey, you okay?" Luke asks, looking worried.

"No" I shake my head. "I'm a mess. I don't know if I can do this anymore," I say.

"Come on Eva in, just one shop left," Luke says, pointing a dingy, crumbling store.

"I know it's hard but we have to do it."

He walks inside and I turn around.

I shudder when I saw an old woman approaching me. She looks like a customer, just going to buy her cakes.

"Destiny" she says, looking straight at me. I have no idea what she is talking about. "Destiny, my dear," she opens her arms wide, walking toward me but I step back into Luke, coming out of the shop.

I shake my head, but she comes to me and pulls me into an embrace. I freeze. Who is she? And why is she calling me by the name of my birthmother?

I pull away from her and stare at Luke, who is as shocked as I am.

"Who are you?" I ask, and she looks at me sadly, as if I should not have forgotten her.

"I'm Wanda, of course. Don't you remember me?" Her voice is old and hoarse. She must be at least ninety years old.

"No, it's the first time I ever met you," I say, and she just stare at me.

Luke joins in. "Hey, you said Destiny, right? Who is Destiny?" Luke told her and she just looked at him, and then walked past him into the shop.

"Man, she looked like she'd have a heart attack, are you sure you don't know her?" Luke says, sitting on a low wall.

"I don't. I truly don't," I say.

Suddenly, the old lady walks out again with a small paper in her hand.

"Look. This is Destiny, " she says, and hands Luke the photo. I walk over to him to have a look, and as soon as our eyes see it, our jaws drop.

"Holy crap. She looks exactly like you" Luke says, and takes the picture from him.

"My name's Wanda, by the way, and If you aren't Destiny, who are you?" the old lady says, and sits next to Luke, smiling at him.

"I'm Eva," I tell her and she sighs and looks down at the sidewalk floor for a little while, and then looks back up at me.

"Well, now I understand,' she says quietly. "You look so much like your mother."

I feel I need to know more. I must know more.

"Please, Wanda, could tell me anything about her. Please? It's really important," I beg," sitting next to her and Luke takes my hand.

"Well, your mother was so beautiful. Your eyes match her so much, I feel like she is looking right at me this instant! But her hair was shorter. I watched her grow up around here, ever since she was twelve." She waves her hands around like she is lost. "I remember that she got pregnant with when she was eighteen, and left this place for two years. I heard she had a boy. I think. Luke was his name."

Luke smiled silently to himself.

"Then, when she came back, she was miserable and sad. I used to talk to her, but I couldn't find a way to help her, especially when she told me the doctors had said that she was pregnant with twins. It must have been you, and your twin," she says, and looks deeply sad. Then she continues.

"Well, your father, Henry was heavily into drugs, but despite this, your grandparents forced him to marry her. But just after they did marry, he got arrested and sent to jail. Which was a relief in a way, she was a lovely girl, but Henry was a bad, bad guy. He beat and abused her, but she didn't listen to me when I told her to leave him."

"Did you ever hear what happened to Destiny," I asked hesitantly, fearing the answer.

"Yes. I'm sorry to say that Destiny died in childbirth. The twins - you-survived. But it was a difficult labor, and Destiny passed away. I am so terribly, terribly sorry."

I am speechless with sadness. I will never meet my birth mother now. Tears trickle slowly down my face.

Luke squeezed my hand, cleared his throat, and continued.

"So, what happened to the twins when he went to jail?"

"Well, the grandparents were too old to cope, so they asked Henry's brother to raise her kids. He had a wife, a good woman. Henry's brother took the babies and I haven't heard anything since. Destiny was as pretty as you are my dear Eva, and I have always wondered what happened to you both. I'm glad I met you," she coughs, and wipes her tears. "I miss her."

"What happened to Henry?" I mutter and she looks at me.

"Well, he got a really long sentence, but I think his jail time has probably ended by now. You will find him somewhere in this ugly old place. But I really wouldn't go there if I were you. Some people are netter left in the past, and he is one of them," she says, with anger in her eyes.

We are all silent for a moment, lost in the tide of the past. And then Luke says:

"Did you ever hear anything about the other twin?" he asks.

"I have no idea what happened to her," she shakes her head. "You can have the photo if you would like," she says, but I hand it back to her.

"It's yours. Please have it back," I but she presses it into my hand, saying her memories are enough.

"My darlings, take care of yourself," she says, and walks back in the shop, returning with two bottles of ice cold water and handing them to us. "It's the only thing I can give you," she smiles and we thank her.

We say goodbye and tell her that we might visit her again soon, and I feel like the world is spinning. We walk in silence to the station, and stand waiting for the train. And my mind is full of questions that may never be answered

Why did I think that I inherited Anderson's eyes, when their beauty was my mother's legacy? And why did I ever hate her? She gave birth to me - gave me her soul, her looks and her heart. Why did I hate her without knowing the real story?

I hate myself for that.

I may always hate myself for that.

Finally, the train arrives, and we sit.

"Eva, are you okay?" Luke whispers and I nod silently.

I feel like my entire world has collapsed once again. I hold on to Luke for fear that I may pass out and start to sob into his chest. My brother hugs me, not saying a word. I whine quietly and cry, he doesn't stop me but rubs his hand on my back and it feels so comforting. I'm crying because every time I get close to the past, it eludes me, like smoke in the wind. I'm crying because Ben is leaving, I'm crying because I am still afraid of Anderson. I'm crying because even my real family isn't a family that we can be proud of. I can guess that Luke feels the same.

We have half an hour to get back to where Ben and Aiden lives, so I just bury myself in silence, and know that Luke won't mind that. We've spent so much time looking for her, and when we finally find out about her, she is dead. Dead for eighteen years now.

Dead.

I pound my fists on Luke's chest and sob even more as the train rattles through the dusty afternoon.

Chapter Thirty-Four

The news of my real mother's death affects me for days. I tell Ben all about it, and he is wonderful and supportive. I cannot shake my dark mood, until one day Ben comes in, smiling his goofy smile, and I can see he is hiding something behind his back

"What?" I say.

He gets down on one knee and I think he is just acting dumb as usual, until he flashes a little red box, handing me a bouquet of beautiful flowers. I hold them tight, afraid of what he will have to say.

"Eva, I know it's impossible that I would ask you for marriage right now. Not because I don't want you, because I'm going back to Germany and you are going to be away from me for some time. You are my everything, the one I will never let go of you, I love you so much. Just waking up to your face and kisses in the morning is love itself, and I am going to give all of me to you and I hope that you will do the same."

"Oh, Ben. That is so beautiful," is all I can manage to say.

He looks deep unto my eyes.

"Eva, I love you. So much,"

I'm crying again, I'm crying at his words and the way his eyes are so full of anxiety.

"For now, this is my ring of promise. A promise to you that I will be back to you as soon as I can."

"Sure!" I cry, and he places a silver ring with a small diamond on top on to my ring finger. He stands up and hugged me to him tighter than ever. He is hugging me like he is never going to let go of me. I love him.

He moves his hands to both sides of my face and rests his forehead on mine, and his eyes are talking for him, I know he is just as broken up as I am and suddenly, I realize that I was just focusing on myself, and I have missed how sad and tired he looks.

"I'm sorry," he whispers and I shake my head.

"Its fine." I hold his hand and pull him closer to me.

I just want to sit with him for eternity.

But eternity isn't a choice that we can have.

Chapter Thirty-Five

The following morning, my phone vibrates. I don't ever want to let go of Ben, but I answer.

"Who is it?" I snap, not too kindly.

"Eva, it's Luke," answers my brother, and I can already tell that something is wrong.

"Hi Luke,' I say, my tone softening. "Where are you?"

"I'm almost at Ben's apartment. Can I see you?'

"Of course, Luke. Give me a few minutes to get dressed."

Ben's eyes open a little at the mention of Luke's name, but he is so tired he rolls over and is snoring in seconds. I caress his brow. He is pale, and a little sweaty, which is unusual, but I put it down to the long night of lovemaking we just shared, and I rise quickly and dress.

I get to the front door as the bell chimes. I open it, and Luke almost runs into the room.

"Eva, I'm sorry, but you have to see this," he stutters.

"What? What is it?" I say, suddenly worried.

"Here you go," he says, handing me a bunch of official looking papers.

"What are these?" I frown. I take a quick look, and I understand little, but there are pictures of my birth mom, Destiny, and I know this because, like Wanda said, she looks exactly like me.

She is standing next to a man who looks plain evil. He has the face of a hunter. He looks truly disgusting.

"I think I can guess who he is." I mutter in disgust.

"Yep. That's Henry," he hisses, and my eyes widen. How fucking filthy he looks. I clench my jaw and look at the other pictures.

"Luke, how did you get these?" I say, and he starts to talk quickly.

"Well, I went back to the neighborhood," he began but I interrupt him.

"You went back? Alone? Are you crazy?" I snap, but he just carries on talking fast.

"Yes, sorry, but I needed to know more, so I went back to see Wanda, and then talked to a few people that she suggested to me. One of them sent me to a barber, saying someone Destiny knew worked there, but I never got inside. At the last second, through the window, I saw Anderson"

My heart almost stops.

"I haven't talked to him" he adds quickly.

"Are you insane?" I cry. "What were you thinking?"

"Hey, it's okay. He didn't recognize me. But he looks so much worse, and I don't think he is in good condition at all."

"He deserves hell and death, that's the condition he deserves," I spit and walk to the couch because I feel like my head spinning. Ben walks in and gives Luke a filthy look, then walks into the kitchen without even looking at me.

I cannot believe that my birth mother fell in love with someone that looked as hideous as him. Ben comes in and mutters something about completing papers before he leaves for Germany, and I smile and wave goodbye weakly.

Luke leaves, but not until I make him promise never to risk going back again. What's done is done, I tell him, and he just shuffles away, as sad and as angry as me.

The past really is another country.

I go back to Laura's place, and I am not alone with my thoughts for long because within an hour, Ben walks in with a large bunch of roses and a sad smile. He places the roses on the table and says. "I am done. All the papers I need to go back to Germany are completed. I have my visa, and they are allowing me to go," he says.

I smile at the flowers, but my heart skips a beat.

Some part of me, deep down, was hoping was hoping that his papers would be delayed for a month more. I am so disappointed. I am a sad soul with a fixed smile and a broken heart

I hug him, acting like I am happy for him.

"Baby, I am coming back you know. I meant what I said."

I bite my lip to prevent me crying and he places his lips on mine without kissing me. "I am coming back," he whispers against my lips.

Why does a still, small voice deep inside me not believe him?

Chapter Thirty-Six

I look around me, and the entire way is covered with flowers, red beautiful flowers. I smile. Everything around me is beautiful. I walk slowly, aware of stepping on the petals. Ben is standing at the end, smiling. He looks so much different. He looks like Ethan. But his body is like Ben. I shake my head but he doesn't change.

This is Ethan. I close my eyes trying to forget this place, but I feel Ethan's hands and his touch sends fear all over me.

"I'm going to fuck you forever, Eva," he snarls.

"No!" I scream, whining with fear.

"Eva!"

I push his hands away and open my eyes.

I am alone.

I climb out of bed and walk to the bathroom, staring at my reflection. My eyes are dark just like my hair. I look pale like I have truly seen a ghost.

I walk downstairs and Ben is sitting with Luke, talking. No fights. Just talking. It strikes me as unusual, but I am too shaky from my nightmare to be worried, and I smile. I want them to be friends so much.

I grab a glass of juice and as I go back to bed I think I see Luke passing Ben a package. I hope it's not a surprise for me, and I've spoiled it, so I look away quickly so they don't see me noticing. I go back up the stairs, lie under the quilt looking at the enormous glass door, and think that I have never actually seen how large it is. Clouds gather in the sky and it looks like it is raining. Or maybe a storm is on the way. I I don't know, and I don't care. I am happy to be sharing this last day with Ben.

"You alright?" Ben startles me from my reverie and I turn around.

"Eva?" he says getting in next to me, "Luke just left. He says hi, and goodbye!"

"Hey there," I whisper in his ear, kissing it. I feel his smile against my cheek.

"We don't have to go anywhere today. We can stay in bed all day," he says and I snuggle into him.

I will miss him. I will miss walking to the park late at night, I will miss kissing him goodnight and kissing him good morning, I will miss the way he calls me babe, I will miss the way he looks at me when I ask him dumb questions, I will miss the way he listens to me while telling him about something that happened to one of my favorite book characters.

I will miss his voice and I will miss his touch. As the countdown finishes, my heart is so fragile and my tears are easily shown.

He senses my discomfort and just starts talking.

"You know, Eva, when I first knew I had heart disease, I locked myself in my room because they told me that I was an angel who had lost his way to heaven. I thought they meant that I was going to die, so I just stayed in my room and hid. I was forbidden from running. I was forbidden from laughing. I was forbidden from any strong emotions, including falling in love. They sent me to a private boys school for years until I was seventeen, to try and stop me from meeting girls.

It was a fabulous school for boys, and I got to do all the things that boys dream about. They taught me how to climb mountains, learn languages, and even how to shoot, and I did get to know other girls outside the school, but to be honest, I never truly loved a girl until I met you. And only now do I understand why they told me not to fall in love. Because falling for you makes my heart beat so fast. And touching you ignites a fire in my soul. And making love to you, I often feel close to death, but I know it would be death in a beautiful way. You have showed me heaven by letting me love you. So maybe, when all is said and done, you are the angel."

I try so hard not to cry now.

"I will be back" he says again and again.

And we make love again and again.

Until I almost believe him.

Chapter Thirty-Seven

Ben doesn't want me to go with him to the airport when he actually leaves. It would be too painful for both of us, too much for his heart, and I would probably cause a scene and run onto the plane with him. So we are sitting on the beach in the minutes before his cab arrives. He is traveling light, the weather is cold but nice, and he has his backpack. I sit next to him and drink in every single detail of his face.

I truly love him.

We take his backpack to the waters edge, remove our shoes and socks and just stand there at the water's edge. The waves lap around our feet as we hold hands and gaze into each other's eyes.

"Your eyes looks so sparkling and alive," he says not looking at me. "I want them to stay forever bright. Then, when I close my eyes, I will feel their warmth," he adds.

"They will. For you, they will," I tell him and he smiles.

I let go of his hand and stand in front of him. "Tell me you love me, and promise you won't fall in love with anyone else as much as you have fallen in love with me," I pout and he moves my hair away from my face.

His touch is so comforting.

"I promise," he whispers.

"And promise me you won't look at any girl the way you look at me," I place my hand on his chest.

"I promise."

"And promise me that when you get back to Germany, you will call me every day and every night so I can hear your voice." He frowns slightly, then smiles, and takes both my hands in his.

"I promise," he says and the waves are getting stronger, smacking our legs, but we don't care.

"And here is my promise to you, Benjamin Eisenberg. I promise to love you endlessly and never forget youand to yell my love out for you to the moon and the stars every night, so at least one of them will sparkle to you, like my eyes are sparkling for you. If I ever write a book it will be about you, and I will never stop loving you until death do us part."

I sob and he wipes my tears hugging me to him. I hug him tight. Burying my face in his neck.

We hug as the sun goes down, and the water freezes our toes.

And then we dress, because the cab has arrived, and as he gets in and sets off for the airport, I think that my heart will break into a thousand pieces.

Suddenly, a strange car draws up.

It's Aiden. He rolls down the window.

"Your lift, madame?" he smiles.

I climb in reluctantly.

"It sucks doesn't it," says Aiden, biting his lip. I think he's going to cry too.

"Did Ben send you?" I ask, knowing the answer before he speaks.

"Yup. That's the kind of guy he is. Always did look out for you Eva. And me too."

And we both sit and watch the tail lights of Ben's taxi fade into the distance. Aiden points, and I see Ben's hand out of the rear window.

Slowly waving goodbye.

Chapter Thirty-Eight

I open my eyes to hear Jacob singing. I haven't heard him signing alone before, without music. He has a pretty good voice. They have been back from their honeymoon for two days and Laura is bustling away, preparing breakfast for us both.

I'm not hungry. In fact, I'm sick to my stomach.

I haven't had a phone call from Benjamin.

Jacob is trying to cheer me up with some singing, and he has checked and Benjamin's flight did arrive in Frankfurt Airport safely and on time, but still no news from him.

I'm in a state of disbelief.

I don't feel like getting out of the bed, I don't actually feel like walking up at all, but someone is cooking breakfast and it smells so nice, so I drift downstairs.

I can smell, eggs, bacon and pancakes. I haven't smelled anything as delicious since they both went away, and my hunger pangs are stirring, I get out of bed, I pull one of the hoodies that Ben left for me, and Laura is cooking! I didn't know that she was that good at it.

"Good morning Eva. I know you are sad about Ben, but I really need to tempt you to eat something" she says kindly, and turns back to the stove. I am famished. When was the last time I ate?

I try to cheer up for Laura's sake, They have had the most wonderful time, and I love her so much I don't want to spoil everything by putting her on a downer.

"Well, it smells so good I can't deal with being sad anymore," I lie, and take a plate from her.

"My baby is a cook," Jacob murmurs, wandering in and kissing her, and I raise my glass of juice in agreement. The food is truly delicious.

"Anything from Ben yet?" Jacob asks softly, and I shake my head and almost stop eating again.

"Who taught you to do this amazing pancakes?" I say, changing the subject, and she smiles.

"Well, I wasn't always a top therapist you know," she jokes. "Besides, pancakes make everything better."

I nod in agreement as I demolish another two of them.

We pass a happy half an hour together, with Laura and Jacob so full of love, and telling me tales of their wonderful honeymoon. I had been so wrapped up with Ben I had almost forgotten how much I enjoyed their company. Then they both finish up their food and rise, simultaneously sighing.

"Ah well, back to reality,' Jacob says, then heads off for school.

"And I will see you later, my precious daughter,' coos Laura, hugging me tight, and running from the apartment.

There goes my wonderful new mother.

Who is always on the run!

My phone rings and I walk to my room. I answer it, and it sounds like Luke. There is a lot of what sounds like wind noise in the background.

"Luke? Hey, Luke!" I shout down my phone.

"Hey, Eva? Are you there?" he yells, and the wind sounds louder.

"Where are you?" I ask, but he doesn't hear me so I have to shout it again.

"Eva? I am going to give you an address and I want you to meet me there right now? Eva?" he shouts and the wind voices disappeared. "Sorry, I was just in the street and the traffic is very noisy" he mutters, and I don't know if he is being honest or not.

"You want me to come now?' I say, not feeling like it at all, but sensing something is wrong.

"'Yes. I have already texted you the address. Come quickly Eva. It's super important that you come soon."

The line goes dead.

I look at the address Luke has given me, and for a second I feel like throwing up everything I just ate.

I recognize it. It is in the old neighborhood.

Why on earth would Luke want me to go there? More important, why would he want to rent there?

I remember the pictures of my real father, Henry, and shudder. He has to be the most horrific guy I have ever seen. And I should ask Luke about Anderson. I wonder if he has found something out about both of them?

This is when I miss Ben the most. He gave me so much confidence that I don't fear walking alone in the streets now. But I do still fear going to that neighborhood alone.

I shake my thoughts away.

On reflection, my brother sounded quite desperate.

"It's super important you come soon," he had said.

He never uses that phrase.

I run to my room, pull on a warm sweater, some leggings and my boots, and hurry for the train station.

Chapter Thirty-Nine

I keep my head down the whole train journey and get off at the nearest station. I take a taxi to the address Luke gave me, and it passes by the house I used to live in. I hunch myself down into the seat. I try to breathe slowly and not have a panic attack.

When I arrive at the house, it looks crappy from the outside. The yard is filthy, full of dog mess, and the grass has turned to a faded brown. What a sad, scary little life we used to live.

I ring the bell twice and no one answers. I am scared to death at this moment.

Then I push on the door, and it swings open with a creak.

My knees are shaking with fear, but my brother needs me, so I pause for a moment, grab the wall to steady myself, then walk slowly down the hall.

As soon as I walk, the wooden floor starts squeaking under me. There is mess everywhere, empty pizza boxes and beer bottles.

I get the feeling that this mess is old.

I turn to the right, into what looks like a kitchen. There is a breakfast bar dividing the room, with a broken chrome barstool propped up next to it.

And Luke is standing there.

"Eva you came," he stammers. He is standing very awkwardly.

I suddenly realize that no one has been here in years and years. I spread my hands and gesture at the mess.

"It's all I could afford," he mutters, staring wildly at me. He is nervous.

Pale. White, in fact.

I don't understand what he is trying to tell me.

There is an open window behind him, and I hear the sound of rushing air as a train sweeps noisily by the window.

Luke stares over my shoulder. His eyes widen.

I suddenly want to leave this place as fast as I can. "What did you want to bring me here for, Luke?"

"This,' growls the voice, and I almost faint with sheer terror.

And then I see the blood.

The blood is pouring like a river from Luke's side.

There is a sudden blur of movement.

A shape rises from behind the breakfast bar, quick as a tiger.

It hits Luke hard, who falls to the floor, clutching his side.

And then I see the man.

Not a tiger at all.

A monster.

"Hello, you dirty little bitch." he spits, and I almost collapse on the spot.

"Ethan," I whisper.

I gasp and try to step back, but my legs have frozen and my heart has stopped.

"Look who's here," the monster tilts his head. "Little Eva. My tiny sex toy."

"You bastard!" shouts Luke. He tries to grab Ethan by the knees, but slips over in his own blood.

"Get off me, you filthy little worm,' screams Ethan, and kicks Luke hard. He smashes his boot right in his face.

"Now it's your turn, my dirty slut. Time to get fucked again."

He moves towards me, slowly.

He is so close that I can smell his disgusting breath. I almost taste that familiar stench of beer and rotten fish.

I jump back, but he moves fast and grabs me violently by the hair in the same old way, pulling me to the ground so that my face touches Luke.

His blood is everywhere. My brother is dying, and there isn't a single thing I can do about it.

"Oh, look! There he is. Little Luke. He refused to call you, even when I tied him to a chair and burned him a few times. Just like I used to burn you, you disgusting little wretch!"

He kicks me hard, in the ribs. I almost pass out. I cannot breathe.

"But I have ways and means of persuading little kids to do what I want. Don't I, Eva? Don't I?' he screams, and I hear him unbuckling his belt.

"Oh, no, please don't," I beg, but he kicks me again.

"I know what you're thinking,' he hisses. "Ethan wouldn't dare to rape me in front of my dying brother. He No one could be that sick. Well. Surprise, surprise! The last thing he will see will be your horrified face as I ride you again, you little whore!"

"Please. No. I beg you," I cry, as he starts tugging off my leggings with his filthy hands.

He starts laughing. The laugh of the truly insane, and I know in that moment that I am going to die. Here. Now. On a dirty floor, my naked body defiled one last time, and then soaked in my brother's blood.

"You thought you were done with me?" he laughs, as if guessing my thoughts. "No baby girl. I am going to end you."

I feel another lash of his belt on my bare buttocks, and then the cold metal of a gun pressed against my neck.

I hear a faint whooshing noise.

And then I swear that I see Luke smile before he closes his eyes forever.

Something falls past me, heavily.

It is Ethan, his eyes frozen wide in surprise.

And half his head is missing.

I turn around, and a tall figure sweeps me up in his arms.

And as I see who it is, I faint with relief.

And my soul cries out with love.

It is Ben.

My Ben.

My avenging angel, come to save me.

Chapter Forty

I t has all been a bit of a blur since then.

We spend the next few minutes trying to resuscitate Luke, but it is too late.

My brother, my poor, protective brother, has gone.

Ben holds me tight, hugging me like he will never let me go, as I weep floods of tears for the brother I have only just found.

And now I've lost him forever.

Ben strokes my hair for what seems like an eternity, until my dry, racking sobs tell him that I can cry no more.

I look up at him through eyes veiled with tears.

"You...you came back for me?" I stammer.

"Baby,' he says softly. "I never left you."

And as the afternoon darkens outside, the evening draws in, and the dogs in this scruffy neighborhood begin to howl, Ben tells me the whole story.

"It was Luke who really saved you, not me. Your brother, little Eva."

"What?' I say, confused.

"Do you remember the day before I left, when Luke came to visit, but you had just had one of your episodes so you weren't really in the mood to talk to either of us?"

"Yes. Vaguely. I remember interrupting you and thinking it was so nice that you were talking."

"Well, yes. It was nice, and I'm sorry that I got him wrong. Your brother was a very nice person."

I start to tear a little again but Ben continues.

"Luke had been back to see that really old woman. The friend of Destiny, the one you met?

I nod.

"Yes. Martha was her name, I think."

"That's right. Well, Luke met with her last week, and she said another guy had been asking around the neighborhood about both of you. Blonde hair. Powerfully built. He was asking especially about you, Eva."

"Oh, my God,' is all I can say.

"It gets worse. Martha has been around the block a bit, as they say, so she took this guy into her confidence and bought him a few drinks. But she slipped a few, shall we say, additives into the mix, and he got really drunk and started to blab. Before he passed out on her shop floor, he confessed that he had escaped from prison that day. He had been due to make a court appearance."

"Oh, my God! Laura!"

"I doubt Laura even knows he skipped court. They were still over the other side of the Atlantic at the time."

"Yes. Of course," I murmur, my eyes still looking down at poor Luke.

"And then, Ethan made the confession that sealed his fate. He told Luke that he knew exactly where you were."

"Oh, my God," I say, utterly horrified.

"Worse, he had been watching you at your fancy new apartment. With your fancy new guardians."

"No. My God, no! I knew I wasn't just being paranoid!" I cry.

"And his last words to Martha were "if I can't have her, none of them can.""

He said he was going to fix you. Fix you all.

I'm trembling again now. I think the shock has finally set in.

"Anyway, as soon as Luke heard this, he had a word with a few of his shadier contacts and came up with a plan."

I shudder again. I just recalled the package.

"He brought you something that day, didn't he?" I ask, straight out.

"Yes, Eva. I'm afraid he did. He brought me this."

Ben reaches around his back and pulls out a large gun.

I've never seen a gun before. Except in the movies.

"What's that thing fixed to the end of it?" I ask, still trying to take it all in.

"Remember I told you I was taught to shoot? Well, that's called a silencer. It makes sure that no one hears the gun go off. Luke thought of everything."

"You mean, you mean Luke planned all of this?"

"Yes. I'm sorry Eva, but he could see no other way to save you. To give you a chance to carry on living the wonderful new life that you've been blessed with."

"He really did love me, didn't he?" I sobbed, looking up from his body.

"Yes, Eva. He truly did. And he always felt guilty about not being able to stop Anderson selling you to Ethan. If he could have, he would. But he was just a kid himself, and there was no way he would have survived. Anderson would have killed him. So as soon as he got away from Anderson, and found you again, he vowed always to protect you. No matter what the cost."

"And he told you all this?"

"Yes, Eva. You were out of it longer than you think that day. He had bought the gun in secret, rented this house in the old neighborhood using a fake name, and then took me here while you were out of it. When you came down the stairs that day and caught us talking, we had only just come back."

'But why...why did you let me think you were going? Why did you let me think you didn't care about me?" I wailed, and pounded his chest with my fists weakly.

"Because, my darling, we knew by this time that Ethan was watching your every move. But every time you left the apartment, I was with you. There was no way he was going to make his move with a big, fit young German hanging around, now was there?"

I shake my head. I know he is right.

"Luke said that his days being a slave to Anderson taught him that Ethan would never ever stop looking for you. He would stalk you and hunt you down until the day you died."

"And Luke was right, wasn't he?"

"He certainly was. Ethan was even there the day we said goodbye. At the beach."

"What?' I cried.

"I saw him. Over your shoulder when I waved goodbye."

I am too shocked by this to even speak.

Suddenly, a door opens behind Ben and a figure looms into view.

I almost have a heart attack.

"And that's where I come in," said the familiar voice.

And Aiden is standing there, smiling.

But his smile quickly fades when he sees Luke lying dead on the floor.

Chapter Forty-One

O nce Aiden has discovered the whole story, he springs into action.

"Okay guys," he says. "There's a full change of clothes in here. You need to move now."

He opens one of the two large backpacks he has carried in, and throws clothes at us. He smiles, bows, and turns his back as I strip out of my gear.

"Ever the gentleman," I think, as I hurriedly disrobe and then don the shapeless, dark gear he has brought for both of us. We both get hoodies, which we pull up, and dark scarves, which cover our faces. It's cold outside now, so a casual observer would not think it strange that we are wrapped up so well.

While we are doing this, Aiden is searching Luke and Ethan. I notice he too is wearing a pair of rubber gloves while he does this.

I know what he's doing. He is taking every single bit of identification from their bodies and dumping in it plastic bags, which he then shoves in the rucksack.

"What about these?" I say, pointing to our old clothes, now discarded on the floor.

"It's okay sweetie, don't worry. It's time to go," Ben says, and helps Aiden unpack the second rucksack.

And suddenly I understand, as they pull out a large tin of gasoline, and some fire lighting material.

"Go, lovers. It's time to go. Your car is a couple of blocks away, Ben. In that alley you showed me. The one with no street cameras," says Aiden, pulling a couple of cigarette lighters from his pocket.

Now I understand.

"I'll make sure this place is really ablaze, then I'll scram. That will buy you some time to get out of the area."

"What will you do?" I say, suddenly worried for him.

"Oh, dear sweet Eva. Always worried about someone else," smiles Aiden.

"It's okay Eva. We hid a bicycle a few blocks away. Aiden will walk calmly away, with his scarf and hoodie up the same as us, and then cycle the back roads home. We checked the route thoroughly a few days back. There are no street cameras there either."

"Now, will you two get the hell out of here?" says Aiden. "And by the way, did I say that I love you guys?"

I run to him and hug him. And so does Ben. We all clasp each other in a group hug, and I swear Ben is crying.

Aiden laughs again. "Get out of here, you big jerk. And Eva?"

I turn to him.

"What'? I pout.

"Don't forget not to write."

I stare for a second, puzzled, and then turn and run as Ben pulls my hand.

As we leave through the darkness of the back yard, I see Aiden's indistinct shape moving fast, and I know he is drenching the place in gasoline.

"Come on baby,' hurries Ben. "Let's get out of here."

Chapter Forty -Two

We've been on the road for two months now.

As arranged, Aiden sent a clipping of the newspaper report to a distant motel agreed by both Ben and Aiden almost nine weeks ago.

It showed that the house rented by Luke in a false name had burnt to the ground that night. The fire was so intense that they had difficulty identifying the two bodies found there.

The neighborhood was so tough it was simply assumed that two homeless drifters had been squatting in there.

And no one cared very much.

Aiden also left a typed note in the package, saying that he had visited the lovebirds and they were devastated, but completely understood once they had been told the whole story.

"The lovebirds" had been Ben's code for Jacob and Laura.

Aiden added that the lovebirds would contact us in the same way at the next drop off point.

And only Aiden and Ben knew where the next point was.

As far as anyone else who would be interested was concerned, Ben was in Germany.

But because Aiden had gone to see the lovebirds so quickly - the day after the fire, in fact - they had never reported me missing. And no one had yet made the connection between me, and the badly charred bodies that had been found in the derelict house.

Enquiries had probably been made. But I knew from experience that people in those neighborhoods rarely, if ever, talked to the police.

They were too scared of some of their neighbors.

I turn over in the warm motel bed. It is nowhere near as luxurious as my bed in Laura's, but I know that I will return to that bed one day.

All I know right now is that our love isn't over. I look at my lover.

The kind young man, who fixed the broken girl and helped that girl to fly.

I can feel his slow heartbeats, the thrill of his skin on mine, and I feel safe in the strong grasp of his gentle hands

I know now that I am truly blessed.

And I know that we will be on the road forever.

Heading down the highway of hope, and daring to dream.

And I am smiling, because I know.

I know for sure that our story is not over.

Acknowledgment

I am grateful to the people with open minds and a supporting soul. Thank you to the ones who encouraged me and told me to keep on going with the writing hobby.

First of all:

Thank you dad, mom and my beloved family for supporting me and believing in me. Thank you dad so much.

Thank you, my dear friends for you words that helped me to keep on writing and never give up!

Thank you to all the amazing English teachers, the ones that gave me hope and taught me to speak English. Especially Sir Nasser, you did great with me in the past years.

Thank you, Ameena, Mothey, Mariam, Reem, Dalal, Fatima and my internet friends, every single one of you. I love you guys for waiting patiently to read this book.

Sara Al-Haider

Thank you, thank you and thank you Mr. Steve. For all that you've done to me.

And a special thank you to a person who stayed with me for a month but taught me a lot, M you know who you are.

Thank you to my little annoying sister who handled me on the nights that I kept on writing, my late night partner.

Thank you to the people who told me not to give up on this.

Thank you to the ones who read this book, and appreciated my work.